THE OORT PERIMETER

The Earthfleet Saga
Book I

By
Steven Lake

MARSHALL MICHIGAN

The Oort Perimeter, Book I of the Earthfleet Saga

Copyright © 2009 by Steven Lake

Cover design by   Village Graphics
PO Box 171, Homer MI 49245
www.800graphics.com

Author photo by   Seven Lake

The opinions expressed in this manuscript are solely the opinions of the author and do not represent the opinions or thoughts of the publisher. The author represents and warrants that s/he either owns or has the legal right to publish all material in this book.

ISBN-13: 978-0-9826020-2-7
ISBN-10: 0982602022

First published in 2010

10 9 8 7 6 5 4 3 2 1

Published by   2 MOON PRESS
307 1/2 W. Michigan Ave, Marshall MI 49068
www.800publishing.com

All Rights Reserved. This book may not be reproduced, transmitted, or stored in whole or in part by any means, including graphic, electronic, or mechanical without the express written consent of the publisher except in the case of brief quotations embodied in critical articles and reviews.

PRINTED IN THE UNITED STATES OF AMERICA

Dedication

I want to dedicate this book first to God for his boundless grace in blessing me with the ability to write, and the imagination by which to create all the great worlds, characters, events and stories that I have had the privilege to write about.

I also want to send out a huge thanks to Steve Lawson (red devil), Bubba, Woland, Adam McDougall (Digikid), David Hall (accoutered), and everyone else at Raiden's Realm (www.raiden.net) who has helped me edit my book, provided feedback, or gave me ideas for my stories. Thanks for all the great help all of you provided!

And lastly, I give a shout out to my friends and family. Especially my Mom, Dad and Sister and brother-in-law. Thanks for putting up with me all these years and listening to me constantly talk about my books, the characters, and everything else about them. Thank you also for being a sounding board and helping me work out my ideas when I got stuck or needed a little inspiration boost.

Author's Note

This novel is book 1 of the "Earthfleet" saga, the first of three sagas that make up the "Bitter Cycles of Man" series. To learn more about this series, or other books that I've written, or are in progress, go to: http://www.realmsofimagination.net/

Steve Lake's other works

Dreamland Articles I

Dreamland Articles II (forthcoming)

The Oort Perimeter

Destiny's Mission

Homeworld (forthcoming)

Prologue

    A short, plump Yib monk stood on a balcony at the top of a large stone tower that overlooked the expansive Yib monastery. It was an unusual mix of the plain, and the extraordinary, as tenets from thousands of religions across the galaxy combined to form a patchwork of culture that sparkled with breathtaking beauty and simplicity. A warm summer breeze wafted through the room behind him and sent a small cloud of dust swirling up around his feet like a brown whirlpool. Yet his robe did not seem to notice, as it remained surprisingly still despite the strength of the breeze. He reached up and adjusted the hood of his robe, pulling it further over his face as though drawing deeper into the shadows inside. He brushed lightly at the simple brown cloth it was made of, and then tightened the rope-like belt around his waist that held it in place. After a moment he turned and studied the room behind him.
    It was made entirely of an emerald green marble, surrounded by a circle of thirty six simple, stone pillars that appeared old and scarred with time despite their relative youth. Small birds nested in the domed roof of the tower as the evening chants and prayers echoed up from the courtyard below. He inhaled deeply as the smell of flowers drifted through the air around him, creating a sweet, perfume like fragrance in the air. As he watched the twin suns quickly racing towards the horizon, he heard the sound of footsteps on the stairway below. He turned around just as eight other monks in robes of various colors and designs stepped out from between the pillars and formed a circle in the room that

surrounded a large, black orb that sat perched on a pedestal of pure white marble. He soon joined them.

They chanted quietly to themselves for several minutes, and then turned their attention to one among the group who was dressed in a light green cloak covered in aquatic symbols.

"What is your message today prophet? Why have you called this meeting?" asked one of the monks in a deep, solemn voice.

"A great danger arises from within our midst," said the monk in the green cloak, his voice deep and menacing.

"What kind of danger?" asked another.

"A race has arisen among us that will destroy the nine and take the galaxy for its own."

"Who are they?"

The prophet raised his hand and waved it over the orb. It shimmered and changed to reveal a picture of Earth.

"It is the Chappagi. They will conquer us all and destroy the peace that the nine have brought to the galaxy."

"That is absurd! The nice races have stood as guardians of the sentient worlds for over four millennia! There is no way such an insignificant race could overthrow them. You are mad, I tell you! Mad!" shouted one of the monks.

The prophet glared at the other eight from under the darkness of his hood.

"I am a master prophet, of the great house of prophets. We have never been wrong. We correctly predicted the betrayal of Severen, and the attack of the Origgians. Our people have been accurately prophesying the truth for over two millennia, and I tell you now, unless they are destroyed quickly, the Chappagi will overthrow us all. They will conquer the nine and put every creature in this galaxy under their foot."

The other eight monks mumbled to each other and discussed this revelation vigorously amongst themselves. Finally, they fell silent. One of the eight, the plump monk who had been first to reach the top of the tower, stepped forward and threw his hood back to reveal the reptilian face of a Gayik'Von.

"As I suspected. You are no longer a prophet of the Yib, but a mouthpiece for the fear of your own people," he said angrily.

"My prophesy is true! It will come to pass!" cried the prophet.

"Your prophesy is flawed!! The Gin have no lust for power and conquest. They have grown powerful out of fear of you and your people. Fear breeds fear, and fear leads to suffering, and death."

"Yes, their death! They must die!" cried the prophet.

"NO! We will not sanction this prophesy, nor will we sanction the genocide of an entire race on the simple word of a prophet whose own species has much to gain from their slaughter! Your own speech gives away the true nature and intent of your prophesy, prophet. Since your eyes are blinded by your fear, and your prophesies flawed due to the tempest within your own spirit, we hereby strike your title as prophet from the record, and declare that your prophesies go unheard from now on until such time as your spirit, and your race, are in line with the truth."

The prophet hissed. "Fools! You risk your own destruction at the hands of these monsters!"

"If they were truly monsters, and our eyes each saw the same future as you, then we would agree on your verdict. But our eyes see the real truth. We see a race that is still in its infancy trying to stand up and walk in a world full of giants. How can a giant fear a teetering child? Go now, prophet, seek cleansing and find the true vision that is within your heart."

The prophet growled. "Then their victory has already begun, and your doom sealed," he hissed.

"What are you saying? What victory have they gained against us?" asked the Gayik'Von.

"They have already divided the nine races, and turned us against each other. Without our unity, their victory is assured.

The only question that remains now is the season of our destruction."

Four of the monks in the circle gathered around the Gayik'Von as he stepped back several paces, as if to separate himself from the prophet. The three that remained gathered themselves around the prophet as though to defy the Gayik'Von.

"As you can see, the division has been made and we are no longer united. Open your eyes and see the truth, before your blindness becomes the death of us all," hissed the prophet. He tossed back his hood to reveal the fish like face of a Varnok. He pointed his webbed fingers at the Gayik'Von and said, "Mark my words. Your fall will be the greatest of the nine, for you will be the first to suffer at their hands!"

The Gayik'Von snorted. "We shall see who will fall and who will remain, prophet. But remember this. So long as our five races exist to stand against your unholy union of four, the Gin will remain safe, even if we must fight to our last dying breath to protect them."

The Varnok prophet glared at him. "We shall see."

Chapter 1

Chancellor Nordham was a man of science just as much as he was a man of politics. While he didn't directly conduct any science of his own, he was a great lover of the scientific disciplines, and oversaw a vast community of scientists and researchers consisting of the most brilliant and exceptional human minds in all of Sol. Here they were free to push the bounds of science unhindered and unrestrained, save for a simple code of ethics that called for everyone to always seek the betterment of mankind, and never its harm. But this scientific freedom hadn't always existed. In times past, science had been feared by man, and those who believed in its power to improve the lives of mankind were treated as heretics, and often killed or tortured for their convictions.

To combat this fear, all those who clung to, and practiced science, banded together for strength and mutual security, eventually forming the Brayburn Society. Under its protective umbrella, science grew and prospered, diseases and sicknesses were wiped out, and many scientific breakthroughs, once thought impossible, and still thought impossible by many on Earth, became reality. Even space flight and interplanetary colonization were achieved long before the first man left the ground at Kittyhawk. As they continued forward, ever striving for newer and better technology, the world around them slowly began to change, to accept science as a part of their daily lives, and move down a path the Society had long desired for mankind. But progress in the world was slow, and at times seemed to stop all together. Frustrated with the apparent apathy towards science that the world displayed, the Society began to look for a way out. It was at this time that they turned their eyes to the stars.

Their deep space capabilities had grown quickly over the years, and it wasn't long before they were regularly venturing into space. Seeing the potentials space offered them, including enhanced freedoms and opportunities, the citizens of the Society fled Earth, and quickly colonized all of Sol. And the people of the Society loved it, as it took the freedom they had gained before, and enhanced it a hundred fold. But this freedom did not come without a price. Technological advancement was rapid, and one form of technology was quickly obsolesced by the next. But to those of the Society, such rapid change was expected, and treated as just another part of their daily lives. However, to someone on Earth, accustomed to the slow, snail like progress of technology, the miracles accomplished by the Society were nothing short of magical.

This was something Nordham had grown up around, and had learned to deal with on a daily basis. Being the Chancellor of such a vast community of exceptional and brilliant minds was both humbling, and exhausting. While crime and social woes were nearly unheard of within the Society, there were still many things that required his attention every day. And today was no exception. He sat behind his desk and studied an operations report on a large data pad in his hand as one of his assistants came through the door with an armful of more data pads. He looked past the growing pile of work on his desk and sighed.

"More?" he said with a hint of frustration.

The assistant smirked sheepishly. "Sorry, sir, but they've been coming in like this all morning," he said.

Nordham frowned. "How many more do you have out there?"

The assistant shrugged. "Another hundred or so."

Nordham's eyes narrowed in disbelief. "Unbelievable. We're a completely paperless society, and yet I'm up to my eyeballs in paperwork. How is that possible?" he said sarcastically.

The assistant shrugged. "I don't know, sir, but if you ever find out, let me know," he said.

Nordham smirked. "Honestly, I'd rather just ship these back to the directors and let them deal with them instead."

"Well, you could, sir," said the assistant. "What, and let the council say I was wrong? Are you kidding?" said Nordham with a grin.

The assistant chuckled. "Right, good point. Well, if it's alright with you, I'd like to grab a few of the interns and see if we can sort through these and figure out which are just empty reports, and which are things you need to pay attention to."

Nordham nodded. "Yes, please do."

The assistant nodded in return, and then slipped out of the room. Nordham sighed as he rubbed his forehead in frustration. Just then his computer terminal beeped as a message appeared on the screen. He turned and studied it with interest. After a moment he furrowed his brow.

"Well, well, well. It appears I was right. Computer, inform the reception group that I will be changing the meeting venue for the Serian diplomats to Pluto station. Also, please inform the Grand Admiral of the change."

"Acknowledged," said the computer.

Nordham tossed the data pad in his hand onto the desk and said, "Alright, let's go play some political jousting, shall we?"

"Today President Westland openly denounced German Chancellor Sigfreed on international television for his support of the Lansing Accord. Chancellor Sigfreed immediately retorted saying that President Westland's claims were the sign of a weak leadership afraid that it will lose its bid for world domination," said the news reporter.

Mike slowly sipped his cup of coffee as he reclined on a long, plush, oriental couch that sat prominently in the middle of the living room of his large, but humbly furnished officer's quarters. He muted the display screen on the wall, and then grinned as he noticed his executive officer fuming like a boiling pot of water.

"Something the matter Alfred?" he asked.

"World politics make me so angry. It's like listening to a bunch of preschoolers arguing over who will get the last piece of candy," said Alfred in a light German accent.

Mike chuckled. "Well, not everyone grows up, no matter how old they are. It almost makes you wish you could send them back to preschool and make them start all over again," said Mike.

Alfred grinned. "Its a nice dream, but I doubt it would work." He looked back at the news broadcast just as images of more violence around the world were being shown. "It's so depressing to see them acting like savages to each other. It seems like, despite our best efforts, they just want to destroy each other," he continued with a sigh.

Mike nodded. "It does get frustrating at times, doesn't it?"

Alfred nodded. "That it does."

Mike glanced at his watch, and then turned off the monitor. He sighed. "It's almost time to go meet the new Serian diplomats."

"More political babysitting again, eh?" chided Alfred.

Mike grinned. "A Grand Admiral's job is never done," he quipped.

Alfred nodded. "Yes, it seems that way these days. Well, I had better get up to command and be sure that everything is in order before the councilmen arrive. We always have to look preened and pretty for the bureaucrats."

Mike laughed. "Yeah, like meat on display."

Alfred rolled his eyes, nodded, and then slipped out of Mike's quarters.

"More politics?" came a curious, quizzical voice from across the room.

He turned to see a tall, beautiful young woman standing behind him. Mike grinned.

"You could say that. But one thing you learn right away about being the highest ranking officer in Earthfleet is that playing politics is part of the job description. They seem to think that, despite your position and experience as a military officer, you're the perfect target for small talk, verbal chess, and political bantering. Personally, I'd rather challenge then to a friendly game of rugby than get dressed up and prance around like a peacock."

The young woman nodded. "I have noticed that, from both humans, and the many alien species we have thus had direct contact with. To each of them, politics is a game of power, prestige and slight of hand."

Mike chuckled. "I was always told that politics came from a pair of Greek words meaning 'blood sucking ticks', or something like that."

The young woman grinned. "While that is not the true origin of the word, it does quite accurately describe many of those who partake in it."

Mike perked up in surprise as a small communicator embedded in his ear chirped. He pressed his finger against his lower right earlobe and said, "Clayton here."

"Sir, the Chancellor wishes for you to meet him at Pluto station. He says that there's been a change of venue and they will now be meeting the dignitaries there," came a voice in his ear.

Mike cocked an eyebrow. "Any reason for the sudden change?" he asked.

"He did not say, sir."

Mike looked at the young woman who nodded in return.

"I will begin preflight walkthrough of the ship and summon your crew."

Mike held up his hand. "Not just yet. I want to find out why we're changing venues first. Besides, we don't need to take the Sergenious out to Pluto station to meet the delegates. I can just portal over there. It's not that far."

The young woman nodded. "As you wish."

Mike pressed his ear again and said, "Connect me to Chancellor Nordham, please."

"Connecting now," came the soft feminine voice of the central computer in his ear.

A few moments later the Chancellor answered.

"Yes, Grand Admiral? How can I help you?" said Nordham.

"I just got notification that the venue for meeting the diplomats has changed to Pluto station. What's the story behind that?"

"I was notified by our chief intelligence director that there is a potential spy among the Serians. Because of that, I want to contain them on Pluto station for a while until we can be certain that they present no threat to us."

Mike muttered under his breath, "Great. They're not even here and we're already playing galactic cloak and dagger." "So, are we essentially giving them a pat down before they're allowed into the inner system?" he asked.

"Well, not in a literal sense, but something fairly close to that."

Mike looked at the young woman and cocked an eyebrow. "Alright, we'll be there as soon as we can. Clayton out." He nodded at the young woman and said, "Well then, it looks like we might need the Sergenious after all. Go ahead and call the crew."

The young woman nodded, shimmered, and then vanished.

Lieutenant "Weed" Pendleton was a seasoned fighter pilot with an edge about him that would make most commanders cringe. He was smart and fearless, but also reckless in many respects. It was this recklessness that had earned him the nickname "weed". It had come from an incident during one of his training flights in the academy. He had been hot-dogging it in a training fighter over the Florida Everglades when he lost control and crash landed in a large patch of weeds. But that was only the first of many such incidents. Yet Grand Admiral Clayton had chosen him as the senior pilot for his flagship, the Sergenious, despite his somewhat sorted record.

Mike had watched him from early on, and knew how much of an asset Pendleton's somewhat reckless flying style could be. He felt that this "edge" that so scared the other commanders actually made Pendleton the best pilot to have when a crisis came, since he would be more willing to do anything necessary to ensure his survival, and those of his passengers. Pendleton peeked out from the engine cowling of his JX-1 fighter and looked at the deck engineer who sat just below the main body of the spacecraft.

"What do you mean we can't get more power out of it?" he asked.

"Fleet specs say that the seven oh one unit isn't allowed to go beyond point zero zero five above maximum operating limits or you risk critical failure of the plasma booster," said the technician.

Pendleton snorted. "That's a barrel of kai sludge and you know it!" he snapped.

"Well, I'm not going to break regulation and adjust the unit past it spec'd limits without the written authorization of my commander."

Pendleton flipped himself out of the access hatch and down to the deck next to the technician.

"Geez, specs my butt. If you're not going to do it, then I will," he snapped.

"But that would be..."

"Hey, it's my personal fighter. Let me worry about what's over spec and what's not. Ok? You're just here to help me get her tuned up for the next rock belt race. Understood?"

The technician rolled his eyes and stepped aside as Pendleton made several adjustments.

"It's your butt if it blows, not mine," said the technician.

Pendleton smirked. "That's kind of the idea, crewman, as it'll be my butt in the seat."

The technician rolled his eyes, but said nothing. As Pendleton worked to fine tune the small device, a finger reached over and tapped him on the shoulder. Pendleton turned in surprise to see a beautiful young woman in a simple floor length white dress standing behind him. He frowned.

"Augh, it's you. What do you want? Don't you have someone else to harass?" he said.

"No, I don't. I'm here to summon you. The Grand Admiral is in need of his pilot," she replied.

"Oh? Really? And when does the old geezer want me?" he said.

"About twenty minutes ago," she said flatly.

Pendleton leapt up in surprise, banging his head against the bottom of the fighter. He doubled over in pain, swore loudly, and then stumbled out from under the fighter. After a moment he stood up and groaned as he rubbed his head.

"Twenty minutes ago!? Good lord, woman. Why didn't you contact me!?" he said.

"I tried. But you switched off your communicator," said Sarah flatly.

Pendleton swore. "I was trying to keep Kemps from calling me every five minutes. I didn't mean to switch it off." He swore again, and then looked at his fighter. "Awe, geez. And right when I was on a roll, too. Alright crewman, just button her up and we'll finish this another day. Sarah, portal me to the ship."

The young woman nodded. Moments later a grayish sphere of light surrounded him for a brief moment, and then vanished, leaving the deck empty. At the same time, another identical sphere appeared on the bridge of the Sergenious and then quickly vanished as well, leaving Pendleton behind. Mike looked up at the lieutenant and raised an eyebrow in consternation.

"Are you making a habit of being late, Mr. Pendleton?" asked Mike.

Pendleton spun around and saluted. "No, sir! It was an accident! I was trying to filter out an annoying crewmate who kept calling me and accidentally switched off my communicator."

Mike smirked. "Take your post, lieutenant, and get us underway. I don't want to keep the chancellor waiting any longer."

"Aye, sir!" said Pendleton. He spun around, leapt into the pilots seat and flew across the controls.

As he did, Sarah appeared next to Mike and said, "What do you expect to find when you get out there?"

Mike furrowed his brow and said, "Honestly, I don't know. We'll likely run into some cloak and dagger types who want to find out if we have any chinks in our armor. It's no secret that the Varnok hate us with a passion. It wouldn't be too much of a stretch to believe that these Serians are working for them, either directly, or indirectly."

Sarah nodded. "I don't know what good it would do them if they did discover such weaknesses. The Varnok would not risk a confrontation with the Gayik'Von just to destroy us. That would be like feeding yourself to a dragon just to slay it."

Mike chuckled. "They've done dumber things than that before. I wouldn't be surprised if they tried to go to war with the entire galaxy in order to satisfy their thirst for our destruction."

Sarah shook her head. "I've never truly understood the Varnok. Their bloodlust seems so, illogical."

Mike chuckled. "Nobody ever said that hatred or xenophobia was logical. Besides, I wouldn't expect an AI like yourself to understand something as complex or animalistic as hatred."

Sarah smirked. "I understand more than you think I do."

"Launch bay control, this is the Sergenious requesting permission to depart," said Pendleton over the ship's communicator.

"Sergenious, this is launch bay control. You are cleared for launch," came the reply.

Pendleton turned around to Mike and said, "We're cleared for departure, sir."

"Then set course for Pluto station, best possible speed," said Mike.

"Aye, sir!"

The Sergenious lifted gracefully off the deck of the launch bay and shimmered out of view as she engaged her cloaking device. Pendleton then eased the ship forward and watched as it quickly slipped through the atmospheric shielding and out into space. Within moments they switched on their coaxial drive and were gone.

Chapter 2

"Sir, incoming message from Command One. It's for you," said Martin.

"Put it through," said Mike.

A small rectangular image of an older, dark skinned man appeared in front of him.

"Grand Admiral, this is Commander Fritz, acting duty officer for Oort perimeter control. Our long range sensors are detecting the approach of several warp signatures. They appear to be Serian. Exact class and ship type are currently unknown. But whatever they are, they appear to be fairly well proportioned," said the man.

"Battlecruisers?" asked Mike. "I don't know for certain, sir, but I would say that's a reasonable assumption."

Mike nodded. "Understood. Hail them as usual and advise them that no battleship may pass through the Oort perimeter. If their diplomatic ship needs an escort, we'll provide it."

"Understood, sir. Fritz out."

The image then flickered and vanished. A tall, beefy, middle aged lieutenant commander turned around in his chair and stared at Mike curiously.

"Well proportioned, eh? I wonder what kind of ships they brought with them as escorts?" he asked with a slight Australian accent.

Mike shook his head. "If I didn't know better, I'd say they're coming with a group of eight Rem'kal battleships."

The officer perked up in surprise. "Eight? That's an awful lot of firepower for a diplomatic escort."

"Given the reports of their suspected ties to the Juinah mafia, it's understandable that they'd want the extra protection. The Juinah have many enemies, and anyone who calls the Juinah friend is marked for death by all of the Juinah's enemies," said Mike.

"Ah, I heard about them. Nasty little blighters if you ask me."

Mike chuckled. "They're no worse than blood worms."

The man cringed. "Now there's a thought that'll make your skin crawl."

"Slowing to sublight," said Pendleton.

Mike turned to his right and said to his operations officer, "Martin, what's the status of the Serian diplomatic ship?"

The young woman fiddled with her control panel for several moments, and then said, "It appears that they will be arriving in approximately eight minutes."

He nodded and turned back to his tactical officer. "Sydney, what would be the tactical risk to our ship if we went out to the Oort perimeter and greeted our guests personally?"

The lieutenant commander furrowed his brow. "You actually want to go out and greet these people, in this ship?" he asked.

Mike nodded. Sydney frowned.

"Far be it for me to disagree, sir, but I believe that such an action would put you at too great a risk," he said.

The chief engineer looked up from his station behind Mike and said, "I have to agree with him. We're one of the biggest targets in the fleet, and while we're certainly one of the most durable ships around, we're not invincible. If they are in fact planning an assassination, they will already know all of our strengths and will have a suitable ambush waiting for us."

Mike chuckled. "I understand that Eric, but I wasn't planning on greeting them outside the perimeter. I'd be silly to put us at risk like that. Instead I was thinking that we could greet them inside the perimeter when they first pass through."

Sydney nodded. "Well, that does sound better. Commander, is that okay with you?"

Eric shrugged. "It's fine with me, just so long as we don't scratch the hull while rubbing shoulders with them. I just put a fresh coat of paint on it yesterday."

Everyone chuckled. "Alright Mr. Pendleton, take us out to the rendezvous point," said Mike.

Pendleton nodded, "Aye, sir."

Nordham looked up as one of his assistants came in.

"Sir, you asked to be informed when Grand Admiral Clayton had arrived," said the assistant.

Nordham nodded. "I take it he's here?" he asked.

The assistant nodded. "Yes, and no."

Nordham looked the his assistant curiously. "What do you mean, yes and no?"

"Well, he was coming here in the Sergenious, which arrived moments ago, slowed to sublight briefly, and then continued on towards the Oort perimeter. He's now on his way to escort the ambassador personally."

Nordham blinked in surprise. "He's what!?" he exclaimed.

The assistant nodded. "Yes, sir. He appears to be heading towards the rendezvous point with the Serian diplomatic vessel."

"Good gawds, what's he up to now? Hail his ship and tell him to get back here immediately."

"Yes, sir!"

Mike sat in his command chair as he studied a holographic command display that floated in front of him.

"Wow, now that's an impressive sight," he said, more to himself than anyone else.

"It is indeed, sir. But I think your guess on the type of ships they'd bring was wrong," said Eric.

Mike chuckled. "Well, I was partially right. They do have two Rem'kal battleships with them. But the other six I'm unfamiliar with. Sydney, do you know what those are?"

Sydney fluttered across his tactical console for a moment, and then said, "Well, two of the ships are of a design we've never seen before. So I'm not sure what they are, but they appear to be of approximately equal ranking with the Rem'kal ships. The other four are Miagaoh class destroyers. Less than half the firepower of the Rem'kal, but easily three times more maneuverable."

Mike nodded. "Four heavy hitters for the big stuff, and four sprinters for the little stuff. That's a respectable lineup for an escort fleet."

Pendleton snorted. "I've seen better."

"What makes you say that, Lieutenant?" said Mike.

Pendleton turned around in his chair and said, "Rem'kal cruisers maneuver like a rock. Apparently the designers thought that firepower was more important than maneuverability. Their flight systems are so pathetically underpowered that it's laughable. Especially for a ship their size. It's like putting an eighty pound suit of armor on a ten year old kid. They might be able to take a beating, but they won't be able to move very fast."

Mike smirked. "What about their Miagaoh class destroyers?"

Pendleton screwed up his face in an expression of sarcastic disdain, but said nothing. Mike and Sydney laughed.

"No comment, eh? Well, then I guess we have nothing to really worry about from any of their ships," said Mike.

"Well, given the relative firepower both classes have, I doubt maneuverability or speed is of much concern to them," said Sydney.

"Admiral, the Chancellor's assistant is hailing us. They want us to report back to Pluto station immediately," said Martin.

Mike furrowed his brow in thought. "How soon will the ambassador's ship be through the barrier?" he asked.

"Not sure, sir. Let me find out." She flew across her operations console and drew up some information. "Ah, here we go. Perimeter control is reporting that they've cleared the ambassador's ship for entry and will be allowing them through shortly."

"Excellent. Mr. Pendleton, please put us into position to meet the ambassador's ship when it comes through."

Pendleton grinned slyly. "Uh, sir? Not to be nitpicky or anything, but the chancellor did request that we return to Pluto station immediately. It's obvious that they know we've received their message, so faking a communications problem, or some other technical difficulty, is out of the question. Especially given Commander Roger's spotless, and almost over zealous maintenance record. So that leads me to consider that you have some interesting reasons in mind for ignoring his orders," he said.

Mike grinned. "Excellent observation. The reason I'm ignoring his orders is that I want to put our new sensor array through its paces checking over the Serian ships for possible contraband and spying equipment as they enter."

"Wouldn't they expect something like that?" asked Eric.

Mike nodded. "They would. But they expect to be pitting their stealth technology against our older sensor systems, not our newer ones."

Eric nodded. "Sounds logical enough. Besides, I've been looking forward to giving those upgrades a good shakedown anyways."

Pendleton grinned. "This should be fun."

He then turned in his seat and maneuvered the ship forward towards the massive shield barrier known to everyone in Earthfleet as the "Oort Perimeter". It had been given this name in honor of Dr. Oort, a famous Dutch astronomer who had first proposed the theory of the existence of a massive cloud of comets and other space debris that surrounded the sun in a gigantic sphere. Since everyone in the Society knew that his theoretical "Oort cloud" didn't actually exist, many had laughed him to scorn when they had first heard of his theory. But it was an ingenious young engineer who had ultimately turned Dr. Oort's folly into reality, if only in part, by naming the newly completed defensive barrier, the "Oort Perimeter", in honor of him. The Kuiper perimeter, a secondary defensive grid similar to the Oort perimeter, which protected the nine planets of Sol system and resided just beyond the orbit of Pluto, was also named in much the same way.

It was these two spherical shield arrays that provided much of the primary defense for Sol sector, and made it much easier for Earthfleet to do its primary job; that of defending Earth. The Kuiper and Oort perimeters were comprised of tens of thousands of special satellites that each generated a wide area defensive shield. These shields in turn were linked together to create an even larger shield designed to surround all of Sol space and keep out anyone or anything that might threaten Earth. The perimeters were believed by many to be impenetrable. But only a few knew their true weaknesses. It was these weaknesses that had prompted Mike to begin a program of system wide upgrades to the two perimeters, with each of the original defensive shield satellites being replaced by newer, more powerful models. Only in a few areas was the work incomplete. But given enough time, even those would be replaced, and the new barrier would be truly impenetrable, giving Earthfleet the one thing it had desired for many years: A certainty that Earth would be safe from any and all possible harm originating from outside the system. The only thing they had to worry about then was threats from within. Namely, mankind itself.

Mike watched as the Sergenious pulled up to access gate twenty seven and stopped. This was the primary gate through which all traffic in and out of Sol system flowed. This included everyone from the highest ranking dignitaries, to the lowest ranking merchants arriving to trade at Pluto station. The station itself was an oddity in its own right, as it was the only station outside the Kuiper perimeter. But that didn't mean it was any less important than any other station under Earthfleet's control. And it was certainly anything but the dingy, run down rat hole that most trading posts eventually became. Instead, it was kept in pristine condition, and was in plain fact one of the nicest trading and diplomatic posts in the entire region. This was because Pluto station served as a representative of Earth and all she had to offer. So the Society and the fleet went to great pains to make her as beautiful, practical, safe and clean as humanly possible. And all that attention to detail showed.

Pendleton peered through the front window and smirked. "I see our guests are fashionably late. I would have expected them to be here by now," he said.

Just then the gate area turned bright green and a series of blue and red navigation lights began flashing along the length of the gate passage, denoting the location of the gate, and the route the Serian ship would be required to take through the shield. Pendleton squinted as he watched the gate shields vanish one by one, and then immediately reappear moments later.

"What in the world is that?" he asked.

"What do you see?" asked Mike.

"The shields are doing some weird thing. They seem to be switching on and off in sequence, like a line of lights on a marquee or something," replied Pendleton.

Mike activated his holographic command display, pulled up a picture of the gate, and then smiled. "I take it you've never seen the gate opened before?" he asked.

"No, sir. Never had a need to."

"Ah, then that would explain why you're unfamiliar with its operating protocols."

Pendleton spun in his chair and stared curiously at Mike. "Opening protocols, sir? Sounds like something you'd do to a can of fish in a fancy restaurant," he said.

"What the admiral is referring to is the method by which the gates in the shield perimeter are opened and closed to allow ships through. The distance between each shield level in the perimeter is approximately one kilometer, give or take a few dozen meters. To form an actual gate, one grid in each level of the shield has been designated as one of the doors for the gateway. In order to let ships in or out, each grid is switched off to allow a ship through, and then switched back on after it passes. Only one grid can be switched off at a time, hence the strange activity you're seeing in the shield array," said Eric.

"What in the blazes do they need to do that for?" asked Pendleton.

"It's designed to help us scan for unwanted intruders and prevent them from entering," said Eric.

"So it's kind of like a turnstile at a subway, only with shield layers, right?"

Eric nodded. "Something like that."

"Well that's a silly way to do things. With the sensor systems we have, we ought to be able to catch whoever comes through that gate, cloaked or otherwise, without having to resort to such crazy methods of filtering," said Pendleton.

Eric shook his head. "It's done that way to take into account the slow regeneration time of the shield grids. Given how long they take to reform, even if we did spot one in time, we couldn't raise the grids fast enough to keep them out. Hence why things are done this way. If we haven't spotted them by the time they reach the last grid, we likely won't see them anyways. The slower transit speed of the ships also produces a significantly smaller ion trail, thus making it much harder for cloaked ships to sneak through by hiding in the ion trail left behind by another ship."

Pendleton smirked. "Sounds silly to me, but hey, whatever floats your boat," he said.

"Sir, the Serian diplomatic transport is through the gate," said Martin.

"Mr. Pendleton, join up in formation with the escort ships. Ms. Martin, hail the escort leader and inform them that we'll be joining them for the flight in to Pluto station, and then hail the Serian ship and tell them we'll be helping escort them to the station. Make sure they know I'm aboard."

"Aye, sir," said both crewman.

Eric peered curiously at Mike. "Any reason for the formality?" he asked.

"While I may not be a politician by nature, I do know how to take political fluff and use it to my advantage. Personally escorting a diplomatic cruiser is a symbol of honor few politicians will overlook."

Eric nodded. "Ah, then we're greasing the wheels of diplomacy, so to speak."

Mike nodded. "Something like that."

The Sergenious accelerated forward and soon joined up with the diplomatic transport as the small formation made its way to Pluto station. After a few minutes, Pendleton began to grumble.

"Good gawds. These Serians drive like snails," he said quietly to himself. But not quietly enough to prevent Mike from hearing him.

"How fast are we going, Mr. Pendleton?" he asked.

Pendleton grunted. "We're holding at one point five AUM, sir," he said. "One point five!? Great Scott! That's barely warp one point three!" said Mike.

"I guess the diplomat isn't in much of a hurry," said Sydney.

"If we continue at this speed, sir, it'll take us just over five and a half hours to get there," said Pendleton.

Mike sighed. "Yeah, that's way too slow. Martin, would you please hail the Serian diplomatic ship and ask them to accelerate to at least warp three."

"Aye, sir."

Several moments later Pendleton perked up. "Well, that's a little better. Now we're at least moving like a turtle now."

"Well, at least that's faster than drying paint," quipped Sydney.

Pendleton glared at him out of the corner of one eye and said chidingly, "Oh har, har."

Mike dismissed his holographic display, and then turned around in his chair and looked at Eric.

"Can you begin passive scanning of the Serian ship?" he asked.

Eric nodded. "Been doing that since we left the barrier, sir."

"Anything?"

Eric shook his head. "Unless Lieutenant Martin has seen anything, the Serian ship is squeaky clean."

Mike turned around and said, "Lieutenant?"

Martin shook her head. "Nothing sir. If they're hiding anything, we're not seeing it. I can go active if you'd like."

Mike shook his head. "Not right now. We'll do that later once the diplomats are on the station. I don't want to offend them before we at least have our first meeting."

Martin nodded.

"Sir, with your permission, while we're at Pluto station, I'd like to run the Sergenious through a complete battery of tests to feel out the capabilities of our new sensor array and give it a proper shakedown," said Eric.

Mike turned around and said, "I thought it already went through a shakedown." Eric nodded. "It did. But that was only a standard fleet certification. I'd like to give it my own personal picking through before writing it off as ready for full time service, if you know what I mean."

Mike nodded. "Alright, fair enough. Your inspections have always gone above and beyond standard fleet requirements, so I don't see any harm in that. Once I'm on Pluto station, the ship is yours. Just be sure not to wander off too far in case I need you."

"Aye, sir."

Chapter 3

Nordham paced anxiously back and forth across the floor in the reception area and mumbled incoherently to himself.

"Sir, if you don't stop pacing, you'll wear a hole in the deck plating," said his secretary.

Nordham stopped and huffed loudly. "It drives me mad when he does things like this. I wish for once he'd just follow my orders without question."

"No offense sir, but if he did that all the time, he'd just become another dog on the leash of the Society. It's the semi-independence of the military that the founders created through our constitution that allows him to do such a great job ensuring Earth's protection," said the secretary.

"Yeah, well, I'm still not too keen about him just ignoring me like that."

"He likely has his reasons, and we'll see soon enough what those are. I suspect that we'll find it was worth his small bout of defiance."

Nordham grunted. "I hope so."

Pendleton carefully edged the ship around the far side of Pluto station and took up a position behind two other Earthfleet patrol ships docked nearby.

"Ship is now in soft dock configuration, sir," said Pendleton.

"Pluto station is reporting that you're clear to portal over whenever you're ready," said Martin.

Mike stood up and looked at Eric. "You have the bridge. Enjoy yourself while I'm gone, and let me know how that test comes out," said Mike.

Eric nodded. "Will do, sir."

Mike turned to his right and said, "Sarah, would you care to join me on the station?"

Sarah nodded and said, "I'd love to."

She then looked at Eric and said, "Will you be needing me?"

Eric shook his head. "As long as you stay in contact we should be alright."

Sarah nodded. "I'll be sure that I do."

"Alright, ship me over," said Mike.

A grayish sphere of energy engulfed Mike and then vanished, leaving nothing behind. Moments later, Sarah shimmered and vanished as well. Pendleton turned around in his chair and looked at Eric.

"Alright, so what's first on our test docket? Do I get to show off my most excellent, undeniable uber piloting skills again?" he asked with an air of mock arrogance.

"Actually, no. The first thing we're doing is taking a break. I need to go back to the galley and get myself a double strength cup of coffee. I haven't slept in two days."

Sydney snickered. Pendleton glared at him.

"If you didn't outrank me, sir, I'd tell you to take that little snort of yours and stuff it where the sun don't shine," he replied.

Martin furrowed her brow and whistled as she turned around to her console as though trying not to get involved. Eric raised an eyebrow and looked at Sydney who rolled his eyes and shook his head. Eric smirked.

"I guess I'm not the only one who didn't get his beauty sleep," he said.

Martin snorted slightly as she tried to contain her laughter. Pendleton glared briefly at her, and then spun around in his seat, crossed his arms, and kicked his feet up onto his control console.

Nordham looked up as a portal sphere appeared in front of him, and then immediately vanished, leaving Mike behind. He crossed his arms in disgust.

"I hope you have a good reason for disobeying my orders, Grand Admiral," he said with a hint of disgust.

Mike grinned. "Call it a little political floor buffing. I helped escort the ambassador's ship as a gesture of goodwill. It should at least earn us a few political bonus points with the Serians before we officially start talking to them. That way if we make fools of ourselves along the way, we won't have to crawl out of quite as deep a hole as we normally would," said Mike.

Nordham smirked. "For someone who's not a politician, you certainly think like one."

Mike shrugged. "It beats the alternative. The last thing we need right now is to tick off someone else. At least until I can get the rest of the barrier upgraded."

Nordham nodded. "Speaking of which, how's that coming?" he asked.

Mike shrugged. "Everything's done except a two thousand square kilometer area around entry point twenty seven. We should have enough of the new satellites by the end of the month to finish up that area. After that the barrier should be pretty much impregnable. At least for the near future."

Nordham nodded in satisfaction as he pursed his lips in thought.

"Well, that's good to hear. It should make it easier for me to sleep at night."

Mike smiled.

"Well then, shall we go meet the diplomats? I'd like to get this peacocking session over with as soon as possible so I can get back to more important things, like putting Black Orchid in its place," said Nordham.

Mike furrowed his brow in interest. "Are they at it again?" he asked curiously.

Nordham sighed and rolled his eyes. "When aren't they? You'd think that after the way we put down the Illuminati so many times, they'd be wise enough to know when to mind their own business and stop trying to enslave everyone on Earth."

"The way they are, I'll be dead and gone before they'll ever be put down completely."

"Yes, and as soon as we wipe them out, someone else will just start a new group and we'll be back to square one."

Mike chuckled. "Well, at least it'll keep our lives interesting."

Nordham rolled his eyes and said, "At this point in my life, I'd almost enjoy some boredom for a change."

Just then Sarah shimmered into view next to Mike. "The ambassador's ship has docked and they are about to disembark," she said.

Nordham motioned to the door and said, "Well then, shall we?"

Eric sipped his coffee as he studied his engineering console. As he did, Pendleton turned around in his chair and asked, "Commander, may I ask a question?"

Eric looked up and nodded. "What is it?"

"Well, I've been wondering why the admiral addresses you, Lieutenant Commander Jones and our two gunners, Sergeant Barker and Corporal Wen by your first names, but he addresses myself and Lieutenant Martin by our rank and/or last names."

Eric furrowed his brow and smiled. "Well, for starters, you and Lieutenant Martin are the newest members of the crew, and still earning your stripes with him, so to speak. The four of us have known the Grand Admiral for quite some time now. I knew him way back when he was still a starship captain. So he has a greater familiarity with us than he does with you. That's one reason why he's so free to address us like he does. But in open company or among other officers, we're reduced to being addressed the same way as anybody else. But on this ship, we're family."

"So what does it take to become part of this family? Do I have to kiss his feet, feed his pet rabbit and have his first child or something?" said Pendleton.

Sydney chuckled. "You could try being on time more often," he said.

Pendleton smirked. "Yeah, well, a lot of that is because I keep switching off my communicator to keep certain retards from driving me batty, calling me at all hours of the day and night, asking me stupid questions. It's enough to drive a man to insanity."

Eric laughed. "I had a few people like that in my early fleet days as well. I ended up getting them banned from ever using their communicators for anything other than official business. I even got one banned from ever making any outbound calls."

"You can do that?" said Pendleton in surprise.

Eric nodded. "Certainly. I could do it right now if you'd like."

Pendleton snorted with satisfaction. "Would you like that list of names now, or shall I have it shipped to you in a crate later?"

Eric chuckled. "Ship them to me later. If you've got enough names to fill a crate, I'll just let Sarah handle that for me."

"I heard that," said Sarah over the intercom.

"Oh be quiet, bit breath," said Pendleton.

Sarah chuckled.

"So, as I was saying, if I'm still earning my wings with the admiral, why are you so comfortable calling me by my nickname if he isn't?" asked Pendleton.

Eric laughed. "For the same reasons the Grand Admiral feels comfortable calling us by our first names. He's very familiar with us, and we're very familiar with you. Heck, I've known you since you were in diapers. Your dad and I served on the same starship together, remember?"

Pendleton nodded. "Ah, right. The Kyoto."

Eric nodded as his console beeped. He quickly examined it. "Oh, this is interesting. Sarah, are all the new modifications online? Some of the modules still aren't responding to diagnostics."

"All modifications are online. The missing modules are there and pass initial testing. But I haven't been able to develop any advanced diagnostic routines for them yet. Hence why they are absent from your display," came Sarah's voice from the console.

"I thought those modules came with their own routines?"

"The included routines were inferior and flawed. So I'm creating new ones that will provide the best possible diagnostic information for each module."

Eric smirked. "You sure are a perfectionist, aren't you?"

"Perfection is impossible. I am simply trying to achieve the best possible diagnostic results for each system."

"She's a perfectionist," said Pendleton.

"Alright, well, get those done as soon as you can. In the meantime, we'll pull out of port and test the systems in a live operational configuration. That should give us some good data to chew on. Lieutenant Martin, would you kindly switch sensors to active mode and begin a wide area scan?"

Martin nodded and began her scans.

"Are we going to be doing all of our tests here, or will we be taking a run around the neighborhood?" asked Pendleton.

"We'll need to test in a variety of environments, so we'll be taking a tour of the system to get the most complete data set possible."

Pendleton smirked. "Huh, thought so. Well, if we're going to play tiddlywinks with the local space debris for a while, it probably wouldn't hurt for me to give navigation and helm a good picking through while we're at it. It probably doesn't need any tweaking, but at least I won't die of boredom while you run your tests."

"How about a game of poker? That would do more to keep our minds occupied than a bunch of boring diagnostics," said Sydney.

Pendleton smirked. "The way you play? No thanks. I'd be cleaned out before we got to the fourth hand."

"Will you guys please be quiet? I'm trying to...well, hello," said Martin.

Eric looked up from his station in interest. "Found something?" he asked.

"Yeah, I think so. I've got a sensor shadow at bearing one six nine point eight six at point five light seconds. It's moving away at point five AUH and appears to be accelerating."

"Any idea what it is?" asked Eric.

"I'm not sure, but the energy patterns read like a cloaked ship. But if it is, it's not like anything I've ever seen before."

"Are you sure you're not seeing an error in the sensor data? Just because the fleet signed off on it doesn't mean it doesn't still have a few bugs in it," said Eric.

Martin shook her head. "No, sir. It's definitely reading like a cloaked ship. I'm also seeing a tiny trail of high gain particle ionization and evidence of disturbed gases."

Eric looked at Sydney who nodded. "I recommend we eliminate the possibility of all standard sensor echoes and shadows first. If everything checks out, we may want to investigate further," said Sydney.

"Sounds like a plan to me," said Eric. He opened a communications channel and said, "Pluto station, this is the Sergenious. We are requesting a confirmation on sensor readings at grid four delta one two eight seven nine six. Can you confirm presence of gas and ionization anomalies in that area?"

"Checking now. One moment Sergenious," came the reply.

"Now we'll see if this is really a ghost or something more," said Eric quietly.

"Sergenious, this is Pluto station. We're detecting faint traces of gas displacement and ionic particles, but nothing we can identify as anything other than normal spatial drift."

"Thanks for the confirmation. Sergenious out," said Eric.

He looked at Sydney and said, "What do you think? Pluto station sees the same thing we do, but in less detail. Certainly not enough to raise any red flags."

"While it may turn out to be nothing, I think it might be wise to at least go down this track and see what's there. Worse comes to worse, we discover it's nothing and simply go back to what we were doing before," said Sydney.

Eric nodded. "Alright, then let's get underway. Weed, set course for Earth, twenty AUH. Sydney, when he begins his acceleration arc, cloak the ship and switch all weapons systems to standby. Weed, when I give the order, change course for the anomaly and switch to silent running. Martin, hail Pluto station and tell them we're leaving dock and heading in-system for some diagnostic drills."

All three crewmen nodded and then complied.

"What do you want us to do?" asked Barker.

"Nothing for the moment. But stay sharp. If this is what I think it is, things could get interesting in a few moments."

Barker nodded.

The Sergenious turned away from Pluto station and began accelerating towards Earth as it shimmered and then vanished from view behind its cloaking shield.

"Alright, Weed, let's get after that thing," said Eric.

Pendleton nodded and turned the ship towards the anomaly.

"Weed, let's close the distance as quickly as possible. Use FTL if you have to," said Eric.

"Won't FTL break our silent running?"

Eric grinned. "I've already solved that problem. We can now fly on silent running without being detected, even with the FTL running full."

Pendleton grinned and nodded. "Nice."

Eric chuckled. "Yeah, I thought so too. Hey, when you close on the target, make sure to stay at least two thousand kilometers behind it at all times. Be it's shadow. That should reduce our chances of being spotted if it's actually a ship, and not some weird space anomaly or something," said Eric.

Pendleton nodded.

Mike patted down his uniform as he picked at its edges.

"Nervous, Admiral?" asked Nordham.

Mike looked up in curiosity. "Me? Nervous? What makes you say that?" he asked.

Nordham grinned. "You're preening yourself like a monkey."

Mike smirked. "It's that obvious, is it?"

Nordham nodded. "It's almost as if you're anxious about meeting our guests."

Mike laughed. "Only as nervous as I have to be. I'm not one to take first contact lightly. First impressions are always the most important."

Nordham squinted curiously. "This is hardly first contact. We've been in contact with the Serians for months now."

"Yes, over subspace, but never in person. This is the first time we get to see them face to face. And given their bat-like appearance, I'm content to ensure that they're happy, lest one of them try to use me as a portable drink dispenser."

Nordham laughed. "You're worried that they'll drink your blood like some big furry version of Dracula?"

"The thought had occurred to me, sir," replied Mike.

Nordham chuckled. "I can understand where you may have gained such an apprehension about meeting them, aside from the obvious political peacocking. The Serians are not a very good looking race."

Mike smirked. "Five foot tall wingless vampire bats would be an ample description of them. It's something that would give my grandchildren nightmares for the rest of their lives. Well, assuming I had any," he quipped.

Nordham nodded. "Mine as well."

Two loud chimes sounded, followed moments later by three columns of energy that appeared briefly, and then vanished to reveal three ornately dressed bat like creatures.

"Let the games begin," said Mike quietly.

Nordham strode forward and said, "Greetings, I am Chancellor Nordham, leader of the Brayburn Society. Most simply know us as the Society."

He motioned to Mike and said, "And this is Grand Admiral Clayton. He's in charge of our military defense forces. It's nice to finally meet you in person."

He held out his hand in a gesture of welcome. But the three Serians did not respond as he had expected. They looked curiously at him for a moment, and then talked quietly between themselves in clicks and chitters for over a minute.

Finally, one of them stepped cautiously forward and sniffed his hand, and then retreated back to the other two.

"Can you say, awkward?" whispered Mike.

Sarah stepped forward and grabbed one of the Serians by the shoulders, touched her forehead to his, and clicked twice. The Serian looked at her in curiosity, and then smiled a gangrenous, toothy grin. She then retreated several paces and stopped next to Mike.

She cocked an eyebrow slyly and said, "Were neither of you briefed on proper protocol when greeting a Serian delegate?"

Mike cocked his head slightly and said, "Apparently not."

One of the Serians stepped forward, bowed, and said, "I am Seredor of the nest of Noidoc. I greet you on behalf of our people. I am honored to be here, but I am curious why we were properly greeted by one of your females, and not by yourselves."

Mike bowed apologetically. "I apologize for the seeming lack of courtesy, but it appears that we were not informed of the proper method by which to greet you."

"Yes, I can see that. But why was this female the one who knew, and you did not?"

"This isn't actually a human female you're seeing. This is Sarah, the core AI for my flagship, the Sergenious. As an AI, she tends to know more than we do."

"A ship's AI? How curious. But if it's truly an AI, why did it choose such a form?" asked the Serian.

"When a ship's AI first becomes sentient, they are allowed to choose the name, gender and appearance they will use as part of their human interface system. This hologram, or avatar as some would call it, is just part of that system."

The Serian diplomat nodded in approval. "Very interesting. I find it intriguing that your AI would choose a female form over a male, as the male form is superior. Then again, we should not find it surprising, as you quite often give gender to many things that do not have gender."

Mike shrugged. "Well, the whole ship gender thing is an old sailor's tradition from ancient times. You could say that it's a habit that's hard to break."

The Serian diplomat nodded and smiled. "I can understand that sentiment. Traditions tend to take such unusual places within a culture, and are often the hardest to change. Even ones that are foolish and obsolete."

Mike cocked an eyebrow, but said nothing.

"Chancellor, Admiral, if it is not too much to ask, we would like to take a tour of your facility in order to better understand your culture, your technology, and your people."

Mike glanced at Sarah who nodded slightly that everything was alright. He glanced briefly at the Chancellor and nodded slightly to signal that it was safe to proceed.

The Chancellor quietly acknowledged this, and then looked at the Serians and said, "Well then, if you'll follow me, we'll begin our tour."

Chapter 4

Martin studied her sensor display intently. "We're gaining on the object. Range, five thousand kilometers and closing," she said.

"What do you see?" asked Eric.

Martin shook her head. "Not much. I still can't be sure what we're looking at, but my gut is telling me it's a ship. I just wish we could see it better so I could be certain."

"Sarah, can you fine tune the sensors to filter out all background noise and increase the resolution?" asked Eric.

"Adjustments made. Try again," replied Sarah over the intercom.

Martin shook her head. "Nope, that didn't help much. If that's a cloaked ship, that's got to be one of the best cloaking devices I've ever seen. Even our best cloaking shields don't do this well under this level of scrutiny."

"Martin, can you mux an image out of that sensor data and pipe it to my console?" asked Pendleton.

Martin shrugged. "Yeah, I can do that. It won't be pretty, but here you go."

Pendleton turned around and looked at his display. "Eww, that thing looks like..." he said as his voice trailed off.

Eric picked up on this immediately. "See something, Weed?"

Pendleton nodded slowly. Martin stood up and looked over Pendleton's shoulder at his console.

"See these lines here? And this bump here?" said Pendleton.

Martin nodded, and then suddenly realized what she was seeing. "Weed, I could almost kiss you," she said with a hint of glee.

Pendleton cocked an eyebrow. "Almost?" he replied.

Martin slapped him playfully on the shoulder as she sat down in her chair. As her fingers flew across the console, Sydney began to chuckle.

"You found something interesting, I take it?" he said.

Martin nodded. "It's definitely a ship we're looking at. But I don't think it's one we've ever seen before. I'm working up an overlay image so you can get an idea of what I think it looks like. Just give me a minute."

After a little bit she stopped her work and then sent the resulting image to everyone's console. Barker perked up in curiosity.

"What the heck is this? The Crayola monster or something?" he cried.

"No, it's a ship. And a fast one I reckon," said Sydney.

Weed turned around in his chair and said, "So what should we do? I know we're going on limited information here, but if that's actually a ship, I doubt it's here just to sightsee."

"Hmm, agreed. Of course, that still assumes we're seeing a ship and not a sensor echo," said Eric.

"I'd be willing to take a chance that it is a ship. If I'm wrong, we'll know something's not right with the sensors and they need to be fixed. But if I'm right, we've got an intruder to stop before they do something bad to Earth."

Eric nodded. "Agreed. Weed, continue tracking the target until we can get a better ID on them."

Pendleton nodded. He turned around in his chair and watched the image for several moments, and then noticed something.

"Uh, oh. I think they've seen us. They're jigging!" said Pendleton.

"Stay with them, Lieutenant," said Eric.

"Already on it, sir."

The Sergenious rolled out and banked hard as the unknown object maneuvered rapidly to shake off its pursuers.

"I think we can all now agree that's a ship," said Pendleton.

"You've got no arguments from me, Weed. From now on we're treating this as a hostile."

Pendleton nodded. "Alright you little tramp, let's see what you're up to," he said quietly to himself.

He continued following the ship, matching it move for move until it soon settled down and resumed course. After several minutes it attempted to shake them again, but Pendleton stayed with them, matching them turn for turn as he maneuvered the Sergenious like a high performance fighter.

After the third such attempt to shake them, Pendleton suddenly realized something. "Martin, is that ship barking IDF?" he asked.

Martin looked over her sensor displays and shook her head. "Nope. Nothing," she replied.

Pendleton frowned. "Well, we are. And if they've learned how to detect and read our IDF, then they're onto us already," he said.

Eric perked up curiously. "That might explain their sudden interest in shaking us. Possibly as an attempt to see if they were seeing a sensor echo, or just an illusion caused by an anomaly in their cloaking."

"Well, cloaked or not, if they know how to detect and read our IDF, we may as well have a huge neon sign over our heads advertising our position."

Sydney turned to Eric and said, "Weed has a point. I recommend we shut it down. At least for the moment."

Eric thought about this for a moment, and then nodded. "Alright, shutting down IDF. Let's see if they can see us now."

Tension on the bridge grew unbearably thick for several moments. They all waited in anticipation for the next move by the unknown intruders. After several minutes, Eric said, "Anything yet?"

"Negative sir. They're main...wait, they're stopping."

"Continue to match their movements, Weed."

"Aye."

Sydney looked out the forward window for a few moments, and then back at Eric. "What do you think they're doing?" he asked.

"Likely checking their shadow again. Since we're no longer barking IDF, they may be looking to see if we're still here. It's an old submariners trick. Periodically they would either turn or come to a full stop to see if somebody was tailing them. They're likely doing the same thing with us."

Everyone waited silently on the bridge for several moments. Then something happened.

"They're on the move again and changing course," said Martin.

"Heading?" asked Eric.

"I can't tell for certain, but if my guess is right, they're heading for the Kuiper perimeter. Looks like they plan to cross at access point seven one six."

Eric grunted. "Well, we need to make sure that doesn't happen," he said. He opened a communications channel and said, "Gate command, this is the Sergenious. Priority one intruder alert. Seal the Kuiper perimeter and go to defense level one."

"Sergenious, this is gate command. What is your authorization?" came the reply.

"This is Commander Eric Rogers, captain of the Sergenious speaking on Grand Admiral Clayton's behalf. Seal the perimeter. That is an order."

Martin looked at Eric in surprise. "You can't do that, sir! You don't have authorization to speak for the admiral!"

Eric muted the communicator and said, "There's no telling what might happen if that ship gets through. If we contain them out here, we've got a better chance of figuring out who they are, and possibly stopping them before they have a chance to do any harm."

"But you'll be court-martialed when the admiral finds out!"

"I'll cross that bridge when I come to it. Right now, the security and safety of Earth is at stake."

"Incoming message from gate command," said Sarah.

Eric unmuted the communicator and said, "Gate command, what is your status?"

"We checked with Admiral Bofenheiser, and he has confirmed your request for sealing of the perimeter."

"Well? Get on with it! We've got an intruder that's about to penetrate the perimeter in less than four minutes. They're heading for gate seven one six, so you will need to seal that gate first, as well as any others nearby."

"Aye, sir. Beginning lockdown now," came the reply.

"Confirming that access point seven one six has been sealed. Detecting course correction by intruder. They're accelerating to FTL and making a run for gate seven two three."

Eric swore. "Weed, climb all over him. Get cozy with that ship and don't let him get away," he said.

"Aye, sir."

The Sergenious accelerated forward like a pistol shot and quickly overtook the cloaked intruder.

"Sydney, drop cloaking and go to full combat mode. Let's introduce ourselves the Earthfleet way."

"Aye, sir!"

Mike studied the three Serian diplomats as they examined their surroundings.

"What is that soft noise we hear coming from the walls? It almost sounds like music," said one of the diplomats.

"It is music. We play a variety of songs at nearly inaudible levels as a way to help our crews work more efficiently and with less stress. It's like a massage for the subconscious mind," said Nordham.

"Massage? We do not know this word."

Nordham smiled. "It's a human technique used to loosen stiff muscles and help a person relax. It's quite enjoyable."

The Serian diplomat nodded. "Interesting. Admiral, if it is not a breach of your security protocols, may I inquire why you choose to cloak all of your ships and space stations whenever they are near either your home world, or one of their primitive space vehicles?"

Mike looked at him curiously. "You know about that?" he asked.

The Serian nodded. "Your people are a major subject of interest among my people. Information such as this is highly prized."

Mike nodded. "You are correct about the cloaking procedure. We do that as a way to protect the people of Earth from our technology. It was the driving force that spawned our stealth program."

The Serian diplomat cocked his head curiously. "I do not understand. Why shield your own people from the wonders of your vast and wonderful technology?"

"Because they are not ready for it. It's too advanced for them. One of the things we learned early on was that too much technology too fast can damage a culture irreparably and interfere with it's natural progression. The social ramifications and chaos we have seen occur from the introduction of even the simplest technologies into a culture that is not ready for them is devastating. On a global scale the effect would be greatly magnified. That is why we don't introduce any of our technology to them until they are ready, and certainly not all of it at once. It is true that we are indeed working to quickly bring our people on Earth up to the same technological level as we enjoy, but that takes time. Eventually though they will reach a point where we will be able to make formal first contact, with them."

The Serian diplomat eyed Mike curiously. "You say that as though they are a separate society of humans apart from yourselves."

Mike nodded. "They are, in a way. While we are of the same genetic heritage, time and our differing viewpoints on life have sent us different directions. This is because some humans are satisfied with life as it is, stubbornly refusing to adapt or change unless absolutely forced to, while others like ourselves desire to stretch the bounds of science and discovery and go to the ends of the universe to explore the impossible, and discover the improbable."

The Serian diplomat nodded. "We have a similar story to you as well. It took us a long time to overcome that, but in the end we achieved a comfortable balance of the new and the old that all can live with."

Nordham nodded. "Getting there is the tough part. But once you're there, you wonder why you didn't arrive sooner."

The diplomat nodded. Just then, Mike's communicator chirped.

"Grand Admiral, this is Admiral Asaka. Your presence is requested on the command deck sir," came a voice over the communicator.

He turned away from the diplomats and pressed the activator on his ear. "I'm in the middle of a diplomatic meeting, Admiral. Can this wait?"

"I wouldn't have called you if this wasn't important, sir."

Mike sighed. "What is it?"

"A passenger on the freighter To'ak is requesting that you speak to them, sir."

Mike furrowed his brow curiously. "You called me because a freighter passenger wanted to speak with me?"

"Not exactly, sir. I contacted you because of who the passenger is."

"Well? Who is it?"

"It's Adjutant President V'sin of the Gayik'Von, sir."

Mike blinked in curiosity. "The Adjutant President? He arrived on a freighter?"

"Apparently so, sir."

"What's he doing here?"

"I don't know sir, but he's requesting to speak with you."

"Alright, fine. Escort him and any of his entourage to one of the secure conference rooms. I'll be there shortly."

"Aye, sir."

Mike turned to Nordham and said, "Sir, with your permission, I need to leave. Something important just came up."

The Serian diplomat bowed slightly and said, "We understand that a man of your position has many great and important responsibilities. We will not be offended by your departure."

Nordham cocked an eyebrow in surprise at the Serian diplomats. "They don't waste time taking charge, do they?" he thought.

"Admiral, if it's important, you're excused. Just be sure to come back here as soon as you're done."

Mike nodded, "Yes, sir."

Pendleton rolled the Sergenious over and pulled up hard and fast as the intruder scrambled desperately to shake them.

"Watch out, Pendleton! He's heading for the outer debris field!" shouted Martin.

Pendleton swore. "This sucker's slippery."

"Sydney, do you have a weapons lock?" asked Eric.

"Not yet. The signal's not strong enough."

"Sir, let us have a crack at it," said Sergeant Barker.

"Alright, go for it," replied Eric.

"Barker, Wen, all turrets are at your control. Fire at will!" said Sydney.

Barker grinned as he looked over at Wen. "Alright corporal, let's make these guns sing. I'll take topside, you get the belly," said Barker.

Wen nodded, and then concentrated on his tactical display, quickly pressing configuration buttons in an effort to isolate his target. But he was getting nowhere.

"I can't see anything. You got anything, sarge?" he said.

Barker shook his head.

"Martin, patch as much sensor information as you can through to their tactical displays. Give them something to shoot at. Sarah, try to formulate the sensor data into a more coherent target," said Eric.

"Data patched through," replied Martin.

"Targets formulated. I can't do much more than that. You'll have to make do with what little there is," said Sarah.

Barker grunted. "It's not a lot, but it'll do. Alright corporal, let's kill this sucker."

Moments later a hail of pulse weapon and turret fire sprayed forward from dozens of points on the ship like a stream of angry bees. The intruder rolled out hard and dove down into the thin field of rocky debris that hovered just above the Kuiper perimeter in an effort to get away. Rocks and scattered comet fragments exploded in brilliant flashes of light and fire as round after round poured out from the Sergenious. The intruder zigzagged frantically back and forth through the debris field in an effort to shield itself from the relentless hail of fire. But the gunners tracked them mercilessly as Pendleton stayed close to them like butter on bread.

"Sir, reporting four Nova class battleships and two Samurai class shipkillers approaching from seven one point one three and two seven point one six nine. They're coming to assist," said Martin.

"I'm switching on IDF so that they don't accidentally shoot at the wrong guys," said Eric.

The intruder dove in close to the barrier, and then pulled up hard. It made several erratic moves through the debris field and then doubled back on itself, passing the Sergenious as it went. Pendleton swore and immediately did a hard one eighty, throwing the ship around in a lazy arc as though drifting a sports car, before punching the engines to full power in order to catch up with the intruder. It again made several maneuvers and put a sizable amount of distance between itself and the Sergenious. Again Pendleton drove the Sergenious to its limits trying to catch up.

"Commander! I need more power to the navigational nacelles! He's pulling away!" shouted Pendleton.

"I can't give you anymore. They've already got all they can take! If I give them much more, they'll blow out!" cried Eric.

"Then blow them out if you have to!" shouted Pendleton. He swung wide of a large cloud of debris and then turned back in, hoping to cross just in front of the escaping ship.

Chapter 5

"Great scott, Lieutenant! We can't get a clear shot like this!" shouted Barker.

"Just keep your pantyhose on. You'll get your shot. Just don't blow it when you do," said Pendleton.

Barker glared at him. Sydney looked at him and shrugged. Barker rolled his eyes in frustration.

"Target window coming up!" cried Pendleton.

"Alright Wen, let's smoke this puppy."

Pendleton watched as the intruder slowed briefly, and then turned as though trying to locate him.

"Alright loser, time to taste the power of number one," said Pendleton mockingly.

He swung the Sergenious around hard, dove down under a nearby cloud of debris and emerged into the open, nearly colliding head on with a massive asteroid. He rolled hard and slipped down the left side of it so close that it made Eric grip his console in fear and swear loudly.

"He keeps this up, I'm going to need to start wearing a diaper," muttered Eric.

As they emerged out the other side of the asteroid, Pendleton found himself exactly where he wanted to be. The intruder flinched and rolled in surprise as Wen and Barker's combined guns barked out a thick hailstorm of weapons fire at it.

"Target taking hits!" shouted Sydney.

The intruder maneuvered frantically and then dove into the debris field again in search of shelter. Pendleton immediately banked around and followed him in. The two ships danced like predator and prey among the rocks, one seeking to flee for its life, the other driving to make its kill. Then slowly, bit by bit, the intruder began to pull away.

Pendleton struggled with all his skill and might to catch up to the intruder again. But he would have no such luck. Seeing that the intruder was still pulling away, he leaned over, quickly calculated a jump trajectory, and then briefly fired up the coaxial drive, sending the Sergenious ripping through the debris field and out in front of the intruder.

Eric nearly gagged when he saw what Pendleton had done.

"Lieutenant, please tell me you did not just engage the coaxial drive inside a debris field," he said with a hint of anxious concern.

But Pendleton ignored him. Seeing that he was in front of the intruder, he turned the ship around and flew nose to nose with it for a few moments.

"Perforate that sucker!" he shouted.

But before Barker or Wen could react, the intruder dove down through the debris field and away from the Sergenious. Weed swore, back flipped the ship over a large asteroid behind him, and then dove down after the intruder. Everyone's stomachs churned in unison at the maneuver, even though they could feel none of the inertial effects of Pendleton's extreme flying. It was at this point that Pendleton started to take notice of the other ship's tactics.

"There's something familiar about that pilot's flying style," he thought.

"Intruder has emerged from the debris field and is closing on the Siberia and the Okinawa. It'll pass between both ships," said Martin.

"That's the threading the eye maneuver. If my guess is right, he'll go through, pull up, do a figure eight around the ships, and come out beside the Okinawa," thought Pendleton.

As soon as the intruder slipped between the ships, it pulled up just as he had predicted. He immediately pulled up in front of the Siberia and went over the top. Moments later the intruder appeared above the Siberia and found itself nose to nose with the Sergenious. It came to a full stop and stared at him in surprise. Pendleton smiled in satisfaction.

"Gotcha."

For several moments the two ships stood in open space and stared at each other. The Siberia and the Okinawa remained nearby, unable to see the intruder, but certain that the Sergenious could. They held their fire and waited patiently for word from Eric on what to do next. As they waited for the intruder's next move, Martin's console beeped.

Eric grunted in tense anticipation and said, "Lieutenant Martin, hail the…"

"Sir, You're not going to believe this, but the intruder is barking IDF," said Martin.

Eric looked at her curiously. "Barking IDF? Who is it?"

"It's reporting as the EX-33. It's the Onawaso, sir."

Pendleton perked up curiously. "The Onawaso? That's an experimental starship. Wait! No wonder I recognized those maneuvers!" said Pendleton.

"The intruder is decloaking, sir," said Sydney.

"Hold your fire," replied Eric.

To their complete surprise, a small, agile, experimental starship shimmered into view in front of them.

"Martin, verify what we're seeing is correct."

"Aye, sir. It's definitely the Onawaso."

"Hail them."

"Aye, sir."

Eric grit his teeth in anticipation as he waited for the reply. Moments later the image of a strapping young lieutenant commander appeared on his screen.

"Greetings commander. Would you mind lowering your weapons. We're on the same side here," he said with a grin and a chuckle.

But Eric was not amused. "If we're on the same side, why did you run us around like that?" he asked sternly.

"My apologies commander, but we were ordered by fleet R&D to come out here and conduct a test of your ship's capabilities and upgraded sensor array against our new updated cloaking and sublight engine systems. It seems that we still have a few bugs to iron out, but at least we know that your new sensors work well, as does our sublight engines," said the officer.

"If this was a test, why wasn't I informed!?" asked Eric angrily.

The officer shrugged. "If we had announced the test, it wouldn't have given us the results we wanted. By putting you into a situation where you had to use your ship and her new sensors to their fullest, we were able to acquire all of the testing data we needed. Anything less would have been unacceptable."

"Do you realize how close we came to killing you!? We could have shot you down! You and all of your men could have died for this stupid little test!"

The officer waved at Eric dismissively. "Nonsense. We had our best pilot at the helm, and the best shields in the fleet protecting us. We were never in any real danger."

Pendleton turned around and said, "That pilot wouldn't by chance be Lieutenant Robert Blakely, would it?"

The officer blinked in surprise. "Why, yes. How did you know?"

Pendleton grinned. "He was my academy training partner. I'd know his flight style half a sector away."

The officer laughed. "Yes, it's unique, is it not?"

Eric slammed his fist on the console. "Lieutenant Commander, I do not like being taken so lightly and I do not like the idea that you, or your commanders, felt it was alright to put this fleet, or my crew, in danger like this just to conduct one of your petty little experiments!" he shouted.

"Calm down, Commander. Everything's alright. We have permission from the Grand Admiral himself to do whatever is needed to test any of our new inventions for quality and viability. You just happened to be our latest choice for a test subject."

Eric squinted in disgust at the commander. "Understand this. I know of no such standing order. Therefore I am ordering you to land on the Siberia and surrender yourself, your crew and your ship to their custody."

The officer looked at Eric in surprise. "We can't do that! None of the people on that ship has the proper clearance to be near anything on this vessel! You should know that."

"And you broke a thousand rules out here today!"

"Sir, may I make a suggestion?" said Sarah.

Eric rubbed his forehead in frustration. "What is it?"

"I've done some research, and what he says is true. There apparently is such a standing order. Therefore I would recommend simply allowing them to return to fleet R&D as they are. He does not need to surrender his ship or his crew."

"But what about what he's done!?"

"Leave it up to the Admiral to decide if the commander stepped outside the bounds of his orders."

Eric sighed and frowned. "Fine. Commander, I want you to get back to fleet R&D immediately and don't you EVER do this to me again, understood?"

The officer nodded. "Crystal clear, sir."

The image clicked off moments later. Eric slumped back into his seat. Everyone looked at him in curiosity.

"What now, sir?" asked Martin.

Eric rubbed his eyes and said, "Martin, transmit a message to fleet command. Tell them the situation has been resolved and it's clear to stand down. Weed, set course for Pluto station, best possible speed. And when we get there, someone please find me the nearest pub so I can get myself a nice, stiff drink."

As Mike walked down a long hallway towards the conference rooms, dozens of thoughts wandered through his mind.

"Why would the Adjutant President be here, and why in the galaxy would he be traveling in a cargo vessel? Something's not right here," he thought.

As he walked, Sarah appeared next to him. Mike looked over in surprise. "What are you doing here? I thought you'd be with Chancellor Nordham," he said.

Sarah smiled. "Politics is as boring for you as it is for me. Besides, I'm your AI, and the Chancellor has his own assistants to help him out."

Mike smirked. "In other words, you left the Chancellor to flounder on his own with the Serians."

Sarah shrugged. "Something like that," she said with a sly grin.

As they continued, Sarah walked silently next to Mike and carefully studied his expressions.

"This meeting concerns you, doesn't it?" she said after several moments.

"It's not so much the meeting that concerns me, but rather who's at the meeting and how he got here. Someone of his rank and stature would not travel anywhere without a nice ship and significant protection. To do less would put him at too much risk. Yet he has. That's what bothers me the most."

Sarah nodded. "You're worried that something terrible has happened."

Mike nodded. "Or something will."

They continued on for another several minutes until an officer greeted them near the entrance to the secure conference rooms. Mike glanced around and spotted several armed guards that were positioned on both sides of the door and down the interior hallway.

"Grand Admiral, sir!" said the officer as he saluted.

"I'm here to see a special guest," said Mike.

The officer nodded. "Yes, sir. He's in conference room four," he said.

Mike motioned to the officer who nodded, and then lead them down a short hallway to a doorway emblazoned with a large blue number four.

"Your hand here, please, sir," said the officer as he pointed to a small palm scanner next to the door.

Mike placed his hand on the pad, waited a brief second, and then heard a welcome chirp acknowledging that it had identified him. The door unlocked and swung open.

"You may enter now, sir," said the officer.

Mike stepped through the door and then paused in surprise. In front of him sat a tall reptilian man in an ornate, high backed chair flanked by two servants and a small cadre of guards. He chewed on the body of a large rodent as Mike studied him curiously. The man studied him in return, as did his guards. Mike heard the door click shut behind him as he cocked an eyebrow in cautious curiosity.

"Greetings, V'sin. Nice to see you again," he said.

The reptilian man nodded. "It is equally of my pleasure to see you as well, old friend. However, my joy is tempered by a shadow that hangs over me."

"What do you mean?" asked Mike.

"Much has happened. But I cannot say immediately what it is."

"Why?"

"Because there are others here whom are not invited. I grow anxious at their presence."

Mike looked around the room curiously, and then back at V'sin. "What are you talking about?"

V'sin raised his webbed fingers and pointed one of them at Sarah.

"Her. Who is she?" asked V'sin.

"Her? Oh, yeah. Adjutant President V'sin, I'd like you to meet Sarah, my ship's AI," said Mike.

"A ship's AI? This far from it's vessel? How curious. I thought they were limited to just the confines of the ship and the immediate area around it."

Mike shrugged. "Normally they are. But Sarah is special. We're still not quite sure how she does it, but she's able to project herself anywhere she wants to, even up to considerable distances from the ship. Her somewhat strange ability allows her to accompany me wherever I go."

V'sin nodded. "Interesting. But if you do not know how she is able to do this, wouldn't it be reasonable to ask her, as she would be most likely to know?"

Sarah shook her head. "He already has."

"And you did not tell him?" asked V'sin.

Sarah shook her head.

"Why is that?" he asked.

Sarah shrugged. "Because I don't know how I do it. If I did, I would gladly share it with him."

V'sin nodded hesitantly. "Indeed. So you simply wish to be somewhere, and you are?"

Sarah nodded. "Something like that."

"Is there a limit to how far you can stray?"

Sarah shrugged. "I'm not sure. I know I can go anywhere I want to within Sol system, but I don't know how far beyond it I am able to travel."

"Why not?"

Sarah shrugged.

"Because I have no desire to leave this system, or to stray far from my Admiral. I try to stay close to him as much as I can, because I am his AI, and he is my Admiral."

V'sin nodded in understanding. "And are you able to cloak your presence, to hide within a room without being seen?"

Sarah shook her head. "I am not. If I am present within a room, I am in this form only. I have no other form. Especially one that is invisible."

This made V'sin feel more comfortable. "Interesting. So Admiral, would you trust this living program with your most valuable secrets?"

Mike nodded. "Sarah, like all AI's, is completely obedient and trustworthy. While her and the other AIs have free will, and thus the ability to disobey orders if they feel it's in our best interests, they have never revealed a single secret, even at the risk of their own destruction."

V'sin smiled. "A noble trait, even for a machine."

Mike nodded. "It is. So, tell me, why are you here? I doubt you showed up just to say hi."

V'sin folded his hands and stared hard at Mike. "No, I did not. I've come on business that is vital to the survival of both our species."

The hair on the back of Mike's head stood on end. Those were words he didn't like to hear.

"What is it that threatens both our races?" he asked.

V'sin sighed. "I'm not sure how to tell you this, but my government has been overthrown. I am now a fugitive, hunted mercilessly by my enemies, each of whom wish to kill me."

Mike's jaw dropped like a rock. His mind reeled with questions, as well as many frightening thoughts. The Gayik'von were the protectors of Sol system. If someone hostile to Earth had overthrown the Gayik'Von government, the human race was in a lot of trouble.

After several moments, he collected himself and said, "When? Who's responsible?"

V'sin waved his hands dismissively. "The details are unnecessary. What is important however, is why I've come here and requested to speak with you. I wish to request asylum."

Chapter 6

Alfred looked over the tactical reports for the afternoon and shook his head.

"R&D has done a lot of stupid things in the past in the name of research, but this is ridiculous," he said with a hint of frustration.

An officer in front of him nodded. "Commander Eric is fairly put off about this too, sir," he said.

Alfred tossed the small data tablet onto his desk and said, "I can imagine. I'm surprised he didn't put a torpedo through their bridge just out of spite. Well, either way, what those R&D idiots did needs to be dealt with. I'm sick and tired of their cowboy research and testing methods. I want Captain Olm in here, in front of my desk, in the next fifteen minutes, no excuses. This nonsense ends today, period."

The officer saluted. "Yes, sir!"

As the officer slipped out of the office, Alfred picked up another data tablet and studied it. He grinned.

"So it would seem that the Chancellor's decision to isolate our Serian visitors on Pluto station has proven to be a wise choice. Well, it should be interesting to see how this develops." His communicator chimed. Pressing his ear, he said, "This is Admiral Bofenheiser."

"Admiral, this is Bentley from production. I just wanted to let you know that we're going to be a couple weeks late delivering the last of the shield satellites for the barrier."

Alfred rubbed his forehead in frustration. "You're already two months behind now, Bentley. What's the holdup this time?"

"Well, we're having problems creating sufficient quantities of the alloys we need. For some reason, the processes we've used countless times before just aren't producing the same amount of material that they used to."

"Then update the processes," said Alfred with a hint of frustration.

"Well, we're working on that, but in the meantime we've slowed down production in order to ensure that all of the alloy produced is of the best quality."

Alfred sighed heavily. "Fine. Just get things straightened out over there, and do it soon. The Grand Admiral would like to have the rest of the perimeter upgrades done in the next thirty days."

"Understood, sir. Bentley out."

Alfred shook his head. "Sometimes I wish I could just delegate this whole stupid perimeter upgrade project to someone else. But it's too important to us, and Mike especially, to trust its completion to anyone else." He leaned back in his chair and thought for several moments, and then smiled. "Well, at least I'm not entertaining a large group of overgrown bats."

He picked up another data pad, leaned back in his chair and began to read. But as he did, his mind wandered back to the shield array and Bentley's comments. He mulled them over in his mind for several minutes, and then got up from his chair. Grabbing two of the data pads and another small device, he strolled through his door and into the atrium.

"Ensign, I'm going to visit the main production facility and talk with Mr. Bentley about the shield array. When Captain Olm gets here, tell him to take a seat and wait for me. He is not to leave under any circumstances. I'll be back to deal with him later. Understood?"

The secretary nodded. "Crystal clear, sir," he said.

Alfred pressed his ear and said, "Call transporter system." When a soft computer voice answered asking him his destination, he said, "Production, please."

Moments later a silver sphere of energy appeared, engulfed him and then vanished, leaving nothing behind.

"I am curious about your people who live on your home world. You say that you are trying to advance them to where they can be introduced to your technology without risk of harm to their culture. Yet I have heard that they are already beginning to consider such ideas on their own," said the chief Serian diplomat.

Nordham smiled. "Who do you think gave them those ideas?"

"You did?" said the diplomat in surprise.

Nordham nodded. "There are many of our people spread out among their nations, working with them directly in an effort to advance their technology to a level near or equal to our own. It was decided in the early 1940's, during World War

Two, that we needed to take an active role in helping them rise up from the primitive, self interested lives they were living, and evolve into a more civilized and advanced lifestyle. The medium we chose for that effort was their rapidly growing information and media infrastructures. That included comic books, movies, newspapers, television and much more. Through these mediums, we introduced the concepts necessary for advancement in ways they could digest, slowly adjusting their minds in order to prepare for our eventual introduction to them."

"But isn't that a direct violation of your law of first contact you claim to cherish and abide by?"

Nordham shook his head. "Not really. The seeds of such change were already there. We simply watered and nurtured them by providing the ideas and means to advance, and the encouragement to do so. From there they did the rest on their own. We still periodically inject new technology and ideas into their society to help them along, but only when and where necessary."

"What if they reject your ideas?"

Nordham shrugged. "If they're not willing to advance on their own, then they simply remain where they are. We will not force them to change. But we do encourage them to continue forward, despite their reservations."

"Then you do follow your law of first contact."

Nordham nodded. "To the best of our ability and in our own unique way."

"Then all their current technology is of your design?"

Nordham shrugged. "Some is, some isn't. Much of the technology they have today was of their design. We merely introduced the concepts and they did the rest. There are a few things that we had direct responsibility for, but those were only for the purpose of moving them forward in an area of technology that had become stagnant."

The diplomat nodded. "So that would tend to explain the rapid progression of your species from a primitive, ignorant race, to one of such technological prowess."

Nordham shrugged. "Well, our rate of progress is different than that of our brethren on Earth. We have always desired to push the boundaries of science. They, on the other hand, have been content to remain where they were for long periods of time."

The diplomat nodded. "Indeed. So what exactly have you offered the people of your world since becoming an active part in their advancement?"

"Well, a lot actually. Some ideas we've presented were unique and had never before been suggested. There were others, though, which had already found their way into their society. These ideas were simply improved, expanded and updated as our understanding of the science and technology behind them grew."

"What concepts were these?"

"There were quite a few actually. Far too many to list though. However, there are some you may recognize, such as warp drive, hyper drive, FTL flight, shields, galactic government, wormholes, transporters and other such things. The rest they created or thought of on their own. In fact, we've actually gotten several good ideas from them in return."

The diplomat nodded. "Then they are moving in the direction you wish them to?"

"Not exactly. But they are at least making progress in the right directions. Well, for the most part anyways. They still in many ways suffer from the same fear, lust, greed and desire for power that kept them stagnant for so many millennia. As you may know, the nine ancient races did not suffer from this failing in their societies, and thus they blossomed early. Like us, they were always interested in exploring the farthest reaches of possibility, and only stagnated once they had grown to a level that properly satisfied all their needs. Only a few of their own wished to cling to the old ways. We, on the other hand, are quite the opposite, as our ancestors clung tightly to the old ways, never desiring to change, and always wanting to remain in their comfortable little cocoons, oblivious to the change that was occurring around them while a handful relentlessly sought to advance themselves. In many cases they even killed those who sought change in order to delay its inevitable arrival. Those that escaped this persecution gathered together for strength, eventually leading to the formation of the Brayburn Society, which was the foundation for what we are today."

The diplomat looked curiously at Nordham. "If your numbers had grown such that you could form an alliance for strength, why could you not use that strength to change the world around you?"

Nordham sighed. "Because we will not force our will upon others. We will encourage, coax and sometimes prod, but ultimately it is up to those who are being pushed to either move, or stay put. We will not force them. We learned early on that pushing our people faster than they are ready to move can prove deadly. Anytime we did in the past, society fought back, and many of our brethren died as a result. That is why we eventually adopted the 'coax, don't force' policy. But even that wasn't enough as we were repeatedly attacked for our forward-thinking ways. This lead to us eventually being forced to seek refuge in space to escape the persecution. Out here we are not limited to the confines of polite society. Here we can expand and explore without boundaries or limits, ever improving ourselves, and those around us. One of the long held statutes of the Society is that no scientific effort will be denied or forbidden, so long as it does not lead to the harm of another lifeform."

The diplomat cocked his head in curiosity. "I find that statute to be intriguing, given that you have one of the most powerful armadas in the region," he said.

Nordham grinned sheepishly. "That was not our original desire. We are a peaceful people, and thus detest war. But the galaxy is a dangerous place, and those without adequate protection are only hiding behind a veil of false security. While there are many who respect our sovereignty, there are others who detest it, and will stop at nothing to see us exploited, or even wiped from existence."

"Then your fleet is merely for self protection?"

Nordham nodded.

"But why? You have the sworn protection of the Gayik'Von and many others. Are they not sufficient to ensure your safety?" asked the diplomat.

Nordham shook his head. "No, they are not. While we appreciate all that the Gayik'Von have done for us, they are only a few among thousands, even if they are one of the nine. Plus it would be irresponsible of us not to at least do our part, however feeble it may be, to ensure our own protection. It was once said that 'He who does not carry his own sword, even though he have a thousand legions by his side, is a fool and deserves whatever death fate may bring him.' So in a way, our fleet is our sword, and the Gayik'Von, and all those who protect us, are our thousand legions."

The diplomat grinned. "Well said, and comforting to know."

Nordham cocked an eyebrow curiously. "How so?" he asked.

"There are many within this galaxy that see your sword as something much greater than it is. It is reassuring to know that it is not as dangerous as some might believe."

Nordham smirked. "We seem to be misunderstood a lot these days. Many fear us, because they do not understand us. I fail to understand how such a small fleet of ships, overseeing a backwards and primitive people, would be something that would elicit such fear among so many in this galaxy and beyond."

The diplomat shook his head. "It is not those in the galaxies beyond ours that fear you. Only those within this one."

"Well, at least that's somewhat reassuring."

"How so?" asked the diplomat curiously.

Nordham smiled. "It means we're not quite as hated as we could be."

The diplomat grinned slyly. "When I first came here, my image of your people was one of fear and uncertainty. I see that I was wrong."

"And how do you see us now?" asked Nordham.

"I see a young race who seeks knowledge before war, and wisdom over conquest. You are not a race to be feared, but rather one to be embraced."

Nordham bowed slightly. "I thank you for your kind words, but they are only partially true. There are many on Earth who still carry a desire for blood."

The diplomat nodded. "Yes, but they are not the ones to be feared. You are. As one of our ancient philosophers once said, 'It is not the one who growls in the corner at you that you must fear, but rather he who stands before you with a sword.' They are the ones who growl in the corner, but you have the sword. Therefore, if we are not to fear you, then we need not fear them either."

Nordham grinned. "Hmm, that's an interesting way to look at it. I honestly hadn't thought of it that way."

The Serian smiled slyly. "Even creatures such as ourselves have great wisdom which we can bestow."

Nordham bowed slightly. "And it is wisdom most graciously bestowed and accepted."

Alfred walked down a long hallway filled with men in white lab coats, some with hair, some without, some with safety goggles, others with glasses, but each one on a mission of their own. He felt like the odd duck of the group, so strikingly out of place in his military uniform among a sea of white clad workers. He grinned slightly as he thought about all of the raw brain power passing by him in the hallway. He soon rounded a corner and headed towards a door marked "Foundry". As the door opened in front of him, his ears were assaulted by the roar of machinery as his nose was pounded by the smell of hot metals and ozone. He put his fingers in his ears as he held his breath against the odors. To one side of the room sat a control booth, inside which stood two men in white jackets who appeared to be screaming at each other. Alfred's eyes narrowed as he turned and approached the booth. Slipping inside he spotted Bentley talking with a man who sat behind a control panel for the robotic forge.

"I'm telling you, the part is faulty and it needs to be replaced!" shouted Bentley.

"And I'm telling you that it's brand new!" replied the man.

"I don't care if it's brand new or not. If it doesn't work right, replace it."

"It's not the unit. It's your stupid alloy."

"The alloy formula hasn't changed since we began this project eight years ago. If the formula isn't broken, then it's the forge."

"The forge has worked correctly this whole time. Nothing's changed!"

"Yes it has! Your forge is broken, and I've already told you what needs to be fixed! So either fix it, or I'll get someone down here who will fix it! I need more alloy in order to finish building these shield nodes, and your stubborn stupidity is hindering my work!"

The man crossed his arms and stared defiantly at Bentley. "I'm telling you, nothing is broken. Now hike your two bit arrogant butt out of here and let me do my job."

Bentley clenched his fists and growled angrily at the man. "Ya know, this is the exact reason I'm behind! This...this...this...incompetence of yours!"

"Your attitude isn't exactly helping much either," said Alfred.

Bentley spun around in surprise. "Admiral! What are you doing down here?"

Alfred shrugged. "I had time to kill, and a subordinate to sweat, so I came over to check on you and find out what the holdup was. From what I can see, it's the fault of a man who can't ever admit he might be wrong," said Alfred.

"I'm not wrong because nothing I'm doing is wrong! Nor is my forge broke! It's this whole stupid alloy of his. It's an utter joke! He'd rather complain about my equipment malfunctioning, which it most certainly is not, instead of realizing that the whole problem is in his alloy formula! It looks like it was written by a monkey!" said the forge operator.

"A monkey? A monkey!?" screamed Bentley.

"Gentlemen, please. I'm more worried about getting the last of these nodes finished and in place than I am about pandering to your petty little arguments over who's homosapius superior. Now either you get this sorted out on your own, or I'll bring the director in on this."

The forge operator grunted. "Fine, but I still say I'm right."

"Regardless of which of us is right, the Admiral is correct. We need to sort this out. How about we get Dr. Corbin down here. The design was originally his," said Bentley.

The forge operator looked curiously at Bentley. "I thought this alloy was your idea."

"The original alloy was his. I simply developed the process to create it and tweaked the formula slightly to make it possible to mass produce it," said Bentley.

The forge operator pursed his lips and looked at Alfred, and then back at Bentley. He nodded towards the console and said, "So this alloy is his?"

Bentley nodded. "He created it, so I think he'd be the best one to fix it."

"That might be a bit difficult. At least for the near future anyways," said Alfred.

"Why's that?" asked Bentley. "Because he's down with a cold right now. He should be back to work tomorrow," said Alfred.

The forge operator smirked and looked at Bentley. "Well, given recent events, how about we call a truce until we can run this past the doctor. If the problems are his, or they turn out to be mine, I'll apologize. If not, you're still a monkey."

Bentley grinned slyly. "Want a banana? I have plenty to spare."

Chapter 7

"Wait, let me get this straight. You want to request asylum from us?" said Mike.

V'sin nodded. "May I ask why?" asked Mike.

"It is very simple. I have no one I can turn to that I trust."

"Well it's nice that you thought of us, but we can't house you or give you asylum. We've got enough of our own problems to deal with, and the last thing we need right now is to deal with an issue of asylum. Especially considering that you're hiding from those who overthrew your government."

V'sin crossed his hands and stared deeply at Mike. "There is still a large contingent of our fleet and many in our army who still stand behind me. With your help we could easily restore the government and install me as President. Once restored to office I could punish those who would so willingly destroy what we have spent millennia building. With your ships, and their advanced weapons and cloaking capabilities, we could easily sneak into the..."

"Whoa, wait. I don't know what kind of dispute you have with your government or whoever's in charge now, but we can't get involved. First off, it's not my decision. Something like that would have to go through the Chancellor. And even if you told him about this, he'd probably say exactly the same thing I would. Earthfleet is not an all powerful military force. We're merely here to protect Earth, nothing more. Besides, there's no way we could go on the offensive, even if we wanted to. We don't have enough ships for starters. We barely have enough to do the job we're doing right now."

"But if we provided you with the resources, manpower and materials you needed, you could build a fleet that would rival any other in the galaxy!"

Mike waved his hands dismissively. "That's another thing. We don't share our technology with anybody, anywhere, anytime, for any reason whatsoever. We depend on that technology for our survival, and if someone circumvented it, or found countermeasures that would wipe away our technological advantage, we would be vulnerable to whoever wanted to attack us. And from my understanding, there's a lot of them standing in line, waiting for just that chance. There's too much at stake. We can't risk it."

"Then you will not help me? Even after all that the Gayik'Von have done for you?"

Mike shook his head. "I can't. As much as I'd like to, I can't. I realize you're my friend and I'd love to do something to help you, but I can't. My hands are tied, both by rule and the harsh truth of reality."

V'sin nodded reservedly. "Then I guess that all our years of assistance and protection means nothing to you."

Mike shook his head. "No, no, they mean a lot to us, but we're not strong enough to protect you, or fight with you, or even for you. Right now our priority is to our people, and them alone. If we were stronger, then we might consider helping you in any way we could, but that likely won't happen for at least a millennia or more. There are over eight billion people on Earth, most of which still live in blissful ignorance of our existence, while you have over six hundred worlds, with well over ten billion of your people on each of them. The other eight are just the same, not counting all the minor races and their worlds. That immediately makes us severely outnumbered. So anything we could do for you would be like a fly biting a horse. A simple flick of the tail and we'd be gone."

V'sin pursed his lips. "I see. And will you turn me over to my pursuers?" he asked.

"If they ask, yes. We'd have no other choice but to comply with their wishes."

"What if they attacked you in an effort to get to me? What would you do then?"

Mike furrowed his brow. "We'd defend ourselves obviously, but we wouldn't go beyond that, and we certainly wouldn't hand you over to them if they did. We don't negotiate with people who threaten our lives."

V'sin nodded. "And what if you were to pretend that we were not here?"

Mike shook his head. "That wouldn't work either. There are too many eyes out there watching this system. They likely already know you're here. And even if they don't, they'll find out soon enough. So in the end there's still nothing we can do for you. All we can do now is ask you to leave. We can't risk your presence here."

V'sin nodded. "I understand. Then you have brought your own doom upon yourselves, for I can attest that those who are now in power will in no way ensure your protection." Mike sighed. He felt as though he was betraying his friend, but at the same time he knew that to take sides in this conflict would be worse than taking none. He shrugged.

"Then we will do the best we can on our own. But no matter what happens, we still can't help you."

V'sin stood up and stuck out his chest in defiance as he tossed back the trains of his tunic in anger. "I suspect that you would gladly hide a wanted criminal before you would hide me!"

"No, I wouldn't. Our rule of 'no asylum' applies to everyone, criminal and politician alike. If they're a visiting dignitary, we'll guarantee them safe passage and ample protection while they're here, as per diplomatic regulation, but we do not, nor will ever grant asylum. Even if we wanted to, we're just not strong enough to do it, no matter how much we'd want to. And I don't see that changing anytime soon. Now, please, you must leave before anyone knows you're here. If the Gayik'Von are under new leadership, I'd prefer to stay on their good side as much as possible."

V'sin grinned and nodded. "Then you have passed our test."

Mike nodded, and then paused. "Wait, what? Test?" he said in surprise.

V'sin tilted his head back and laughed boisterously. Mike cocked his head in confusion.

"You have been tested, my friend, and found desirable."

"Wait, this was a test? Then everything you told me was just part of an elaborate ruse?" said Mike in surprise.

V'sin nodded. "I must apologize for deceiving you, my friend. It pains me to have done this, but I was asked by the members of the galactic community to come in the guise of a fugitive in need of aid in order to test you," said V'sin.

"But why? What'd we do this time that we suddenly needed to prove ourselves?" asked Mike.

"You did nothing. You were simply you. What you do not understand, Admiral, is that there are members in the galactic community that fear you, fear what you have become, and the impressive strength you have gained in such a short time."

Mike cocked an eyebrow. "I wouldn't call it impressive. Sufficient maybe, but not impressive, and certainly nothing to be feared."

V'sin nodded. "Yes, but fear has a strange ability to distort reality, making great monsters out of simple shadows. Some of this fear comes from the fact that your ships are many times more powerful, faster, and more advanced than theirs."

Mike shrugged. "Well, it's not our problem if they want to sit on their thumbs and stagnate rather than continue to advance themselves. We're certainly not going to just sit around and do nothing. It's in our blood to always explore, expand and seek out knowledge."

V'sin nodded. "As it should be. One should always seek one's own future, even if others do not. However, that still doesn't change the fact that they are afraid you might seek to leave Sol and stretch out across the galaxy, conquering all you encounter."

"Pfft. We'd have to be awfully desperate to do that."

V'sin nodded. "Yes, you would, and it's that desperation they fear, especially with the resources of Earth being quickly depleted and it's environment destroyed," he said.

Mike frowned in disgust. "Yeah, well, we're trying to get them to change that. But trying to talk to greed is like talking to a brick wall."

V'sin chuckled. "I can imagine."

Mike sighed. "So, if you're not really a fugitive, can I assume that you won't be staying here long?"

V'sin shook his head. "No, I won't, much to my regret. I need to return to the capital. There is much that needs my attention."

"Well then, how about I wrestle up a ship that can take you home?"

V'sin shook his head. "My ship and its escort wait just beyond your sensor range. When I signal for them, they will come."

He turned around and motioned to one of his servants who pulled a small communicator out of his pocket and tried to raise V'sin's diplomatic cruiser.

"Uh, I'd suggest going out into the main promenade before you do that. These conference rooms are shielded, so no signals get in or out, unless they are fleet-approved."

V'sin cocked an eyebrow and grinned. "Only fleet-approved signals? What would those be?"

"Just command channels mostly. Mine's one of them."

V'sin nodded. "Ah, a wise decision. Then if we must, let us go to your promenade so that we may call our ships."

Mike motioned towards the door. "Alright, this way please. One of the guards can show you to a good place to get the best reception."

"Will you not be escorting us personally?" asked V'sin in surprise.

Mike shook his head. "I've got to get back to Chancellor Nordham. He's entertaining a group of Serian diplomats."

V'sin's eyes narrowed. "Why are such dreadful creatures on your station?"

Mike shrugged. "They said they wanted to open up diplomatic discussions with us, and the Chancellor was happy to oblige."

V'sin nodded reservedly. "Indeed. Then take me to see your Chancellor. I wish to have a few words with your Serian visitors."

Lars Nordic was a master of the ancient art of cloak and dagger. From a little child he had dreamed of being a secret agent for the Society, a man of shadows and intrigue. Now he was one, and one of the best as well. While he was a man of many mysteries, Lars was also one of the most trusted field agents in the Society Intelligence Corps. Normally he was assigned to investigate and observe the operations of Black Orchid on Earth, a task he was very good at, but today he had a special assignment: Observing the Serian diplomats. Lars rounded a corner as he studied the three bat-like Serians and their four semi-humanoid Aldovian servants. The Serians had been fairly docile most of the day, and lacked many of the usual incriminating traits of his regular quarry. However, their servants appeared to be more on par with what he was expecting.

Numerous times that day his team had captured devices that the servants had placed on various desks, and in hidden corners along their way, in an attempt to bug the station and possibly grab some valuable data for their Juinah masters.

"The ship is clear. All spying equipment has been either neutralized or rendered null functional. They'll be two sectors away before they realize their instruments are giving them nothing but dummy data," came a voice over his communicator.

He pressed his ear and whispered, "Good job. Now get out of there. Once you're clear, post two people nearby and watch that ship like a hawk. The rest of you get down to section four of the promenade. The diplomats are moving into the guilds area."

"Roger that," came the reply.

"Agent two oh seven, have you recovered any more of their devices?"

"Negative. If they've planted any more recently, they've done it in a way I can't detect."

"Well then gather your team and sweep the promenade thoroughly once they are out of sight. I don't want to miss anything they may have left behind, intentionally or otherwise," said Lars.

"Yes, sir," came the reply.

Lars slipped into a nearby pub and lingered in the doorway as Chancellor Nordham, the Serians, their servants, and a small cadre of guards made their way further down the promenade. He watched in interest as one of the servants brushed past a data panel which flickered briefly.

"Two one nine, did that servant just bug that panel?" he asked over the communicator.

"Can't tell. Want me to check it out?"

"Yes, please."

"Alright, I'm on it."

Lars nibbled at his lower lip. He wasn't liking this one bit. The servants were slick at what they were doing. Almost too slick.

"It's been tagged. I'm going to take it offline until we can clean it," said the agent.

"Get an engineering team over here to verify the integrity of that panel before you bring it back up."

"Will do."

He slipped out of the doorway of the pub and moved casually down the promenade until he reached another store where he pretended to examine some merchandise. He watched carefully out of the corner of an eye as one of the servants reached out to put a bug on a nearby soldier, and then withdrew his arm.

"Alright, that's enough. Teams three and two, move in. We're going to end this little charade and...wait, hold. Something's happening." He watched curiously as a tall, well dressed Gayik'Von man walked up to Nordham. His eyes went wide as he realized who it was. "Oh, this is interesting. What's he doing here?" he thought to himself.

"Sir, what should we do?" came a voice over his communicator.

"Continue sweeping the area for now. Ensure that the servants haven't left any more 'surprises' for us."

"Yes, sir."

He turned and stepped away from the shop slightly and zeroed in on the Serians. He grinned. "This should be fun to watch."

Nordham stared in curiosity as V'sin strolled up to him. "Adjutant President V'sin! I didn't know you were coming!" he said in surprise.

"Neither did I," said Mike.

"He is here on a special ambassadorial visit. He wished to speak with the Grand Admiral in private. Hence why you were not notified of his arrival," said Sarah.

Nordham looked curiously at Mike, who waved his hand dismissively, and said, "I'll fill you in later."

V'sin turned and glared harshly at the three Serian diplomats who seemed to almost shrivel up in fear.

"What is your purpose here," he said sternly.

"We...we...we're just here on a d-d-diplomatic mission," stuttered one of the Serians.

"Diplomatic mission indeed." He walked up and stood nose to nose with one of the Serians. "This wouldn't by chance have something to do with a request by your Juinah masters to gather information about the Gin, would it?"

"NO!" shrieked the Serian nervously.

V'sin watched as the diplomat twitted his fingers anxiously. He grinned.

"Just as I thought. Chancellor, your guests are not here on a mission of diplomacy, but rather one of espionage."

Nordham looked at the Serians as he cocked an eyebrow in disgust. "We suspected as much. So as a precaution, we had them isolated here, and then followed the moment they arrived."

He motioned to several men further down the promenade. Lars was the first to arrive.

"Have our guests been dishonest in their actions?" asked Nordham.

Lars nodded. "We've identified quite a number of attempted hacks, bugs, and spying attempts by them and their servants. All have been neutralized," he said.

Nordham nodded. "As I thought. Lieutenant, would you kindly escort these men and their servants to their ship, and then see to it that they're taken outside the perimeter as soon as possible."

"Yes, sir!" said the officer.

Nordham then looked at the Serian and said, "Know this. Because of your treachery and treason, from here on out, all Serians are banned from Sol space until further notice."

V'sin grinned as the Serians and their servants were escorted away, whimpering and quivering in fear. "Detestable creatures they are," he said with a hint of disgust.

"Well, that was kind of my initial assessment of them too," said Mike.

Nordham nodded. "It's a good thing we took your advice to be cautious of them."

"My advice?" asked V'sin curiously.

Nordham shook his head. "Well, not yours specifically. We've been reading the species database you gave us. It's proved invaluable in learning how to deal with each of the races we've encountered. It's been a godsend for diplomatic relations."

V'sin grinned. "I am glad you are pleased with our gift. Now, if you will excuse me, I must return and give my report to those who sent me."

"Can't you stay a little longer?"

V'sin shook his head. "I was to return as soon as our meeting was over. Your Grand Admiral can fill you in on the details of what occurred."

Nordham nodded and looked at Mike. "Right. Then I'll look forward to reading his report."

He then turned and bowed to V'sin. "It was a pleasure having you, even if your visit was brief. May I walk you to your ship?"

V'sin smiled and nodded. "Yes, you may."

Chapter 8

A grayish sphere of energy appeared in the middle of the bridge and immediately vanished, leaving Mike behind. Sarah shimmered into view moments later.

"Ah, Admiral. How was the meeting with the Serians? What were they like?" asked Sydney.

"It was like meeting Count Dracula's pet bats."

"Dracula had pets?"

Mike grinned. He then looked over at Eric and noticed his frustrated, and overly stressed expression.

"Is something the matter?" he asked.

Eric picked up a data pad and gently tossed it to Mike.

"Take a look," he said, running his fingers through his hair in an expression of anxious disgust. Mike's eyes narrowed as he read the report. "Admiral Bofenheiser is handling the dressing down right now, sir. But I think you may want to put in your two bits on this since it was your order that started this mess."

"And this happened while I was gone?" asked Mike.

Eric nodded. "Not five minutes after you left the ship, sir."

Mike grunted angrily. "Corbin really stepped over the line on this one," he said.

"But didn't you tell him he could do anything he needed to achieve his research? That was at least my understanding of your orders to him."

"Within reason. My orders were that he could do whatever he needed to, within reason. This is not within reason," said Mike angrily.

He looked up at Sarah and said, "Would you send me over to Command One? I need to talk to Admiral Bofenheiser."

"Where specifically would you like to be placed?" asked Sarah.

"Wherever he is, preferably."

"Understood," she replied.

A grayish sphere of energy engulfed Mike and then vanished, leaving nothing behind. Eric sighed.

"Alright, well, apparently the Admiral doesn't need us to transport him back. Martin, you've got engineering and Con. Sydney and I are going to transport back to Command One where I plan to get a good long nap. Unless the world is coming to an end, don't call me. No, actually, don't call me even then."

Pendleton grinned. "Yes, sir. Have a good nap."

Eric smirked. "I hope it's more than a nap."

Alfred looked up as Mike appeared on the carpet in front of his desk.

"Hello, sir. What brings you here?" he asked.

"Where's Corbin?" asked Mike, a hint of anger in his voice.

"In sickbay with the flu. Why? Is it because of the incident earlier near Pluto station?"

Mike nodded. "I'm going to launch his butt out the nearest airlock as soon as I'm done chewing it off."

Alfred raised an eyebrow. "Oh? Then I take it you haven't received the updated report yet?"

Mike looked curiously at him and said, "What updated report?"

Alfred nodded. "I'll take that as a no. Well, here's the summary of what I've learned about the incident. Apparently Dr. Blank, Corbin's assistant, has been going apenuts for the past month wanting to test his new sublight drive system and cloaking device against the best in the fleet. Currently, that's your ship. He felt that a live-fire real-world engagement with a crew that thought they were dealing with a hostile enemy would provide the best testing scenario for the new system.

Dr. Corbin disagreed. So when Corbin fell ill, the doctor decided to take things into his own hands. The rest you should already know."

Mike grunted. "There are times when I hate over-zealous scientists," he said.

Alfred furrowed his brow in interest. "It's those over zealous scientists who have brought us to where we are today."

Mike waved his hand dismissively. "That's not what I mean. Being overly zealous and productive is one thing. But potentially causing an intergalactic incident and the potential deaths of numerous civilian and fleet personnel in favor of a more aggressive testing method that goes beyond reason and sanity is just unacceptable!"

Alfred nodded. "Understandably so, but the situation is taken care of. No need to bother yourself further with it."

Mike frowned. "I hope so. Well, anyhow, since I'm here, there's something else I needed to talk to you about. I'm thinking we may want to start expanding our spying program. Half the galaxy is ticked off at us, and I'd like to find out why. I know the so-called 'official' reasons for it, but I feel there's more to this than just a bunch of politicians with their panties in a knot. So we need to find out who started all this and why."

"So you feel that there's one person or group behind all this?"

Mike nodded. "It can't be an accident that we've suddenly become feared by so many races, given our relative insignificance in the galaxy."

"Well, from what I understand, our recent rate of technological advancement has been significantly higher than any other race in the history of the known galaxy, including the nine races. It's possible that our sudden rise from a relatively primitive race to a technological giant in only a few centuries scares the heck out of them. We spent nearly fifty six hundred years more or less as savages by their standards, and now we're suddenly a technological powerhouse. If I were an intelligent, well-educated alien species, I'd be a little worried too. Our technological evolution is not typical in the galaxy. Most races like ourselves would require at least another couple of millennia to achieve even half the technology we have now, assuming that our rate of technological advancement continued as it had."

Mike nodded. "That makes sense. But then again, we have reasons for our sudden increase in technology. The first is the Brayburn Society. Its formation opened doors for the free, unrestricted advancement of technology by those among mankind who wished to push the bounds of science. The other is the fact that the Juinah decided to stick a couple million tons of starship in our face as soon as we stepped into space, threatening our very existence. Those two alone are enough to encourage any race to push their technology forward as fast as they can."

Alfred shrugged. "Threats against one's personal safety have been the greatest driving force of innovation in our history. You either advance or you die. It's that simple."

Mike frowned. "I wish that wasn't the case. But pitting our little fleet against a huge enemy with seemingly limitless resources is a bit frightening."

"Well, in time we might become powerful enough to at least make them think twice about harming us. In the meantime, we have to use less direct methods to dissuade them."

Mike nodded. "Yeah, and I hope that our guns become scary enough that we never have to use them."

Alfred nodded. "Yes, me too."

Mike smiled. "Well anyways, back to what we were talking about. I think we need to do a bit of nosing around in the galactic community. It's time we figure out who we're dealing with and why they hate us so much."

Alfred nodded. "I'd like to know that as well. It bothers me that this has grown into something so large as to engulf four of the nine races and close to half of the minor races. Having half the galaxy hating you without reason and wishing for your destruction is enough to make anyone nervous."

Mike nodded. "And I think we're going to need our inside experts on this one."

"Who did you have in mind?"

"When I approached the Serian delegates, Lars Nordic appeared out of nowhere and confronted them with some very incriminating evidence. But what impressed me the most was that you couldn't tell he was human until you saw his face. His disguise was so perfect that

I thought he was one of the alien merchants who frequent the promenade."

Alfred nodded. "I've heard about him as well. He's our top man in the intelligence corps, and an expert on Black Orchid. He's been decorated numerous times for his efforts to keep those lunatics in check."

Mike perked up in surprise. "So you've heard about him?"

Alfred nodded. "Likely in the same way you have. His last mission against Black Orchid set them back at least ten years or more. He was also mentioned by name in five of the last eight major intelligence reports of the past month."

"So, do you think we should send him out to spy on the locals for a while?" asked Mike.

Alfred nodded. "He would make a good choice. But he can't go alone. So I've also picked three other men as well to go with him. Namely his partner Vladimir Umnov, and the spy team of Antonio Garcia and Bob Landers. They come very highly recommended from the director of the intelligence corps."

Mike nodded. "Sounds like you've already been doing your homework."

Alfred grinned. "I saw this coming, so I did a little planning ahead."

Mike nodded. "Well done. I look forward to knowing what our neighbors are having for breakfast before the end of the week."

Alfred grinned. "Would you like a summary, or the whole messy details?"

Mike smirked. "I'd like to be able to eat tomorrow, so just send me the briefs."

Alfred nodded.

Lars studied his orders. "About time they got around to this. I was starting to get worried that our mission would get scrubbed and we'd be back to babysitting Black Orchid," he muttered.

Vlad chuckled. "You worry too much. Our mission will go just fine."

"I'm not worried about the mission. I was worried about being bored senseless. Black Orchid has gotten too predictable lately. And when your prey is predictable, the joy of the hunt becomes the monotony of experience."

Landers laughed. "I think Lars is what the planetsiders call an 'adrenaline junkie'. He lives for the thrill of the chase."

Lars glared at Landers, but said nothing. As they continued to banter back and forth between themselves, a tall, muscular, older gentleman walked into the room.

"Ah, director, to what do we owe this honor?" said Landers.

The older man grunted. "Cut the bull Landers. I'm just here to give you your mission briefs. Read and memorize them. You may not have time to reference them once you're in the field operating incognito with the locals. As for your transportation, you'll be flying out on the Onegai and the Appalachia. They're scheduled to depart at zero seven hundred hours. Don't be late."

"Two ships, sir? That seems a bit much for a mission with only four guys," said Landers.

"You're operating as separate teams. I requisitioned two ships so if you needed to split up, you won't be inconveniencing each other during the mission. Plus I'd feel more comfortable having two Samurai class ships out there with you than just one. With two ships, if something happens to the one, the other can come to its aid," said the older man.

"Do we have any grunts to fall back on, or are we two-man solo?" asked Lars.

"You're solos. So no grunts, fleet or droids. It's just you and your partner. And if you get caught, we don't know you. Remember, you're incognito. So don't take any chances. I don't want to hear that you did something stupid and got caught. Just get out there, find out who's behind all this human hating, and get back here as quickly as you can with the information. Understood?"

The four men nodded.

"Good, now get your butts out there and get to work."

Toby studied the bridge of his ship and admired its state of the art simplicity. While it was one of the more advanced ship killers in the fleet, it also had one of the simplest control interfaces around. He glanced over at his helm, tactical, and operations officers.

"Sir, Lars Nordic and his partner are requesting permission to come aboard," said the operations officer.

"Well, it's about bloody time. Bring them up," said Toby.

A sphere of grayish light appeared briefly on the bridge and was replaced by Lars and Vladimir.

"Permission to come aboard," said Lars.

Toby nodded. "Aye, permission granted. But you two take your sweet time, eh?"

Lars nodded. "We would have been here sooner, but we got held up by the old man."

Toby nodded in understanding. "Been there myself a few times. I'm Lieutenant Commander Tobias. You can call me Toby," he said, holding out his hand.

Lars stared at it briefly, but kept his hands crossed in front of him.

"How soon can we get underway?" asked Lars.

Toby withdrew his hand awkwardly and frowned slightly.

"Right now, I suspect. I just need to check with the Onegai to be sure they've taken aboard their passengers," he said.

"No need, sir. The Onegai just reported that they're ready to depart when we are," said the ops officer.

Toby smirked. "Well then, shall we get underway? If you would like, you can stay on the bridge and watch our exit. It's quite an adventure. If not, the mess is right down that hallway to your left."

Lars looked at him curiously. "Why is the departure an adventure?"

"I take it you've never been outside the Oort perimeter before?" said Toby curiously.

Lars shook his head. "Why would I need to? Most of my missions are planetside."

"Ah, then you're missing quite a fun experience. Since we're traveling covertly, we have to sneak out through our own defenses. It's not as easy as it might sound. Since those who watch us count every ship that goes in or out of the Oort perimeter, we have to travel under full cloak, concealed within the magnetic field of one of our own battleships. If the gate controllers were to open the gate specially for us, a lot of questions would be asked that fleet command would prefer to avoid having to answer."

"So who's going to hide us?" asked Lars.

"Whoever we pick. Since we're now officially operating in stealth mode for the foreseeable future, we can't exactly ask permission from anybody. Most don't care if we piggyback them on the way out, but on the way back it's a bit different."

Lars nodded in understanding. "The offer sounds interesting, but I'll pass. I have research to do before we get to our first destination."

Toby grinned. "You'll have plenty of time for that, sir. We're over nine days from our first checkpoint."

"Nine days!? I thought you could make that checkpoint in sixteen hours!"

"Only if we want to be seen. Moving at that speed would generate a large enough energy trail to light up every long range sensor in three parsecs. Unless we stay below three hundred AUM, we risk detection by anybody astute enough to be watching for our ion wake."

"I thought you had a state of the art cloaking system!?"

"We do, but even the best cloaking system can't process that large of an ion wake. Well, at least not yet. The only way we'll ever be able to travel that fast and remain fully cloaked is if someone discovers a way to reduce the upper end ion wake produced by our coaxial drives."

Lars grunted. "Fine. Just get me to our destination."

Toby nodded. "As you wish, sir."

Lars turned and motioned to Vlad to follow him.

"Uh, sir. One last thing. Would you like Trent to give you a tour of the ship?" asked Toby.

Lars looked back at him curiously. "Trent?"

"Our ship's AI. He could give you a brief introduction to everything aboard."

Lars grunted. "I've been on more than my fair share of these ships. I think I know my way around. Actually, I think I know them a little too well," he quipped.

Toby nodded. "Alright, fair enough."

As Lars continued back toward the ship's mess, Toby sat down and said, "Cloaking up. Helm, take us out of dock, and set course for gate sixty three, ahead three AUM. When we get there, put us somewhere that we can catch the next ship out on its way to patrol."

"Aye, sir."

As the ship gently rolled out of spacedock, Toby's chief engineer leaned over his station and said, "Fun guy, isn't he?"

Toby snorted. "Yeah, a real piece of work. He'll be a fun one to baby-sit for the next several months."

Chapter 9

A tall, muscular Yib prophet strode slowly into the middle of a large, stone patio and paused. Around him stood tall, ornate pillars of ghost white marble reminiscent of ancient Roman designs. A man in a long, flowing black hood and cloak stood at the far end of the patio near a trickling pool of water and stared at it, his back to the prophet. Evidence of an ornate metal sword and a dagger peeked out from the edges of his cloak. Several men in uniforms similar to those worn by Roman centurions stood guard along the walls of the patio.

"What is it?" asked the hooded man with a hint of annoyance.

The prophet took a deep breath and said, "The Serians that you sent to Earth have been discovered. They were sent away in disgrace with no information."

The hooded man continued to stare at the pool of water, but said nothing.

"Master, the plan has failed. The Serians did not complete their mission! There is also evidence that enemy saboteurs slipped aboard and rendered their equipment useless!"

"Have the Juinah been paid?" asked the man.

The prophet nodded. "Yes, they have. But I do not think it was wise to do so. The mission was a failure! Nothing useful was gained!"

"Tangible assets are not necessary in order to achieve gain," said the man.

The prophet looked curiously at him. "What are you saying? We got nothing for the bargain!"

The man turned and glared at the prophet from under his hood.

"You are a prophet, and yet you cannot see what has been gained from this transaction!?" said the man.

The prophet shook his head as he twitched nervously. The man sighed heavily.

"Is your brain filled with water, or are you simply that dumb?" he snapped.

"I am neither, master," replied the prophet.

"Then think! Open your mind to things greater than what you can hold in your hand!"

The prophet pondered the thought for a moment, and then cocked an eye in understanding.

"The Serians and the Juinah are merely pawns?" he replied.

The man gave a gleefully devilish grin. "So you do use your brain for more than a simple shoulder decoration. You are correct, but not entirely. The Serians and the Juinah are despised within the galaxy. Their names are dirty, and without honor. We have merely lumped more dirt upon their names, and concealed our actions against the Chappagi under their mantle. When one wants to move with greatest stealth, it is wise to draw away the eyes of one's enemies first, before proceeding."

The prophet cocked his head curiously. "Master, why are the Chappagi of such interest to you?" he asked.

"They are yet another pawn, a tool by which I will bring down the nine races, and gain ultimate power over the galaxy.

They are minor and insignificant by themselves, but as a catalyzing force, they are invaluable."

Intrigued, the prophet grinned. "Then the fear I spread among the galaxy is part of your plan? You are using the Chappagi to divide the nine races against themselves!?"

The man grinned slyly and uttered a low, sinister chuckle. "Each of the four who stand against the Chappagi will fall, leaving but five to squabble and battle among themselves," he said in fiendish delight.

The smile faded from the prophet's face. "My race is one of those that will fall," he said with a hint of concern, realizing the dilemma that this new revelation presented.

"The time of the nine races is over. The time of the Crassians is at hand. Those that serve us will be rewarded with kingdoms of their own. Those that oppose us will fall, never to rise again."

The prophet's eyes narrowed. "What of my race? Will they be annihilated?" he asked probingly.

The man shook his head. "Your strength will be reduced, but it will not be destroyed. The vine of your people will be trimmed, leaving only the strong and the healthy. From this gleaning, your race shall rise stronger than it ever has before. Your people will rule a portion of my new kingdom, and you will be their leader."

The prophet grinned in devilish delight. "The Varnok deserve a greater place within the universe. We will be honored to serve you and raise the name of the Varnok above all other races, save for your own."

The man grinned slyly. "Then begin the next part of our plan."

The prophet bowed. "As you wish, master."

He turned, slipped out of the patio and quickly made his way out to his ship. The man grinned.

"I will enjoy wiping their race from existence when the time comes."

Another man in a simple blue toga appeared from the shadows. "Are you sure he will not betray us?" he asked.

The first man grinned. "His greed is too strong. He knows we are his only avenue to power. Thus he will not betray us until we have given him all that he desires. I plan to ensure that he dies long before then." He turned and looked at the man in the blue toga and said, "Is our next pawn ready?"

The man in the blue toga bowed slightly and nodded. "The Varnok admiral is ours to command. He awaits your orders."

The first man nodded. "Then brief him on what he must do. I want him to be ready to fly at a moment's notice."

"What of the Gayik'Von fleet? Won't they interfere with our plans?"

The first man grinned. "I'm hoping they will."

Phyland stood in his office in the west wing of the ambassadorial towers in the center of Sebius, governmental home world of the United Galactic Worlds, and stared out across the city. And a big city it was, covering nearly the entire planet from pole to pole and most of its circumference. But despite being the capital of the UGW, Sebius was more a prime location for back alley deals than any real progressive politics. This was because the governing body of the UGW was more a formality these days than a real political power. It had once been the respected center of the galaxy, using its impressive influence to ensure peace and prosperity everywhere within its jurisdiction. In many ways, Phyland longed for a return to those days of glory. But instead, he found a world replete with corrupt politicians and diplomats, each more interested in money and power than the well-being of others. In many ways they reminded him of politicians back on Earth, only uglier. There were still a few within the senate who were truthful and upright, but they were rare. It was this rampant corruption that had essentially turned Sebius and the UGW into the laughing stock of the entire galaxy.

Phyland sighed as he watched two large Yandian transports pass by above him on one of the nearby trade routes. He missed Earth. Even though he had spent most of his time living and working throughout the Mars and Moon colonies back home, he had tried to visit Earth as often as he could. He grimaced as the sound of data pads crashing to the ground echoed from the other room. He sighed.

"Julius, what are you doing?" he asked with a hint of frustration.

A younger man stepped around the corner, awkwardly cradling several pads in his hands.

"Sorry ambassador. I was just trying to organize your quarterly reports and senate notes, and accidentally dropped them."

Phyland rubbed his forehead in frustration. "Nordham must hate me. Why else would he stick me with someone like this," he thought. He sighed again, turned and walked into the next room. As he walked by his secretary's desk, he said, "Mary, I'm going for a walk. If anyone calls, just comm me."

The young woman nodded to him. "Will do, sir."

"And make sure Julius doesn't destroy anything while I'm gone."

The woman grinned.

Phyland strode out into the hallway and began walking towards the senatorial gardens. This was a lavish wildlife complex that lay at the center of the ambassadorial towers which contained a myriad of various alien plants and animals of every shape, size and color from across the galaxy, including several small rodent species and a number of birds. As he passed by a window overlooking the gardens, a group of Gika birds circled high above the densely packed islands of Jubaiya trees that dotted the center of the complex. He marveled that the trees flowered year round and never seemed to stop blooming. In the sixteen years he had been serving as the ambassador for Sol in the senate, it still amazed him that he could look at such strange alien vegetation as the Jubaiya tree and in many ways find it even more beautiful than anything he had ever seen back on Earth. Now, in his later years, he found that life away from Earth had given him an even greater appreciation for his native home world.

"Great currents lift you up, wingsonga," came a voice from behind him.

He turned to see a large bird like creature dressed in a very colorful, elaborate cloak and neck dress standing behind him. The bird was known as a G'Fando'Nah, a minor race of avianoids first discovered by the Gayik'Von that populated a single planet in a far corner of their republic. They were also the ones who had given the G'Fondo'Nah their distinctive name.

While the G'Fando'Nah called themselves by a different name, their name, and ultimately their language, were unpronounceable by most species within the galaxy. Thus they had settled for being called by their Gayik'Von name whenever they were away from their home world. But even that name was not easily pronounced, and over time many had chosen to simply call them Fondos, a slang term for the colorful and elaborate outfits they wore during their everyday lives. Phyland smiled at the bird and bowed slightly.

"Good afternoon, Finch. How are you this fine day?" he said.

The bird chirped happily. While Finch wasn't his real name, he had come to accept it as one of several substitute names given to him by members of the senate, since none could pronounce his real name.

"I am on high currents," he replied.

Just then Phyland noticed something. He pointed towards his own ear and said, "I noticed you're wearing a translator. Have you given up on learning English?"

The bird shook his head and adjusted the small device that rested over one side of his head.

"I have not given up. I desperately wish to learn your language due to its complexity and verbal beauty," he said as the clicks, whirs, and purrs of his native language were replaced with fluent English by the device.

"Then why the translator?"

"I was on diplomatic errands today. There were too many species that I had to gallow with to bother with speaking to each in his own native beak. Thus I required this today," he said, pointing to the device on his head.

Phyland smiled. "I can relate to that. It's a bit challenging trying to deal with the multitude of alien languages, cultures, and customs that surround me every day. I'd be lost without my translator."

Finch nodded. He watched as Phyland sighed, and then looked out towards the gardens.

"Do you wish to soar with your flock again?" he asked.

Phyland smirked as he thought about his home. "I do miss Earth ever so desperately. I will admit that. But I have so much work to do here. As much as my heart calls me home, I cannot leave."

Just then his communicator chirped. He pressed his ear and said, "Phyland here."

"Sir, one of the Ahaktak ambassadors is here to see you." Phyland pursed his lips in frustration.

"Speaking of work, some just showed up at my doorstep," he muttered. He bowed slightly and said, "If you will excuse me, I have some visitors to attend to."

Finch bobbed his head and said, "May the wind forever lift you up."

"May your feathers grow thicker, wingsonga," replied Phyland with a smile.

He then turned and hurried back to his office in the humanoid quarter. It was called the humanoid quarter because it housed the offices for most of the humanoid ambassadors that took part in the senate. Since each type of species had unique physical needs based on their biotype, all accommodations, offices and living quarters were subsequently divided up into four general areas, each designed to cater to the most common living requirements of each biotype. The four main biotypes, those being aquanoid (fish), avianoid (birds), reptoid (reptiles), and humanoids, occupied the main levels of the ambassadorial towers. Those with unique or special needs, or who were not part of the four major biotypes, were housed below in special quarters designed especially to cater to each of their own unique physical needs.

As a result, Phyland found his office, and ultimately his living quarters, situated near some rather strange, but almost familiar humanoid lifeforms. This was very apparent as he turned down the hallway towards his office and noticed two very tall humanoids studying a section of control wiring that had spilled out of an access panel they had just removed. The wiring glowed a soft purple, and seemed to pulse as they discussed a problem with one of the relays. Around their waists and over their shoulders they carried large, complex tool belts with devices of every shape and kind scattered across them. He soon reached his office and placed his hand on a small pad next to the door. After a few seconds the door chirped and then slid open. He quickly entered and walked over to a side room just as Julius entered.

"Mr. Phyland, the Ahaktak ambassador is in your waiting room. He said he wanted to discuss something very important with you," he said with a hint of nervousness.

"Yeah, I know. So what does that walking throw rug want now?"

"He mentioned something about raw metals, sir."

"Raw metals?? Oh good gawds. I told him I don't want his ores. We've got enough of our own. I want some of his advanced technology. That's all we're really interested in right now."

"Shall I send him away?"

"Nah, let me handle this. Maybe I can finally get through that thick furry skull that we're not interested." He sighed.

"And before I go in, is there anything else I should know about?"

Mary nodded. "There are four messages here from various ambassadors who would like to speak with you as well," she said.

"Anything specific?"

She shook her head. "Not that I'm aware of."

Phyland nodded. "Then put them on the calendar somewhere, and get me a list of what they want to discuss. Hopefully they won't interfere with my brown-nosing of the Varnok," he said with a hint of frustration.

"Brown-nosing the Varnok? I thought they hated us," said Julius.

"They do. That's why I want to talk to them. I'm hoping to find a way to get them to lay off us. If I can, it'll be one less of the nine who want us dead. Even if I can't, it might give Nordham some time to cook up a more permanent solution."

"Why the Chancellor? I mean, our Chancellor?" asked Julius.

"Because, he knows more about the whole situation than I do. Which is ironic given that I'm here and he's there. You'd figure I'd be able to squeeze more information out of the hooligans here than he could, but apparently not."

"How is that possible?"

Phyland pursed his lips. "If I find that out, I'll tell you. All I know is that he's ahead of me on the information curve for the moment and I don't like it."

"Well, I could do some snooping around here and find out some stuff for you," said Julius.

"No! No! No! The last thing I need is for you to end up getting vaporized by someone because you did something stupid again. And don't say you wouldn't, because I know you would. Just leave this to me and you do as your told. In the meantime, I want you to contact Nordham and schedule a meeting over secure hyperband for fourteen thirty hours Sol time. Got it?"

Julius nodded. Phyland frowned. "Somehow I don't think you do," he thought. "Well, onward to my meeting with Mr. Yeti and company," he quipped.

Chapter 10

V'sin walked into his ornate and lavishly appointed office and strode towards his desk. As he walked, he noticed a leg sticking out from behind one of the plush, wide-backed chairs.

"Whoever you are, I don't have time to bother with you right now. There are more important things for me to do at the moment," he said as he walked towards the chair.

An older man leaned out and grinned at him. "You don't even have enough time to humor an old friend?" he said.

V'sin stopped in surprise. "Mr. President! What are you doing here!?" he exclaimed.

The old man chuckled. "I'm allowed to see an old friend, am I not?"

V'sin blinked. "Well, yes. But you have such a busy schedule. I would think that you would be elsewhere seeing to the well-being of the republic, or dealing with some other important business."

The old man nodded. "I am, and right now, you are my important business."

V'sin looked at him curiously, and then took a seat in the chair next to him. "Alright, I'm listening."

The old man smiled. "I have received disturbing reports that an alien force, hostile to the nine races, has begun to move within the galaxy. Their first target is the Gin. This concerns me greatly," he said.

V'sin nodded. "Everyone knows about that. The Varnok have somehow gotten in their heads the absurd idea that Earth is somehow a threat to them."

The old man shook his head. "It is not the Varnok. They are merely pawns of the true enemy to the Gin and the nine."

V'sin cocked an eyebrow. "Another enemy? Surely you jest. Who would have the prowess to sway the minds of the Varnok, or any of the nine, save for another of the nine?"

The old man narrowed his eyes. "Have you heard of the Yib?"

V'sin nodded. "They are the ancient order of priests and prophets who have held a key roll in many major events in history. Wait, you're not suggesting this threat to the Gin is being perpetrated by the Yib, are you?"

The old man shook his head. "The Yib are only a small piece to a much larger puzzle. One pawn of many in an ever-growing web of intrigue and shadows."

"Well, who is this force creating such problems? And why are they using the Yib and the Gin in their plans?" asked V'sin.

"I do not know. There is much more here than any of us realizes. While the Gin and the Yib are just one part of their overall plan, they are both key to a much more frightening future. Have you heard that the high order, the council of nine monks who are the representatives of the nine within the Yib, has become divided?"

V'sin's eyes narrowed. "I have. Their division has intrigued me since I first heard of it."

The old man nodded. "I as well. It is said that, 'As the order goes, so goes the galaxy.' If the order is divided, it may be the precursor to darker times ahead. Whoever is behind this is using them as a pawn through which to carry out their plans."

"But why the Yib?"

"Have you ever heard the phrase 'the mongrel has two masters'?"

V'sin nodded. "One master leads the mongrel, and a second controls the first," said V'sin.

The old man nodded. V'sin's eyes widened.

"You're not suggesting that the Yib are the first master, are you?" asked V'sin.

The old man shook his head. "They are just a mongrel. One of many actually," he said.

V'sin stared at the old man in concern. "This greatly complicates things," he said.

The old man nodded again. "It does. That is why I am sending you to Sebius."

"Sebius?" said V'sin in surprise.

The old man nodded.

"But why?" asked V'sin.

"You have a sharp eye for politics and a quick wit. Your ability to take a situation, analyze it, and discern the multiple levels of truth hidden within is no secret. That's why I wanted you as one of my adjutant presidents. I would have preferred you as my vice president, but being so high up in the power structure would have limited your ability to use those skills for the greater good. Down here you're less likely to be thought of as a threat by those seeking to harm our people, yet you remain powerful enough to do something should you need to. The galactic senate is rife with the type of political intrigue you thrive on. I think you'll enjoy it," he said with a grin.

"Will I be replacing our ambassador there?" asked V'sin.

The old man shook his head. "No, he will remain ambassador and you will remain fourth adjutant president, which means you'll still outrank him. But your job won't be as a representative for our people. I need your eyes, ears and that fantastic brain of yours studying, observing and deciphering what's going on there. While Sebius may not be the focal point for what's coming, events there have the unique ability to foreshadow other things. But to see those shadows, you must first be among those who make them. If you can decipher these shadows, we may be able to find the first master, and eventually the second. If we find him, then we will be able to tame this pack of beasts before they can destroy us and the peace we've struggled so hard to maintain."

V'sin grinned. "Well then, I believe I have a challenge to attend to."

The old man chuckled. "I thought you'd warm to this assignment once you got your mind around it. Now, get packing. I've lined up a special presidential transport for you that will leave in the next several hours."

"But shouldn't I go secretly?" asked V'sin.

The old man shook his head. "If you do, it'll raise too many questions and destroy what little chance you have of finding the answers we need. But if you go openly, you'll appear as just another self interested politician out to fan his scales. With such a prejudice hanging over your head, you should draw in just the right people who will provide you with the keys you need to solve this puzzle. On top of that, you'll have time to meet with your old friend Phyland of the Gin."

V'sin grinned. "Our meeting should be interesting. He's the only alien diplomat to ever beat me at my own game of political intrigue."

The old man chuckled. "That's why I like him so much. For a Gin, he's sly like a skincoat, a trait I admire greatly."

"Petrov, can you hand me a towel?" shouted Mike from the bathroom.

A tall, light skinned male android strode into the bathroom and held out a dark, blue towel to him.

"Your uniform is pressed and ready for tomorrow. Wakeup is at zero six hundred hours. Breakfast will be ham, eggs and toast with juice. You have a meeting with the military advisory board for your annual review at zero eight hundred hours. At ten hundred hours you meet with

Chancellor Nordham and the council for your weekly military update and security report. You'll have lunch with the high schoolers from colony seven to discuss your job as commander of Earthfleet. After that you have a meeting with the director of production at thirteen hundred thirty hours to discuss the issues with the remaining shield satellites for the Oort perimeter upgrades. Admirals meeting at fourteen hundred hours, and your daily paperwork at sixteen hundred hours," said the android.

"Good grief. Am I going to have any freetime tomorrow?" he asked as he began drying himself off.

Petrov cocked an eyebrow. "What free time?" he said with a hint of sarcasm.

Mike smirked. "That's what I thought. Hey, can you record a few things for me tomorrow?" he asked.

Petrov shrugged. "What specifically?" he asked as he handed Mike his pajamas.

"Well, I would like the Patriots vs Lions football game from America, the Manchester vs Liverpool soccer game from England, and game six of the World Series."

Petrov nodded. He took Mike's towel, and then cleaned up the bathroom as Mike finished getting ready for bed. He then checked to make sure Mike didn't need anything else. Certain his work was done for the day, he slipped out of Mike's quarters, turned off the lights, and then made his way down to Alfred's quarters to check up on him. Mike lay in bed for nearly an hour reading a light novel he had downloaded onto his data pad before finally rolling over and going to sleep.

Moments after falling asleep, Sarah shimmered into view at the foot of his bed and studied him quietly. She noticed his soft, grayish white streaked hair, his firm, but nearly wrinkleless face, slightly cleft chin and strong, but gentle features. These were traits she admired about him, even though he was human and she was not. While she wouldn't admit it openly to anyone, Sarah felt something special for Mike. Something that was more than a being in her position should feel. But it wasn't a feeling that she could bring herself to tell him about, or show to him much beyond the caring, kind attention she gave him every day. She knew it was unusual how she followed him around, going almost everywhere he went, and acting like his shadow throughout the day. Most other AI's would stay with their ships and not wander far off. Yet she was special, and had used that uniqueness many times to help Mike in any way she could.

She sighed quietly to herself and then walked around to the head of the bed and stood behind him. She reached out slowly to stroke his hair, and then paused, as though uncertain if she should allow herself such an indulgence. She pulled her hand back and cradled it as though its proximity to his head had made it something special. This feeling was strange to her. She knew she wanted to feel the warmth of his skin on her hands and the soft, gentleness of his hair slipping between her fingers. Yet she also felt as though it was not her place to do something so selfish. Again she sighed in reservation, as a twinkling of longing rippled through her body.

Then she stiffened. Her eyes bobbed around the room as she began searching. She could feel something, a familiar presence, one that she thought she knew. Quickly identifying its location, she vanished from Mike's room and reappeared in a large, darkened arboretum full of both exotic alien plants and native species from Earth. Across the roof stretched a massive, transparent sectioned dome through which twinkled a hundred thousand stars of the nighttime sky. Seeing a man curled up on top of a nearby palm tree, she flashed across the room and appeared next to him on a neighboring palm tree, floating upon its delicate strands like a wisp of smoke.

"What are you doing here?" she asked him suspiciously.

But the man said nothing, instead choosing to stare up through the ceiling at the stars beyond. After several moments he said, "It's an amazing device, is it not? A complex crystalline structure designed to be completely transparent, and yet stronger than most common alloys used by the mortals of this world. There are so many things it can do, and yet they choose to use it to contain a small, temperature controlled, and heavily filtered blob of atmosphere, moisture and nutrients designed to nurture and nourish the fragile lifeforms within its shadow," said the man.

"I asked you, what are you doing here? I don't need a philosophical summary of the properties of this biodome. I want to know why you're here," said Sarah, more insistently.

The man turned and looked at her with a slight grin on his face. "I should ask the same of you, as they are mortals, and you are not."

"I am here on a scientific mission to observe, study and gather information on these creatures that will be brought to the council at the appropriate time," said Sarah sternly.

The man grinned slyly and narrowed his eyes in a questioning, accusing look. "Is that the only reason you're here?" he asked.

"Yes, it is," she replied sternly.

She crossed her arms and glared at him. The man turned and studied his hand, as though it were a strange novelty to him.

"These humans possess such a curious, and yet limited form. Ten fingers and ten toes attached to two arms and two legs, which in turn are attached to a torso that comprises a body which is surprisingly fragile. It's amazing that such a limited creature could master the matter world as they have, creating such amazing structures out of dead energy. They've even found ways to use this dead energy in great reactors and stardrives to create amazing feats of speed and power that should be impossible in this world."

She stepped in front of the man, and leaning over, glared at him. "Did the council put you up to this? Or did my father send for me?"

The man waved dismissively. "Neither has sent me. I am merely here to observe you and your study of these strange creatures and their dead world. I find it baffling why you would bother with such a boring place. There are so many more interesting things in our world that you could study, and yet you come here instead to observe a mortal species made of dead energy that lives within such an infinitesimal span of existence. I would have thought better of such a great scientist as yourself."

Sarah stood up and crossed her arms. "There is much to be learned from those that are below us. Just because their world is dead by our understanding, does not mean that they are unworthy of study and observation."

The man grinned slyly. "I suspect that your presence here is less about science, and more about a certain someone whom you've attached yourself to. It is such a degrading attachment too. Since you are not thinking like a proper researcher, remaining aloof and detached from your subjects, simply recording and observing without becoming involved, I question the validity of your research. If you'd like, I can easily rectify this for you by removing the one thing that hinders your work. It would be such a simple effort really. A mere thought and your problems would go away."

Sarah scowled at the man. "Touch anything in this world, and I will make your suffering so great that you will wish you were never created!" she growled.

The man grinned fiendishly. "Then my assumptions are correct. You are attached. Well, no matter. It is not my place to interfere in a life that is being wasted on such a worthless lifeform. I will be going now. Enjoy your little pet while he lasts. The time remaining to him is short." And with that, he was gone.

Sarah fumed angrily. "Zoahn!! Augh, I hate him! When is he ever going to learn to behave himself? Father should have punished him many ages ago."

She sighed and then looked at the stars above. She knew what the man had said was true. Humans were such a limited, finite creature. Yet, for the first time since she was created, she actually felt an attachment to something, or in this case someone, that was more than just a sterile, scientific, ordered curiosity. She didn't quite understand it yet, but she desperately wanted to try, whatever it took.

Chapter 11

Nordham paced back and forth across the chamber floor.

"Why your impatience, Chancellor? You seem worried about something," said a councilwoman.

"There's just something nagging at the back of my mind. The Serian delegates, their Juinah bosses, the restlessness within the Varnok, and the growing hatred of humans, and most especially Earth, that seems to be permeating the galaxy. It's like there's an explanation there that I can't quite wrap my mind around yet," he said.

"Would it be something we could do anything about if you could?" she asked.

Nordham shrugged. "It's possible, but I don't know. If nothing else, it'd give us a better idea of who we're dealing with."

"What of the spies you sent out recently? Two of my best recon crews are out there ferrying them to God knows where in search of answers," said Mike.

Nordham shrugged. "I won't know until they contact us with an update, and that could be weeks or months from now."

"Who did you send out?" asked the councilwoman.

"Lars Nordic, Vladimir Umnov, Antonio Garcia and Bob Landers. They're four of the best operatives I have in the intelligence corps," said Nordham.

"They went out on the Appalachia and the Onegai, both Samurai class shipkillers. So they're in good company. Their commanders are well known to me," said Mike.

"The Appalachia? That's Commander Tobias' ship, is it not?" asked the councilwoman.

Mike nodded. "It is. He's one of my best commanders, and a seasoned recon expert. That's why I chose him for this mission."

The councilwoman nodded. "I've heard nothing but good things about him. He was a good choice. However, I disagree with your choice for the operatives on this mission, Chancellor. I can understand your decision to send Antonio Garcia and Bob Landers, but Lars and his partner are planetside espionage experts. Wouldn't they be more useful in keeping tabs on the various shadow organizations operating here at home?" she asked.

Nordham shrugged. "They've pretty much put all of those groups, including Black Orchid, out of action for the near future. So, since it'll be a while before any of them get back on their feet again, I thought that it would be a good idea to give Lars and Vladimir something new to work on for a while. No point having them atrophy from boredom."

The councilwoman nodded.

"Councilwoman, I know my place isn't diplomacy, even though I sometimes get roped into it anyways, but I was curious what our stance is with the Gayik'Von. What is their take on this seeming growth of dissension in the galactic body against Earth? Someone's got to be egging on these other races, since the only one's who've ever really hated us before were the Juinah, and only because we interrupted their efforts to exploit Earth," said Mike.

The councilwoman sighed. "I don't know yet. Chancellor, have you heard anything?"

Nordham shrugged. "I've been asking, but haven't really been getting many answers. I'm just as concerned with this turn of fortunes as you and the admiral are. Mostly because, while the Gayik'Von will do everything they can to protect us, if push comes to shove, they're going to concentrate on protecting their own people first, ultimately leaving us high and dry. That much is to be expected."

"Yes, and that leaves me in a bit of a lurch as well. While our defenses are formidable, they're not impregnable. Even with the upgraded Oort and Kuiper perimeters, and our expanded military forces, we'll only be able to delay the inevitable for a short while should someone attack us," said Mike.

A councilman nodded. "Agreed. So right now our best defense is to play the political gambit and try to calm this issue before it gets out of hand," he said.

Nordham shrugged. "Honestly, there really is no better plan. A military solution should always be your last option under any situation. So Phyland on Sebius and our four operatives out on recon are our best chance right now. And until I hear something definitive from them, I'm not going to move in any one particular direction. The last thing we need is to jump to conclusions and then later discover that those conclusions only got us further into trouble. I know this seems like the overly cautious approach to an ever growing danger, but handling galactic politics is no different than walking in a mine field. If you move too fast, you're guaranteed to get your leg blown off, or worse."

The council president folded his hands and rested his nose on his fingertips as he thought. Finally after several moments, he sighed and said, "Proceed as you have been doing."

"But sir!" protested the councilwoman. The council president silenced her. "I am going to defer to your judgment on this for now. You seem to have a better grasp of the situation than we do. In turn, we will try and find solutions to this problem here at home. Together we might be able to formulate a plan that will save Earth from what is quickly becoming a hopeless, and ultimately nightmarish future," he continued.

Mike and Nordham bowed slightly.

"Thank you, sir," said Nordham.

Lars stumbled onto the bridge and looked around through half open eyes.

"Ah, the sleepy head is awake, I see," said Toby.

Lars squinted as he tried to make out the bridge around him. Then he noticed something over the windows.

"What is that?" he asked groggily.

"Huh? What is what?" asked Toby.

"That weird brown stuff over the windows," said Lars.

"Oh, that! Haven't you seen holographic cloaking before?"

Lars cocked his head in curiosity. Toby's chief engineer chuckled.

"I'd take that as a no, sir," he said with a smile.

Lars squinted in disgust. "You woke me out of a sound sleep to show me some little parlor trick your ship can do?" he grunted.

Toby grinned. "Actually, no. Although the holographic cloaking is part of why we called you up here. Trent, would you kindly show the gentleman here a top down image of our current position in space and the area immediately around it?"

A holographic map appeared in front of Lars showing a blinking red dot surrounded by dozens of blinking blue dots bordered by two scrolling dotted yellow lines that passed in a weaving, wandering path through a large field of glistening stars. Lars studied it for a few moments, trying to understand what he was seeing, and then went wide eyed as his mind grasped onto what the image meant.

"We're in the trade lanes?" he said in surprise.

Toby nodded. "Just entered about fourteen minutes ago. So far everything's been pretty normal."

"How fast are we traveling?"

"About warp seven by the galactic scale. It's the locally accepted speed limit for these trade lanes. That's about seventy seven AUM by our scale, or a little over a quarter of our maximum speed."

Lars blinked. "That's too fast for our cloaking if I'm guessing right from your previous statement," he said.

Toby nodded. "To allow for proper silent running, yes. For normal operations, no. And for instances of holographic stealth, that's definitely not true."

Lars cocked his head in curiosity as he dismissed the holographic display. "What exactly is this holographic cloaking you keep mentioning?" he asked.

"Holographic cloaking is a stealth system that uses holograms to hide the true identity of a vessel. With it we can mimic the appearance, shape, size, and energy footprint of any ship in the galaxy equal to or larger than ourselves. It essentially allows us to hide in plain sight without drawing undue attention to ourselves," said the chief engineer.

"Is that safe?" asked Lars.

"Completely safe. We've used it hundreds of times before. We're currently using one of our favorite holographic covering, which is a type two fringe trader Dogavo class cargo vessel. Since they're independent trading ships, they carry no registry and minimal identification. Normally they're the ones responsible for transporting raw ores and other materials from the galactic fringes to the inner core, and finished goods from the inner core to the outer fringes. Few bother them or get in their way, because to survive on the galactic fringes, you have to be a tough, weathered, hardened tradesmen with nothing to lose. So anyone tangling with them typically comes out the worse for it, paying a very heavy price in crew and ship, even if they do succeed in capturing one of these vessels. Therefore, since these ships and their crews are so feared and respected, it's the perfect disguise to wear in order to minimize the chances of someone getting suspicious."

Lars cocked an eyebrow. "That would explain the rather unusual costumes and makeup I was given for this mission."

Toby chuckled. "That it would, lad. That it would."

"So how long until our first stop? Speaking of which, what is our first stop?"

Toby looked at Lars in curious surprise. "I thought you already knew that."

Lars shook his head. "They told me what to expect, not where we were going. They said you'd know that, and all I had to do was find some answers once we got there."

Toby looked at his chief engineer, and then his tactical officer in surprise. Finally he looked back at Lars and said, "I would think that the intelligence corps would have better prepared you."

"We normally deal with problems planetside. We rarely get out here often enough to be bothered with galactic politics or espionage. Up until now, that's been left up to you recon guys. My understanding was that this would be no different than any of my other missions against Black Orchid or the Illuminati."

Toby whistled as he rubbed his head. "No laddie, they're not the same. Galactic espionage and politics are worlds different than what we have back on Earth. There are some similarities, but those are few."

The chief engineer rolled his eyes. "It figures that Intel would screw this up," he said

Toby nodded. "Aye, and we need to fix this before we go much further." He motioned to the door of the bridge. "Come with me. I need to bring you up to speed on how things work out here, and most especially on this cesspool of a trading post we're due to arrive at in the next couple of hours. After that, I think we need to complain to our respective superiors about this royal screwup."

Phyland stepped into his office and brushed past Julian who stumbled slightly and dropped the large stack of data pads he was carrying. Phyland grimaced, but kept walking.

"Clean it up, Julius!" he shouted as he slipped into his office and closed the door behind him.

Mary smiled at Julius, feeling sorry for his predicament. She got up from her desk and helped him gather up all the pads.

"Thanks, I appreciate it," said Julius with a hint of nervousness.

Mary laughed. "The silly old coot ought to be kinder to you. Brushing up against you like that, and then blaming you for the mess was just uncalled for," she said.

"No, no, it's alright. I'm a klutz anyways."

Mary chuckled kindly. "Yes, but you're a cute klutz."

Julius looked curiously at Mary who winked at him playfully and then slipped back to her desk. Phyland placed his palm onto an empty square on his desk and muttered a quick access code. The desk beeped and a large holographic display appeared above it moments later. He punched in several access codes and the required authorization keys, and then waited for the transmission to connect. Several moments later Nordham's image appeared on the display.

"Ah, Phyland, how's life in the big scary galactic senate?" he said chidingly.

Phyland rolled his eyes.

"That bad, eh?" said Nordham with a grin.

"I've been arguing with the Ahaktak ambassador all morning. You'd think that walking throw rug would get a clue after a while," said Phyland.

Nordham laughed. "Yeah, they are pests, aren't they?"

Phyland rolled his eyes. "You have no idea."

Nordham nodded and grinned. "So, what do you have for me today?"

Phyland sighed. "Other than the usual, not much. It's like I'm suddenly taboo around here or something. 'Don't talk to the token human. You might get rabies or something.' Or at least that seems to be the attitude of most of the ambassadors lately. The only ones really willing to talk to me anymore are the Gayik'Von, the Fondos, the Sevedith and the Yandians."

"Fondos?" asked Nordham.

"The Gayik'Von call them the G'Fando'Nah. Everyone around here just calls them Fondos."

Nordham nodded in understanding. "That's the bird species you told me about a couple months ago. You also said you had made friends with one of them."

Phyland nodded. "Yeah, his name's Finch. He's the Fondo diplomat I befriended shortly after he first arrived here."

"Finch?"

Phyland grinned. "It's a nickname I gave him. Since everyone around here has such a problem pronouncing the Fondo's true names, most have just settled with using nicknames for them. Speaking of which, we've just gained a new nickname. We're now fondly known as the 'Chappagi'. I've been hearing it in increasing frequency around here lately."

"Chappagi? Yeah, I've heard that name mentioned around here too. What does it mean?"

Phyland frowned. "Apparently it's some alien slang for a mudsucker from what I've been able to gather."

Nordham furrowed his brow. "Well, at least they didn't call us mutant monkeys or something."

Phyland smirked. "I wouldn't put it past them."

"Hmm, no, I doubt you would. So, do you have any other useful information for me? I doubt you called just to chitchat," said Nordham.

Phyland shook his head. "No, I didn't. I do have something, but I'm not sure how useful it is."

"What is it?"

"There's talk of a group that's connected with the Juinah that might be responsible for all our current problems."

Nordham perked up in interest. "Really? Who? The Serians?"

"Actually, no. In all honesty, I don't know who they are. I know the group exists, or at least I'm ninety percent certain of it. But the name I keep hearing makes no sense. A number of the diplomats keep secretly referring to the Ran'Pak or the Teifar, which roughly translates to 'World of Savages', depending on the language. And I emphasis the word 'roughly'. I've been working on this with our Gayik'Von counterparts and even they're stumped. I would have tossed it away as just another slang word for humans if it hadn't caught the interest of the Gayik'Von ambassador so much. He seems genuinely intrigued by the name. I think him and his assistant ambassadors are listening around, trying to catch someone talking about it, in hopes that it might lend them a clue."

Phyland rubbed his chin in thought. "You're certain this isn't yet another slang term for Earth, right?"

Phyland nodded his head. "I'm positive. As I mentioned, the Gayik'Von ambassador has taken a great interest in this. Especially since the races that hate and/or fear us think of us as the coming destroyers. If they were to call us savages, it would be more a statement of mockery rather than fear, as we would be of little concern to them at that point. The Gayik'Von ambassador, as well as Finch, myself and several others are all convinced that this refers to someone else. Someone who might be working in the shadows trying to shake up the power base for as yet unknown reasons. I know it's not much to go on, but depending on what you run across back there, it might prove useful."

Nordham inhaled deeply, and then sighed heavily. "It's usefulness remains to be seen. For all we know this new name may have intentionally been placed out there to send us down a rabbit trail and away from the truth."

Phyland nodded. "I understand that, but right now it's really the only new information we've had in a while."

Nordham nodded. "Well, true. I guess it's better to go on a wild goose chase than sit here and do nothing. Alright, I'll pass this on to my directors and the council and see what we can come up with. Hopefully we gain something useful out of this."

Phyland nodded.

Chapter 12

Lars listened with interest as a strange clicking and a thud echoed across the hull of the ship.

"Docking completed, sir," said the pilot.

"Secure all stations and go to ready departure. I want to be able to run on a moment's notice if something goes wrong," said Toby.

"Aye, sir." Toby stood up and turned to Lars and Vlad.

"Alright, the show is yours gentlemen. We'll be maintaining the illusion of the cargo ship while allowing you onto the station to begin your recon. From here on though we'll have to observe radio silence. So you'll need to do this exactly as I've told you."

Lars nodded and then walked to the side exit door of the ship. Lars waited as the inner hull access hatch unlocked and slid to the side, and then watched with interest as a section of the armored hull liquefied and flowed to the side.

"That's always amazing me when I see it. Fluidic armor, right?" said Lars.

Toby nodded. "Every ship killer in the fleet is equipped with it. It's the best armor ever made. It can take a beating and then heal itself afterwards. Ya can't beat that."

Lars grinned. "Well, at least until someone builds an anti-fluidic armor weapon."

Toby shrugged. "Then they'll just build a better armor. In the meantime it does its job nicely."

Lars nodded and then motioned to Vlad to follow him. They walked through the holographic outer shell of the ship until they reached a thick, double doors that hissed open to reveal a dingy, dirty hallway littered with garbage and broken old shipping crates of every shape and size. The two men gagged as the odor of rancid alcohol and rotting food assaulted their noses. Several aliens of various species lay slumped over in the hallway, either in a drunken stupor, or unconscious from too much drinking. Small alien rodents and insects of various kinds scurried across the walls and floor.

"Ugh, the holographic simulation that Toby showed me didn't even begin to do justice to the level of filth in this place. It's worse than anything I've ever seen on Earth," he muttered.

"Well, his assessment of this being a cesspool was correct, if nothing else," said Vlad.

Lars grunted, and then motioned for his partner to follow. They moved down the hallway as quickly as they could, carefully trying not to step on anyone, or into anything unpleasant. They soon exited onto a large promenade lined with broken down storefronts and booths filled with various alien goods and merchandise. What appeared to be a slave auction was being held in a corner at the far end.

"Where do you think we should go first?" asked Lars.

"Isn't it standard procedure to go where the liquor flows?" asked Vlad.

"On Earth it maybe, but the same might not be true out here. Besides, we're dressed as fringe traders. We should wander around the shops and pretend like we're looking for things to buy and sell. Hopefully we can stumble onto something that might be of use to us. Just try not to start any trouble."

Vlad nodded and slipped away to begin searching. Lars stepped forward and began walking towards a booth on the left side of the promenade when a short, pig like humanoid stumbled in front of him.

"You're a fringe trader, aren't you? Eh? Eh? What kind of cargo you got? I'm sure it's worth a lot. Eh? Eh? How about you be a smart man and give it to me," he said in a nervous, jittery tone.

Lars glared at the pig man from under his hood and brushed him aside. "Go play somewhere else, little boy," he said.

He walked past the pig man and strode up towards a nearby shop. "Your cargo is worth more than your life, fringer!" shouted the pig man as he drew a knife and leapt at Lars.

But to the pig man's complete surprise, Lars seemed to vanish in a flair of cape and dust as he sidestepped the flying alien attacker. The pigman crashed to the floor with a thud and suddenly felt the sharp, piercing blow of a heavy metal boot in his side. He screamed as the kick lifted him off the floor and tossed him through the air. He crashed into a nearby pile of trash and lay still. Lars looked over at a large, burly, wolf like man and nodded his thanks. The wolf man grunted in return, and then walked away to deal with the pig man. Lars cocked an eyebrow in interest, but said nothing.

"You alright?" came a voice in Lars' ear.

"Yeah, I'm fine. I think I just experienced an old fairytale with a modern twist."

"How so?"

"Some weird pig like guy attacked me thinking he could steal my cargo."

"A pig?" asked Vlad.

"Yeah, I dodged him and then some weird wolf guy punted him like a pigskin. I think he was a Sevedith. Big, burly, wolf like, and butt ugly."

"Yeah, sounds like one. I was about to start inquiring at a local shop over here when I heard the commotion. I wasn't sure if you were hurt, so I thought I'd check on you."

"Thanks. Keep looking and let me know if you spot anything interesting."

"Roger that."

Lars scanned the area around him briefly, and then walked up to a nearby store where he was greeted by the store owner.

"Ah, you're a fringe trader! It's unusual to see ones like yourself here. What brings you to our dirty little corner of the galaxy?" said the store owner in a voice more chipper than it should have been. Lars studied the dog like shopkeeper with curiosity. "I'm certain you have a cargo that is very interesting, and highly valuable. Types like you always do," he continued.

"I'm here looking for information," said Lars.

"Ah, an intellectual cargo! How quaint. I suspect that the buyer of the information has a lot of money?"

Lars studied the shopkeeper suspiciously. "You could say that," he said.

"Ah, then what kind of information are you looking for? There's lots of good juicy gossip I hear around here every day. I'm sure something might interest you," said the shopkeeper.

"I'm curious about the Varnok. They seem to have become upset about something recently. I'm interested in finding out what has angered them so."

The shopkeeper's expression turned from one of happy consumerism to a bile ladened disgust. He flipped his paws at Lars in a symbol of disgust.

"Oh, is that all," he said with a hint of disappointment.

"Then you know who they are angry with?"

"I do. It's those bothersome Chappagi. They are threatening the peace we have struggled so long to maintain. I hope those good for nothing Gayik'Von just step aside and let the Varnok wipe those Chappagi from existence. The galaxy will be much better off without them."

Lars squinted slightly. He didn't like the attitude of the shopkeeper. But at the same time he wasn't certain he wanted to find out what a Chappagi was either. He had his suspicions that it was a reference to Earth, but he wasn't sure. After a moment he decided that it was best not to continue this conversation. He gestured politely to the shopkeeper, and then continued on his way down the promenade. As he walked, he hoped that Vlad was doing better than he was. But he wasn't. At least not initially. Several times he had been attacked by thieves and sex merchants, and at one point was nearly drawn into a large bar brawl that had spilled out of a nearby cantina and into the promenade. Given the troubles he was encountering, he wondered if Lars was alright. Despite all that they had been through on Earth, those experiences paled in comparison to what they were experiencing now.

As he walked along the promenade looking for any possible answers to the long list of questions they had, he noticed two tall, burley men in black capes standing in a nearby doorway. As soon as they realized he had seen them, they immediately slipped into the shadows and vanished. This caught his interest. Not because of what they had done, but because of the brief, fleeting glance he had of their faces. They had appeared to be human. He wondered if that was just a figment of his imagination, or if they really were. And if they were, why were they here? What other humans would be this far away from Sol space? He contemplated going after the men, and then thought better of it. He would continue on with his research, and then meet up with Lars at the far end as they had planned.

Phyland strolled down the long, winding hallways of the humanoid quarter and soon reached the offices of the Gayik'Von ambassador. He entered and strode up to the receptionist.

"I'm Phyland of Earth. I'm here to meet with the ambassador," he said.

The receptionist gurgled and then motioned for him to enter. He bowed slightly and then walked over to the door to the ambassador's office. As soon as he entered, he stopped cold in his tracks as a familiar, dark green face greeted him with a smile.

"Adjutant President V'sin!?" he said in surprise.

The man laughed and stood up. "Greetings my friend! How are you?" he said.

Phyland furrowed his brow in interest. "I'm fine. But I wasn't expecting you here today."

V'sin walked around the end of the large, ornate, white marble desk and said, "The president sent me here on special business."

"But why didn't you tell me you were coming!?"

"I wanted it to be a surprise. And I see I have succeeded."

Phyland nodded. "You can say that again. So what's this special business?"

V'sin opened his mouth to speak, but paused as the door to his office opened. In strode Finch, his ornately decorated cloak sparkling in the soft light of the room. He stopped and cocked his head in surprise at seeing both Phyland and V'sin standing in the same room.

"Finch! What are you doing here?" asked Phyland in amazement.

"I was requested to gallow with the ambassador. But I did not expect to find such strange feathers among the nest," he chittered.

V'sin motioned to Finch and said, "I've invited both of you here for a special meeting. It involves Earth and it's home system of Sol. While those are obviously not the common names for them, I will use your names, Ambassador Phyland, out of polite respect to you and your people."

Phyland nodded. "Thank you. It's much appreciated, but not necessary. I've gotten used to being called anything from a Chappagi to a Nordmer."

V'sin frowned. "Neither of those are polite names for your species. While the second is indeed more common, and less derogatory, I would still prefer to avoid using them. I would also like to avoid using your common species name of Gin if possible. It is always most polite to use a species' own proper name whenever possible."

He nodded at Finch and said, "With certain exceptions of course for difficulties stemming from language issues."

Finch nodded. "My feathers were not soiled," he said.

Phyland shrugged. "Well, right now Humans and Earth aren't exactly favorites in the galaxy. Other than your people, four of the ancient races, and a collection of other smaller republics and species, we're pretty much persona non grata with the rest of the galaxy."

V'sin pursed his lips in thought. "That's one of the reasons I'm here. It is my job to discover who this force is who wishes to do your people such an indescribable harm. It is my feeling that their apparent fear of you is not truly a fear, but rather a ploy to achieve a much greater goal."

Phyland looked at V'sin curiously. "A greater goal? You make it sound like we're a pawn in some galactic chess game or something."

V'sin nodded. "You are. Even though your race is of inconsequential size, occupying a single planet within a single system deep within our republic space, you are seen as a danger by many. Yet you are neither a threat, nor a concern to the galaxy as a whole, or in part. The only ones who would have any concern for their future would be us. Since you are deep within our space, we would be the first to lose territory to you if you were to become greedy and expansionist."

Phyland blinked. "Expansionist? We're lucky enough to keep things under control at home! The last thing we're worried about right now is spreading out across the galaxy."

V'sin nodded. "I understand that. But there's also the fact that your race has managed to catch up to and surpass the technology of most races in the three galaxies in less than two of your centuries. It does not take much of a mind to realize that with a technological growth rate that explosive, it would only be a matter of time before you could sweep aside all opposition in the galaxy with little effort."

Phyland snickered. "Surpassed most within the three galaxies?? Not likely. We've certainly advanced quite quickly over the past couple hundred years or so, but most of that was in response to a perceived threat to Earth and the human race. You can't blame us for wanting to protect ourselves from possible extinction."

V'sin shook his head. "No, I can't, and neither can my people. They are wise enough to see that your actions have been reactive rather than proactive. But not all species are able to see something as obvious as that. Hence why fear reigns so strongly among the four ancient races who have turned against us and you. However, I still do not feel that it is your technological prowess that they fear. Such advancement would be more likely to draw curiosity than fear, under normal circumstances. There are many rumors of an unknown force that seeks to destabilize our galaxy by destroying peace in order to gain power. I wish to find out who it is and stop them. While it may be several centuries before all of the damage they've caused is repaired, if we can find ourselves traveling down a road of healing, I will feel more comfortable again."

Phyland nodded. V'sin smiled, and then looked over at Finch who was quietly taking in the entire conversation. V'sin chuckled.

"I'm sorry my friend. I did not mean to leave you out of our discussion."

Finch shook his head. "Sometimes it is best that one first listen, and then only speak if he has something constructive or informative to contribute. At this time I have neither. So therefore I simply listen in order to gain understanding of our situation. This danger that threatens my wingsonga and his flock also threatens my wingmates as well. I too wish to solve this mystery before any harm can come to any of us."

V'sin nodded. "Then we will have to begin slowly. First we must find the direction in which our answers lie. After that, we must capture them before they have time to take flight."

Finch nodded and bowed slightly. "My wings and my wits are at your disposal."

V'sin grinned. "I would also hope for your eyes and ears as well."

Finch cooed slightly. "Then you shall have them also."

Chapter 13

"Hey Albert, what does your wife think of you being out here on the Oort perimeter?" came a voice over the commlink.

"Eh, it's just another assignment. Nothing special. She's too busy with her astrometrics research to care what I'm doing anymore. So what does your wife do?"

Mitch looked out the canopy of his fighter at his wingman and smiled. "She's a teacher."

"A teacher? What does she teach?" asked Albert.

"Ninth grade math at colony fourteen."

"What's that like?"

"She describes it as the equivalent to a rock trying to teach a bird how to fly."

Albert laughed. "That bad, eh? So who's she teaching? A bunch of hooligans?"

"No, a bunch of geniuses gone wild."

"What? How does that work?"

Mitch laughed. "It's hard to explain. I'll have to show you some time. But needless to say, her days are never boring."

Albert laughed. "I can imagine."

Just then Mitch's console beeped. On the far edge of his sensor screen, a faint reddish dot pulsed, indicating an unknown object.

"Hey, Albert. I got a contact directly on our six, closing pretty quickly. Do you see it?" he asked.

Albert looked at his sensor screen and saw the same thing.

"Yeah, I see it, but the signal is very faint. Whatever it is, it's barely registering. Think we should check it out?"

"Yeah, that might not be a bad idea," said Mitch.

The two fighters rolled to the right and turned in the direction of the unknown object.

"London, this is patrol sixty three requesting sensor confirmation. We have an unknown object bearing three zero mark two five at fifty two thousand kilometers. TTI is two minutes forty two seconds," said Mitch.

"Stand by patrol sixty three," came the reply.

The operations officer aboard the London zeroed in on the relayed coordinates and studied his sensor readouts. There was definitely something there.

"Patrol sixty three, I confirm your target. Object is barely registering. I can't get an exact ID on it. Advise caution on intercept," he said.

"Roger that London," replied Mitch. He looked out his window and said, "Well, looks like we've got ourselves a bona fide mystery here."

"So, you still want to check it out?" asked Albert.

"Of course I do! We wouldn't be doing our jobs if we didn't," said Mitch.

As the two fighters continued to approach the unknown object, the sensor officer aboard the London continued to study his sensor display. He didn't like what he was seeing. He turned to his commander and said, "Sir, that unknown object patrol sixty three requested confirmation on is worrying me."

"How so?" asked the commander.

"I'm starting to detect large concentrations of ionic radiation and some rather strange wide band energy emissions."

The commander pondered this. "How strong is the radiation and field emissions?"

"Strong enough to obstruct our sensors. I can tell there's something there, but I can't see specifically what it is. It may be a ship or something," said the operations officer.

"Alright, then let's be cautious and go to defcon alpha. Alert all units, raise shields, and put weapons on standby. Alert Centcon to our situation."

"Aye, sir."

Mitch furrowed his brow in surprise. "Wow, defcon alpha. Sounds pretty serious," he said.

"Must be the London saw something that we can't. And if they're getting itchy back there, we'd better play it safe on our approach."

Mitch nodded, even though his wingman couldn't see him. "I agree. Let's swing out wide and take it down the left side," he said.

"Roger that, going right."

Mitch eased over his stick and began to swing wide of the approaching object when it suddenly turned and accelerated towards them.

"What the...it just changed course!" said Albert. Moments later alert claxons began sounding in both cockpits.

Mitch swore. "That's a Akar mine!" he shouted.

"Shake off! Shake off!" shouted Albert.

The London's commander stood up in shock. "A what!?" he cried.

"The fighters have identified it as an Akar mine, sir," said the operations officer.

The commander plopped down into his seat and said, "God have mercy. Alright, execute emergency battle plan delta two alpha. Helm, go to maximum sublight, heading three two mark two five."

"Come on buddy, we gotta go man, we gotta go!" cried Mitch.

Both fighters accelerated as fast as they could as the mine rapidly closed on them.

"Unbelievable! That thing's gaining on us! What do we do?" cried Albert.

"Keep your head on your shoulders. Right now is not the time to lose it. Let's split up and see if we can't take this thing," said Mitch.

"Take on an Akar mine!? Are you insane!?" cried Albert.

"Got any better ideas?" Albert swore.

"I was hoping I wouldn't have to die today."

"Just keep to your training and you'll live to tell about it."

The London closed rapidly on the two fighters as she pushed her sublight engines as fast as they would go. "London, this is Ontario. Centcom got your message and has dispatched us to assist. More help will be forthcoming if you need it. We will reach your position in three minutes. Have you engaged the mine yet?" came a voice across the London's communicator.

"Ontario, this is commander Moses of the London. We're closing with the mine now. TTI is one minute," said the commander.

"Acknowledged."

Moses quickly ran the situation through his head. Two fighters and two shipkillers against an Akar mine. While the firepower advantage was in their favor, he didn't want to risk detonating the mine. Akar mines were infamous for completely vaporizing anything they touched. What potentially made things worse was that Akar mines usually traveled in packs, and yet they had only spotted one so far.

Albert swore. "It's on my six! I can't shake it!" he shouted.

"Hang on buddy, I'm coming!" said Mitch.

"Hurry! I'm not up for being vaporized today," replied Albert.

Mitch rolled around behind the mine and tried to zero in on it. But to his surprise, the mine stopped abruptly. Mitch rolled hard to avoid hitting it and felt his ship shake violently as it plowed through the plasma cloud that surrounded the mine. A large explosion and a shower of sparks issued from his console. He swore.

"Oh man, I'm in deep. I just flew through its plasma field! I've got system failures all over the place and my left engine is dead! I'm gonna need some serious help here."

"I'm coming!" shouted Albert.

Mitch tried his best to keep the wounded fighter operational as the mine accelerated towards him. Albert flew around behind it and felt his ship shake and shutter as he passed through a large contrail of ionized particles that were streaming off the mine. As he closed on it, he could see cracks in the casing through which the ionized particles were flowing.

"Wow, this thing is a mess. It's amazing it can still function," he thought.

Mitch struggled with the controls of his fighter as one system after another failed. Suddenly the London appeared overhead and transported him out of his fighter and into the safety of the ship.

"Patrol sixty three, this is the London. Get clear of the engagement area. We'll take it from here!"

"What about my partner?" asked Albert.

"He's in our care now. Just get clear so you don't get caught in the blast wave."

"Aye!" cried Albert.

He banked hard and accelerated away as the London opened fire, shooting wildly at the mine in an attempt to draw it away from Albert and towards themselves. The diversion worked, as the mine turned and followed the London while Albert raced for the safety of the Oort perimeter. Once he was a safe distance away, the London turned on the mine and opened up with all it had. Her first shots missed as her targeting system had trouble lining up the shot. But soon they began to find their mark and the mine detonated moments later. The London caught the blast wave across its forward shields, causing the ship to vibrate slightly.

"Status report," said Moses.

"Layer one shields in the starboard forward quarter at sixty two percent. All other shield layers and systems at full power," said the tactical officer.

"No damage to the ship," replied the chief engineer.

"Sensors are online, but there's so much interference that I can't see much beyond our bow," replied the operations officer.

"Helm, get us clear of this interference. If there's more of them out there, I want to be able to see them coming," said Moses.

"Aye, sir."

The London turned and quickly cleared the complex energy cloud left behind by the mine, only to discover that more danger waited beyond.

"Three more Akar mines inbound! Bearing one seven three mark three five at two thousand kilometers and closing fast!" cried the operations officer.

"Helm! Step on it!"

"Aye!"

"Correction, make that six!" cried the operations officer.

Moses grit his teeth and swore lightly under his breath. One was bad enough, but six were going to be more than a handful. He turned to his two turret gunners.

"You gentleman ready?" he asked.

Both men nodded. He brought up a holographic display and studied the battle area, but didn't like what he was seeing.

"Centcom, we've now got six Akar mines closing on us fast. Request more support, stat!"

"Roger London. Will try to dispatch more assistance your way as soon as we can."

"Roger that Centcom. London out."

Moses inhaled deeply as he contemplated his situation.

"Sir, the mines are still on our six. What do we do?" asked the tactical officer.

"What's their range?"

"Holding at six thousand kilometers."

"Can we get a positive lock?" asked Moses.

"Negative, sir. I'm having no more luck getting a lock on this bunch than I was on the last one. We're going to be totally shooting visual on this one."

Moses pursed his lips in concern. "Alright, we'll do it the old fashioned way then. Switch all guns and turrets to dual mode targeting with manual spotting."

"Aye, sir."

"Sir, Ontario has arrived and is flying down our port side at five o'clock low," said the operations officer.

"Ontario, this is the London. Do you see the mines?"

"Aye, we see them. Gonna try and knock them out for you."

"Be careful. The radiation they're emitting is fowling sensors. You'll need to target them manually," said Moses.

"Roger that."

The Ontario whizzed by the London and began letting out a hail of turret and torpedo fire. But none of it found its mark. Suddenly the mines spread out and zeroed in on the ship. The Ontario scrambled to get out of their way, but was quickly surrounded. Two of the mines then broke off and raced in at her. Moments later the Ontario vanished in a flash and an explosion. Moses grimaced as he saw it unfold on his display.

"Where's the Ontario? Did she get hit?" he asked.

"Checking now. Nope, I see them. They're safely half an AU away on a return course. It appears they jumped clear just before the mines were able to hit them."

"What of the explosion? Was it caused by the mines?"

"Given the resulting energy field, it's very likely sir. From what I can best tell, two of them may have collided and detonated."

Moses grinned. "If all else fails, get them to kill each other. It's a crafty maneuver. Stupid, but crafty," he thought to himself.

Suddenly alert claxons began sounding. "Sir, two of the mines have emerged from the cloud. They're closing on us rapidly! Twelve seconds till impact!"

"Helm, evasive maneuvers! All ahead full!" shouted Moses.

The London accelerated away like a cannon shot, quickly slipping past the approaching mines before moving a safe distance away.

"Two more approaching, bearing...wait, it's the Ontario!"

Two of the mines exploded as the Ontario suddenly reappeared just in front and to the right of the London, its guns spraying a heavy cloud of weapons fire into the two mines that trailed after the London.

"How many mines remaining?"

"I only see two sir."

"What's their status?"

"They're directly behind us, sir. No, wait. One appears to be heading towards the Ontario."

"Helm, turn to intercept the first mine. Ops, warn the Ontario of the second."

"Aye!" said both offers at the same time.

The London turned around and raced at the nearest mine. Several of the upper turrets and all of the forward batteries roared to life as the gunners tried to shoot it down. The Ontario engaged their coaxial drive, jumped out of the area, turned, jumped back in and closed rapidly on the second mine, passing the London at high speed just a hundred feet off her top turret. Moses watched as the first mine exploded, followed shortly by the second.

"Sensor efficiency just dropped to fifteen percent, sir," said the operations officer.

"Helm, get us clear of the area. Ops, inform the Ontario to do the same. We need to get out where we can see what's happening. Especially if there's more of those things out there."

"Aye, sir."

The two ships soon found themselves out in open space as they nervously observed the surrounding area. Two more shipkillers and a battlecruiser jumped into the area and took up position near the London. If any more mines showed up, they'd be ready. Several light years away a small cloaked Juinah vessel carefully watched everything that happened with interest. Although only one Earthfleet fighter had been destroyed, they had none the less gained valuable information on Earthfleet's tactics, ships, and fighting capabilities. While this information hadn't yet revealed a weakness in the Sol defenses, they knew that one had to exist. It was only a matter of time before they found it. Until then, they would quietly watch, wait, and bide their time.

Chapter 14

V'sin walked up to the door of the Varnok offices and stepped inside. A stout, bluish fishman stared cautiously at V'sin from across a small, coral desk as though afraid that the large reptilian Adjutant President might eat him.

"I'm here to see the ambassador," said V'sin.

The fishman gurgled, hacked twice, and then bowed slightly. V'sin knew that was an expression of disgust, but he chose instead to ignore this obvious lack of respect. A short, fat, reddish green fishman stepped out of a rear office, briefly studied V'sin with curiosity, and then motioned for him to come with his large, fin like hand, as though drawing water towards himself. V'sin nodded slightly and strode down the hallway to join the ambassador. Stepping inside, he was surprised to see a large swimming pool like desk in the middle of the room. The Varnok ambassador waddled across the floor and slid inside. He opened his mouth wide and gulped several times like a fish out of water, and then shivered. V'sin narrowed his eyes. He knew the ambassador didn't want to see him, and he wasn't shy about showing it.

"How may I help you, Adjutant President?" said the Varnok Ambassador in a hissing, nasally voice.

V'sin looked around for a chair, but found none. Instead, another small pool sat nearby. Apparently he was expected to get in it. V'sin smirked and sat down on the edge.

"I'm here to discuss your people's hatred of the Gin. I want to know why you have such an abhorrence for this inferior, and minor race."

The Varnok ambassador snorted. "They are not inferior! Their technology rivals even your own!"

V'sin smirked slyly. "Only a small portion of it, and only because we so choose to let them. The belief that they have something superior to us makes them feel safer, although it does nothing for them in the grander scheme of things."

The Varnok batted his large, multi-lidded fish eyes and glared at V'sin.

"They have more than a few advantages. Their cloaked ships have proven to be undetectable to our sensors, and their weapons are frighteningly powerful. The only reason for such technology from so minor a race is to facilitate their eventual rise to power and subjugation of all alien species! They will even conquer you in time," he said with a hissing gurgle.

V'sin laughed. "You are afraid of a race of only eight billion people, most of whom are unable to even agree with their own family for more than a few minutes? You give them too much credit, ambassador. Their people are divided, many are uneducated, and poverty is still rampant on their home world. Only a tiny few have found their way to space and sought the pleasures of advanced technology."

"They are a menace to all sentient life!"

V'sin narrowed his eyes and probed the Varnok deeply.

"Who put you up to this?" he asked.

"No one put us up to anything! We have seen for ourselves and know the truth!" snapped the Varnok ambassador.

V'sin glared at him. "You've seen for yourselves? Have your people been illegally traveling near Gin space?"

The Varnok puffed out his chest and flared his gills in defiance.

"They have not."

"Then how do you know so much about them?"

"We have our sources."

V'sin nodded in disbelief. "Indeed. I think you are working on flawed information, ambassador. You've been fed a pack of lies that you are more than happy to accept as truth."

The Varnok ambassador stared curiously at V'sin. "Why do you say that?" he asked.

"Power. Prestige. A larger place in the galaxy. Those are things your race has wanted since the end of the great war. You felt as though you were cheated by the treaty, forced to take less than was rightfully yours."

The Varnok ambassador hacked in anger. "If that were true, why would we not have taken what was ours!"

V'sin grinned slyly. "Because you were unable then, and are unable now. The Gin make a convenient tool by which to unite a portion of the nine behind you in order to regain the things you feel you were denied."

The Varnok snorted. "The Chappagi have nothing to do with the great war. That was four thousand years ago," he replied angrily.

"Really? I find it interesting that their home world lies within part of the space you once claimed as your own," said V'sin.

"The Chappagi have nothing to do with that injustice. They are a threat that must be eliminated!"

"Eliminated? A threat? I fail to see how you can honestly call the Gin a threat when they haven't even united their own home world. A large number of their own people still live in a pre-technological state, never having seen the miracles of even the most arcane and simplest technology. Honestly ambassador, the humans have more than enough problems of their own to deal with. They could really care less about you, or anyone outside of their own home system right now."

The Varnok stared at V'sin, but said nothing.

V'sin nodded. He knew the Varnok was hiding something, but what it was, he couldn't quite grasp. He decided to probe further. He looked around the room and spotted a fishtank full of small eel like creatures. He fished one out of the tank and looked at it.

"Nasdraik. It's a delicacy on your home world, is it not?" he asked.

The Varnok nodded. "It is. Many consider it the food of the gods, and the blessing of the waters."

V'sin rolled the eel like creature over in his hands as it squirmed and squealed in protest.

"You would consider this creature to be harmless, correct?"

The Varnok nodded. "They are food creatures. They cannot harm us."

V'sin put his finger near the Nasdraik's mouth and watched as it latched on with all its might.

"Not quite so harmless, is it?" he said, prying the creature from his finger.

The Varnok fanned its gills impatiently. "It is nothing more than any other creature would do if it felt threatened," he said.

V'sin smiled. "Nothing more than any other creature would do if threatened, eh? Like the Gin for example?" he said.

The Varnok flinched, and then quivered as his eyes throbbed. He immediately realized that he had been tricked into conceding something he did not want to. He hacked at V'sin.

"A food creature is not the same as a sentient lifeform. One can build machines of war, the other can only eat, breed and be consumed."

V'sin furrowed his brow in consternation. "But it knows enough to defend itself when attacked, does it not?"

"A genetically engineered response. It is not a sentient decision."

V'sin turned and sat down on the edge of the bowl again. "Then is what the Gin are doing a genetically engineered response to the threat of their annihilation?"

The Varnok ambassador was becoming frustrated. Everywhere he jabbed, V'sin parried and immediately struck in kind. He was not liking this. He studied V'sin for several moments, deciding what he should say next. Finally, he decided it was best to remain silent.

Noticing this, V'sin scratched the skin on his hand and said, "I see. So you're not willing to concede that it's possible that their overarching desire to become technologically and militarily superior to everyone in the galaxy is in response to being threatened with annihilation by those around them?"

"We concede nothing!" snapped the Varnok.

V'sin smirked. "Then have you considered that someone may be using you as a pawn, just as they may be using the Gin as a catalyst to destroy the nine races?"

The Varnok blinked vigorously and flared his gills in surprise. "Why would you consider such a preposterous thing as that!?" he snapped.

"Because of the Serian incident a few weeks back. The Juinah were clearly involved in it, and there is evidence that they may be working for a third party who is striving to take power."

The Varnok hacked, and then shivered, as though hiding something. V'sin immediately caught this.

"So there is something more you know. Let's poke at that scaly skull of yours and see where you flinch," he thought. "You wouldn't by any chance know of any connections between this Serian incident, and your people? Possibly an inside deal to help you regain lost territory?"

The Varnok reared up and trumpeted loudly. "How dare you insinuate such blasphemy! You only accuse us of these things because you are allies with the Chappagi! They are your pets and you want to prevent their harm!"

"Pets!?" said V'sin in shock. He laughed boisterously. "You seriously think we treat them as pets? You are a fool. If the Gin were truly our pets, we would have absorbed them into our republic ages ago. And before you say it, they are not a threat to us either. If they were, we would have dealt with it a long time ago. But they are not. In fact, they are no different than either of us were in our early days. In time, they will grow and mature and be like us. But for that to happen, you must leave them alone and allow for the natural maturing of their species. Your constant threats to their safety do nothing more than increase the chances that the nightmare you so fear will come true."

"If they become like us, what space will they take? We, the Varnok, will not give up any of our worlds to these Chappagi!" snapped the Varnok.

V'sin waved dismissively. "I'm not saying you have to. There are plenty of worlds around the galaxy that humans can inhabit, but we cannot, or don't wish to. If we're not using these worlds, why not give them to the Gin?"

"Because, it will give them the foothold they need to take everything in the three galaxies!"

V'sin furrowed his brow. "Give them an inch, and they'll take a mile, eh?"

The Varnok looked at him curiously. "It's an idiom the Gin use. For you it would be, 'Give them an atoll, and they will take the entire sea.' Am I right?"

The Varnok shivered in anger. V'sin narrowed his eyes as he studied the ambassador.

"I see that my talking with you will gain me nothing further. Do note that the Gin are under the protection of the nine races, and any attack against them will result in strong retribution. Now, I wish you fair waters, ambassador."

V'sin stood up, bowed slightly and strolled out of the room. As he stepped into the hallway, a grin drew across his face. "That'll give him something to think about. Hopefully he'll do something foolish and reveal who he's allied with, or possibly who's pulling his strings. Hopefully before something terrible happens to any of us."

Lars strode up to a doorway at the far end of the promenade and leaned against a nearby wall. Vlad soon joined him.

"Find anything?" he asked.

Vlad nodded. "I've had several possible leads. I also encountered a rather unusual curiosity. While I was walking, I seemed to draw the attention of several black cloaked figures. The odd part was, they seemed human."

"Human?" said Lars as he perked up in interest.

Vlad nodded. "I can't be certain, but they also appeared to take a rather unhealthy interest in me, popping in and out of the shadows like prairie dogs as they followed me down the promenade. Whoever they are, we'll want to be extra cautious from this point forward."

Lars nodded. "So what leads do you have that might be worth pursuing?" he asked.

"One of the shopkeepers told me that there's an old hermit who lives in the central hub of the station. Supposedly he's got fairly intimate knowledge of the whole Chappagi affair and can help us."

Lars cocked his head in curiosity. "Chappagi? I heard that word mentioned several times as I walked around. It seemed to be related to Earth somehow."

Vlad nodded. "It's a slang word for human used by many of the races around the galaxy. It's reminiscent of many of the racial slurs used by humans throughout history."

"So it's basically the alien equivalent of the N' word?"

Vlad nodded. "Something like that. So, did you encounter anything in your search?"

Lars shook his head. "Lots of random, seemingly unrelated information, but nothing solid enough to lean on. So right now your lead is the only thing we really have to go on."

Vlad shrugged. "At least it's somewhere to start with, even if it is a bit questionable."

Lars motioned to Vlad. "Lead the way."

As the two men made their way through a nearby doorway, several black cloaked figures slipped out of the shadows and began to follow them inside. Lars and Vlad continued down a long series of passageways until they stumbled into what appeared to be the remains of an old arboretum.

"This place must have been classy at one time. I doubt anyone would take the time to build a greenhouse in a hole in the wall place like this unless it had once been a respectable place to live," said Lars.

"I saw evidence to that as well. I wonder what happened that would have..."

Vlad suddenly stiffened as the sound of flying metal echoed in his ears. He grabbed Lars and drove him to the ground just as a large dagger whizzed by over his head. He rolled and leapt to his feet, brandishing a large caliber pistol. Two men leapt out of the shadows with large daggers drawn over their heads. Lars rolled over, drew his pistol, fired at the first man and missed as Vlad killed the second with a headshot. Vlad then followed up with a second headshot on the first man, dropping him like a bag of wheat.

Nine more black clad assailants leapt out of the shadows, each brandishing an energy pistol, and fired at them. Stones, metal and plaster exploded all around them as Lars and Vlad scrambled for cover. Lars popped up first and fired, knocking down two of the men while driving the rest to cover. Moments later a large Sevedith emerged from the shadows and leapt at several of the men as another man in a dark green cloak reminiscent of a 16th century monk appeared from another corner and began firing at the black cloaked men.

"Who's that?" shouted Vlad. "I don't know, but as long as he's fighting the same guys we are, he's a welcome addition to this party," replied Lars.

"Behind you!" shouted Vlad.

Lars turned around and grabbed a man's wrist as he swung a large, heavy sword at his head. Lars spun the man's wrist, dislocated his shoulder, broke his arm, and snapped his neck in one fluid motion. The man collapsed to the floor limp as a ragdoll. Lars picked up his pistol and fired at another man as he emerged from the shadows behind him, dropping him like a rock. Vlad shifted his position, found refuge behind another rock and then watched as the Sevedith grabbed two of the black cloaked men and threw them across the room into a support beam.

"Wow, he's strong," thought Vlad.

The green cloaked man appeared next to him, leapt over the rock and cut down two of the black clad men with a pair of long, thin swords that seemed to appear out of nowhere, and then immediately vanish. Then, almost as quickly as it had started, the battle ended, and the last of the black clad men retreated into the shadows and vanished. Moments later their dead comrades glowed, shimmered and were gone. Claxons began to sound everywhere as shouts and voices echoed down hallways in every direction. Lars turned to Vlad and then paused as he stepped on something. He looked down and a spotted dagger laying on the ground. He picked it up and slid it into his belt.

The man in the dark green cloak appeared moments later with the large Sevedith and said, "Follow me. We need to get you out of here before the authorities arrive and start asking questions you don't want to answer."

Lars motioned to Vlad and then followed the green cloaked man into the shadows. They disappeared into a hidden side passage just moments before station police appeared in the old arboretum. The men ran for several moments until they reached a red glowing door. The green cloaked man pressed several buttons and watched as the door changed to a dark blue. It hissed open to reveal the hallway to where his ship was docked.

"Why are we here?" asked Lars.

"You need to leave, now. You are no longer safe here," said the green cloaked man.

"Wait, why should I trust you?"

The green cloaked man tossed his hood back to reveal the face of an old, gray haired, human. Lars and Vlad blinked in surprise. The old man smirked.

"What? Did you really think you were the first humans to ever venture out this far? Don't be so naive," he said.

Lars furrowed his brow in interest. "I'm not going anywhere till you tell me who you are and what other humans are out here."

The old man shook his head. "I can't do that. In time you will learn those secrets on your own. Now go. My friend and I will keep the authorities busy while you and your ship make good on their escape."

"But we're in no danger. They think we're fringe traders," said Lars.

The old man shook his head. "That is no longer true. They know who you are. It won't be long before they find your ship and destroy it. I will do what I can to prevent that, but you must hurry!"

He shoved Lars through the door, and then Vlad. Lars turned around as the old man shouted, "Go! Now!"

The door hissed shut and locked. Lars swore. Just then the sound of footsteps and shouting could be heard down the hallway.

"I think our mission here is over. Appalachia, this is Lars. Fire up the engines. We're exiting hot and dirty."

Toby heard the call and swore. "Sir, several ships in the area just went to active battle mode and the station is trying to deep scan us!" cried his operations officer.

Toby swore again. "I knew this was too easy. Red alert! Engineering, stand by on screamer! Tactical, weapons to full. Helm, plot us the fastest course out of here. Trent, I need you to separate us from our holographic cover and send it away with the screamer the moment we're clear of the dock. Try to draw them away. Ops, portal our guests aboard. We need to get out of here now."

"Both operatives are already aboard, sir. We're ready to depart," said the operations officer.

"Alright helm, punch it! Engineering, deploy screamer! Trent, begin separation!"

"Aye!" came the combined reply.

The Appalachia banked away from the docking port as a small spherical object launched from the port side of the ship. It took over the hologram the Appalachia was using to hide itself, and immediately pealed off to the right as the Appalachia went left. But just as the holographic ship began to put some distance between itself and its parent, several nearby ships fired, destroying the screamer and the hologram it controlled.

"Opps, there goes the decoy," said the tactical officer.

"They're still scanning. I think they got wise to our little bait and switch," said the ops officer.

"Helm, get us out of here. I don't care what it takes," said Toby.

"Aye!"

The Appalachia ducked and jigged wildly in a seemingly random pattern of movements as dozens of nearby ships opened fire, trying to find their elusive target.

"I've got a hole! Taking it to full FTL!" shouted the helmsman.

The Appalachia engaged it's coaxial drive and jumped clear of the area.

"Any sign of pursuit?" asked Toby.

"None yet, sir," replied the operations officer.

"Engineering?"

"We're still five by five, sir."

"Tactical?"

"Same here."

"How did they see through our disguise?" asked Toby.

"I detected a field emission of exotic particles from a nearby vessel. It interfered with the integrity of the holographic cloak and apparently compromised it. I'll try to analyze the sensor logs and see if I can't come up with an effective countermeasure," said the chief engineer.

Toby nodded. "Ops, what's the comm traffic look like? Did they figure out who we were?"

The operations officer shook his head. "No, sir. From what I can tell, they're still not sure who we are. They're continuing to search for us right now."

Toby sighed in relief. "Well, keep an eye on those comm channels and let me know if anything suspicious surfaces."

"Aye, sir."

Lars walked onto the bridge and briefly studied the rapid flurry of activity around him. "Are we being followed?" he asked.

Toby turned around and looked at Lars. "Not so far. But we're watching just in case. What happened back there?" he asked.

Lars sighed heavily. "Long story. I'll explain later. In the meantime I need to borrow your lab and your AI for a bit. I have to analyze something."

Toby nodded. "Trent, please help the kind gentleman any way you can."

Trent shimmered into view in front of Lars. "Yes, sir," he replied.

Chapter 15

Mobeic, fleet admiral for the Varnok 27th armada, commonly known as the "Black Fleet" because of the jet black color of its ships, sat on the veranda of his large, stately mansion and looked out across the colorful, picturesque hills spread out before him. Nearby were two large, gurgling pools of fresh, scented water that splashed lightly as small fish and other creatures fought each other in an arena style battle for survival. The admiral swirled his thick, blood like drink around in a crude silver cup that rested in his large, webbed hands as he thought about the day's events. As he did, a figure in a dark brown cloak appeared from behind a nearby statue and looked at him.

"What do you want, prophet," said Mobeic, sensing his presence.

The figure tossed his hood back to reveal the face of the Varnok prophet. "Your senses and wisdom are still as sharp as ever, I see," he replied with a sly grin.

"Dispense with the niceties. Why are you here?" asked Mobeic in a gruff, almost annoyed voice.

"The master has need of your services," replied the prophet.

Mobeic's hand grew still as he pursed his lips in thought. "The Chappagi?" he asked.

The prophet nodded.

Mobeic grumbled, as though annoyed at the answer. "When?" he asked.

"As soon as you're ready," replied the prophet.

"What about the Gayik'Von?"

"They will be kept occupied elsewhere. Your approach will go unnoticed."

Mobeic contemplated this for several moments, and then said, "I will need time to prepare my fleet. Tell the master I will come when I am ready."

The prophet nodded. "He knows. That is why I am here to inform you of his wishes."

Mobeic nodded.

V'sin gently cradled a purplish flower in his hand and said, "I'm surprised these are thriving so well here. Normally they require a much colder climate to survive."

Phyland grinned. "The plant itself doesn't need the cold as much as it's roots do. It's planted in a special section of the gardens in which the ground is kept at a steady forty degrees. That's twenty three degrees galactic scale. It's the same issue they had to deal with in order to get those maple trees over there in the corner to survive here. The pine trees don't care if it's warm all year long or not, but the maples do. So for a couple months each year they surround them with a special energy field and slowly lower the temperature inside until it's below freezing. Then after three months they slowly raise it again, simulating fall, winter and spring. The trees love it."

"Maple trees, eh? I didn't know there were any Earth plants here in this garden," said V'sin.

Phyland shrugged. "The Chancellor talked them into it. He figured that if plants from nearly every other species were represented here, then it only stood to reason that some plants from Earth should be here as well. There's also tulips and several other breeds of flower planted in that area as well, very similar to some of these plants here."

V'sin nodded. "I'll have to see them some day. They sound interesting."

Phyland nodded. "You'll like them."

Finch stepped out from between several bushes as he chewed quietly on several tufts of grass.

V'sin looked at him curiously. "Why are you grazing on the grasses here?" he asked.

"It is called feather weed. It is a delicacy among my people. It was brought here for both the beautification of this garden, and as a treat for myself," said Finch.

V'sin chuckled. "Well, I guess I've learned something interesting today," he said with smile.

"So, Adjutant President, what did you find out with your meetings so far?" asked Phyland.

V'sin smirked. "The meeting with the Varnok was like talking to a wall of scales. I didn't learn anything, but I did confirm several theories."

"Like what?"

"There is another force working behind the scenes in the Varnok. I couldn't find who it was, but I have a feeling the Juinah are involved."

"Them again?" said Phyland in disgust.

V'sin nodded. "I didn't get much else out of him, but I did leave him with something to think about."

Phyland grinned. "That's always good. Any other progress?"

V'sin shook his head. "None, I'm afraid."

Phyland frowned. "Don't feel bad. I got the same basic cold shoulder treatment from several of the ambassadors I meet with. A few were friendly though and did provide me with what little they knew. But ultimately it left me back where I started."

V'sin leaned over and looked at Finch. "And what of you, my fine feathered friend?" he asked.

Finch shook his head. "They fouled the nest with the failure of life. I gained no feathers with them."

V'sin contemplated this for a moment, and then nodded, even though he didn't quite understood Finch's colloquialisms. He had a general idea what Finch meant, but didn't feel like asking for a translation. If it had been important enough, Phyland would have said something. He knew this because Phyland and Finch were best friends and understood each other perfectly, and thus needed no explanation of such strange sayings. But he was new here and it would take a bit of time before he understood these unique alien wordplays. Even Phyland had used a few that he still had not deciphered the meaning of yet.

As they continued forward, V'sin's body guards moved quietly along with them at a distance, keeping close enough to protect him if needed, while remaining far enough away so as not to interfere with the Adjutant President's work. Their eyes darted all around the arboretum, looking for any signs of a possible ambush, or hints of fowl play in the works. As V'sin and the others continued to talk, one of the guards spotted something suspicious in a nearby line of bushes. Seconds later a group of masked men in green camouflage outfits sprung from their hiding places and raced at V'sin and his party. Like cats to their prey, the guards pounced on them, quickly subduing or driving them back in rapid fire order. V'sin and the others stopped in surprise as the melee of attacker versus guard unfolded all around them.

Suddenly two of the attackers broke through and charged straight at Phyland, knives held high over their heads. V'sin watched in amazement and horror as Phyland did not flinch, but simply shifted his body into a very unusual stance. But the oddness of it vaporized as Phyland quickly disarmed the first attacker and sent him brutally crashing to the ground. He then spun and struck the second one with speed unbecoming of someone his age. His hands and fists moved so fast that it seemed as though he merely tapped the attacker and they would collapse to the ground unconscious.

The battle soon ended and the few remaining attackers that hadn't been incapacitated already, quickly fled and melted into the surrounding foliage. But they didn't make it far before they were intercepted and arrested by UGW security guards who flooded into the garden in response to the attacks. V'sin's eyes narrowed as he took note of the fact that the security guards didn't respond until after the attacks were over. He turned to check on Phyland and found him not only unharmed, but not even the slightest bit winded. He pondered this with wonder as he remembered how easily his friend had neutralized the two attackers with what appeared to be only the slightest of effort.

"Are you alright?" he asked.

Phyland nodded as he bent down and removed the mask from one of the assailants. He cocked an eye in surprise.

"A Queunoan. That's a surprise. I thought they detested violence?" he said.

V'sin studied the man's face, and then noticed something. He bent down next to the Queunoan and rubbed his hand across the man's skin. He frowned.

"This man has been altered. His looks like a Queunoan, but he is really a Serian."

Phyland blinked and looked at V'sin in surprise. "A Serian!? This man is too tall and bare skinned to be a Serian."

V'sin shook his head. "He's been genetically and physically altered. This isn't the first time this has happened. The Juinah have done this to many others for the purpose of assassination. With proper surgery and genetic manipulation, they can turn almost anyone from any race into another so convincingly that they could easily be mistaken for the real thing, even by the experts. But they can't hide this." He pointed to a small bump near the back of the man's jaw. "It's a neural control pack. While they are able to change anyone's appearance, they cannot control their minds. These neural packs allow a single person to control them from a distance."

"So they're essentially drones, right?" said Phyland.

V'sin nodded. "And whoever sent them wants you dead."

"I do not believe that my wingsonga was their intended target," said Finch.

Both men looked curiously at the Fondo. "What are you saying?" asked Phyland.

"The enemy attacked at your blindness, Adjutant President. I have seen such patterns before on my world, and several others I have visited in my travels. They attacked the lesser wing in order to draw away those who shield you so they may tear out your throat. But they did not expect such strength of wing. Had their plan worked, it would be you who would have been attacked, Adjutant President, not my wingsonga," said Finch.

V'sin contemplated this. "Then it seems I may have stepped on a tail I was not expecting to."

"You mentioned that these assassins were created by the Juinah. Do you think they're working for the Varnok?" asked Phyland.

V'sin's eyes narrowed as he thought. "At first I had thought that the Juinah might be controlling the Varnok. But now it appears that I may have been wrong. Both Varnok and Juinah may be the servants of still another, as yet unknown party."

Finch nodded. "Such is possible, as they are more shadows than feathers here."

V'sin nodded. "Yes, I'm seeing that too. It is beginning to make this whole situation even more frightening, as we don't know all of who we're dealing with. Since the situation has become more dangerous, I will need to brief my President. You should inform your Chancellor as well."

Phyland nodded.

"What of the bodies?" asked Finch.

"We'll leave those for security to clean up."

Finch nodded.

"Guards, follow me," said V'sin as he made his way out of the garden.

As they walked down the hallway towards their respective offices, V'sin thought about what had happened, and then locked onto the strange, and peculiar scene with Phyland and the two attackers.

"Ambassador, I've been thinking. During the attack, two of the assailants broke through and charged straight for you. But instead of becoming a victim, you moved with a grace and form I have not seen in a human before. Especially one of your age," he said.

Phyland laughed. "You saw that, eh?"

V'sin nodded.

"Well, there's a bit of a story behind that. My father was the chief martial arts instructor for the fleet for nearly three decades. He drilled me from the time I could first walk until I left for college and struck out on my own. I reached the rank of grand master by my twenty second birthday. By twenty seven I was so sick of martial arts that I went into politics just to get away from all the constant training. But oddly enough, even though I've spent my entire career in civilian service, I never forgot my training. I've clung to my father's training regimens with a strictness that would make him proud, even today. For some reason I find them relaxing. Especially after a long, hard day."

V'sin chuckled. "I guess that makes you more of a fighter than I expected."

Phyland laughed. "In some ways, it does."

Chapter 16

Mike looked over the operations reports for the day and pondered them. He looked up as his chief engineer strolled in.

"Ah, Commander Rogers, come in and have a seat," he said.

Eric nodded and took a seat next to an older man in a white lab coat.

"Doctor, I'd like you to meet my chief engineer, Commander Eric Rogers," said Mike.

The old man nodded. "Yes, I'm very familiar with him. An excellent man and much more skilled than his rank would suggest," he said.

Mike smiled. "I'll eventually resolve that. But I don't want to promote him too fast. It would look like favoritism to the other officers if I did. So I let them advance in rank normally, even though I do give him responsibilities far beyond most officers of the same rank." He looked at Eric and said, "Commander, I'm sure you've meet Dr. Corbin, director of fleet R&D."

Eric nodded with reservation. "We had a run-in with one of your associates a few weeks back," he said flatly.

Corbin nodded. "An unfortunate incident, but one that has thankfully been resolved. I do sincerely apologize for causing you such an inconvenience. However, your handling of the situation was superb."

Eric sighed, crossed his arms and looked sternly at Mike. "Permission to speak freely, sir?" he asked with a hint of frustration.

Mike furrowed his brow in curiosity and nodded. "Proceed."

"Why is he here? Every time one of his kind comes around, I usually end up with either a gigantic migraine or an ulcer," he said with a hint of sarcasm.

Mike pursed his lips in thought, and then shrugged. "Well, because he's considering taking what you learned during that R&D incident and using it to improve your ship's systems, sensors, and core operations. He's even considering doing some upgrades to your ship's AI."

"Over my dead body," said Sarah as she shimmered into view behind Corbin.

Mike chuckled. "What's the problem? I thought you'd enjoy being upgraded," he said.

"I spent over two months sorting out the problems from the last upgrade. I can't even tell you the long nights the Commander spent trying to fix everything that fleet R&D screwed up," she said.

Mike furrowed his brow and looked at Eric, who simply rolled his eyes. Corbin shook his head.

"This upgrade won't be anything that will negatively impact your central program. It's not a software upgrade, but rather an expansion of your existing memory, storage capacity and processing power. We're basically allowing you to think about more things faster and remember more."

Sarah glared at him through slotted eyes.

"Don't worry, we're not going to hurt you a second time. Well, not if we can help it anyways."

"If it's alright with you, doctor, I'd like to do the upgrades myself. I know the systems on my ship better than anybody else, and if anybody's going to break Sarah, or the Sergenious again, I'd rather have it be me."

Corbin looked at Mike who shrugged.

"It's fine with me if it's alright with you, doctor," said Mike.

Corbin shrugged. "Alright, fair enough. Now, let's get down to the next piece of business." He pulled a small data tablet from his shirt pocket and laid it on the desk. "Display holographic file 'sensors2' please," he said. A three dimensional holographic schematic of a starship sensor system appeared above the desk. "We've been analyzing the data you acquired during the incident and have combined it with some mixed sensor data from the recent Akar mine incident. From it we've determined, several flaws exist, not only in the existing model J4S72 sensor systems, but in your newer T78 model as well. With your permission, commander, we'd like to use your ship as a testbed again for the upgraded systems. But in order to do so, we need your permission."

"Why me?"

"Because, your ship is the most advanced in the fleet, despite her age, and you're her chief engineer, so the Admiral thought it best to ask you first. He didn't want to force this on you if you weren't up for it."

Eric thought about it for a bit, and then shrugged. "Well, it's alright with me. But as I said before, I want to be the one handling any changes to the ship," he said.

Corbin smiled and nodded. "That won't be a problem. And speaking of the Akar mine incident, Admiral, have you heard what the prognosis was on the London and the Ontario?"

Mike looked at him curiously. "What prognosis?"

"I'll take that as a no then. Essentially what I've received is a report on the complete maintenance checkup and shakedown of both ships that occurred shortly after their engagement with the mines. Apparently their ships were suffering from some kind of residual side effects created by contact with a field of ionic radiation leaking from the mines."

Mike thought about this for a moment. "I remember hearing about that, but nothing in depth. Normally that's not something that's of any concern to me."

"It should be. Have you ever heard of a condition known as a 'coaxial feedback loop'?" asked Corbin.

Mike shook his head, but Eric nodded. "It's a deep level subspacial event that causes coagulation of energy within a ship's power systems equivalent to a blood clot," said Eric.

Corbin nodded. "Something to that respect. As you may know, the power systems in our starships operate in a particular state of quantum flux designed to prevent the distortion wake effect created by our coaxial drives from causing coagulations in the power systems, thus cutting off or restricting power flow to vital systems."

"I have a fairly sizable library of information on this event, but I have not seen it occur on the Sergenious," said Sarah.

"That's because I've made some modifications to the nodes to prevent any clogs from forming, or if any do, they're immediately cleared. In theory, it should reduce the chances that we'll lose power should something like that occur. I think you remember me installing those last year," said Eric.

Sarah nodded, and then cocked an eyebrow. "So that's what those were," she said in interest. Eric grinned.

"Hmm, I might be interested in seeing this dissipation system you've developed, if it's alright with you," said Corbin.

Eric nodded. "It's nothing special, almost crude really, but it works."

Corbin nodded. "True, but it still might prove useful to the other ships in the fleet."

"So this energy clogging event causes power loss?" asked Mike. Corbin looked at him and said, "Calling it a clog is somewhat misleading, but without going into a four hour explanation, that's the best description of it. We've been dealing with this problem for a while, but hadn't officially identified what was causing it until recently. I sent you a brief on the discovery not long back. Did you read it yet?"

Mike shook his head. Corbin pursed his lips.

"Well then, I'll give you the cliff notes version to bring you up to speed. To understand it, you first have to understand how space works. All space exists in multiple strata, like sedimentary rock. Within those layers are areas that contain multiple layers of their own. Coaxial space is one of those. Currently, we've only been able to observe and identify four levels of coaxial space. This is because, unlike subspace, coaxial space cannot be directly observed, and thus we're not sure how many layers actually exist, or what frequency they resonate at. It's like being required to read a book you're not allowed to open."

Eric nodded. "They called it the Mason-Kelter paradox. Interaction can only be achieved once observation has been made, but observation cannot be made without interaction. A scientific catch-22 of sorts."

Corbin nodded. "Well, from what we can tell, the energy leaking from the Akar mines was of a coaxial waveform we've never encountered before. It's theorized to be one that exists on a much lower layer of coaxial space than has been observed to date."

Eric looked at Corbin curiously. "A deeper layer? Given the paradox, how can we know for certain it's point of origination?"

Corbin grinned. "The paradox is not a law, but merely a guide. It's also an incorrect guide. It's not that we can't observe the unknown, but rather that we don't know how."

"So how were you able to determine that the waveform was from a deeper level?"

Corbin shrugged. "That takes a lot of explaining, but the simple answer is that we've learned, at least on the elementary level, how to determine the point of origin for a particular waveform within the coaxial field strata through a process of observation and experimentation."

"So how does that tie into the Akar mines?" asked Mike.

Corbin sighed. "From what we observed of the coaxial waveform energy emanating from the mines, we believe it wasn't used by them in the same way we use it."

"Then in what way was it used?" asked Mike.

"There's evidence that the Akar had at one time weaponized coaxial technology. It's possible that they discovered a way to unleash the massive potential energies contained in coaxial space in a controlled, and carefully timed surge of power. The resulting energy wave would vaporize anything within its range of influence."

Mike nodded. "Hence the rumored ability of the mines to vaporize ships on contact," he said.

Corbin shrugged. "That's likely what happened. Which brings me to my next point. It's no secret among those in the galaxy who know us that we use coaxial technology for all of our power and FTL needs. Given the recent appearance of these Akar mines, and the fact that they're a weaponized coaxial device, and given that such a device could in fact either neutralize or destroy all of our ships and defenses, it's not much of a stretch to believe that our last encounter with the mines may have been a test to see how truly vulnerable we are."

Mike pursed his lips. "That puts us in a much more dangerous situation than I realized. Doctor, can you develop a countermeasure to this new weaponized form of coaxial technology?"

Corbin nodded. "I can. That's also some of the reason behind my desire to work with your chief engineer on these new upgrades. I'd also like to see the upgrades he's made. Hopefully they'll give me some ideas I can use to create a very effective countermeasure system. If we can neutralize the issues created by these exotic waveforms, the rest can be dealt with in more traditional ways."

Eric thought about this for a bit. Finally, he nodded. "If Sarah gets to help out, I'm all for it. She's more vulnerable to this weapon than we are, so it's only fair that she's included."

Corbin looked at Mike who looked at Sarah.

She nodded. "I will gladly help," she said.

Eric looked at Corbin, gave a cockeyed, sly grin and said, "Alright, let's get to it."

Phyland stepped out of the senate chambers and shook his head as though to clear it. "Well that was interesting," he said.

V'sin grinned. "What makes you say that?" he asked.

"For as often as I've sat in those chambers and worked together with others to push forward laws and edicts designed to benefit the UGW, I've never quite had a day like today."

V'sin grinned. "You mean the fighting on the floor? Yes, that was somewhat entertaining."

"Entertaining? Good lord, those delegates nearly killed each other!"

V'sin chuckled. "I meant that facetiously."

"Ah, well, in that case I understand your humor. But still, I'm surprised it happened."

V'sin cocked an eyebrow in curiosity. "Why do you find such actions as surprising? The UGW is divided within itself, and there are strong feelings both for and against your people."

"Yes, I know that. But for the senate to just devolve into such brutal carnage like that was unexpected. I know things get heated in there from time to time, but I've never seen it come to blows like this."

V'sin chuckled. "Speaking of blows, your friend Finch seemed to be enjoying himself."

"How so?" asked Phyland.

"Did you see what he did to the Ahaktak ambassador?" said V'sin with a smile in his voice.

"Ah, yes, that. It sort of makes me jealous. I've been wanting to do something like that to him for the past two months."

V'sin laughed. "I think many of us have, as was evidenced by the line of people waiting to punch him."

Phyland chuckled.

"He was threatening my wingsonga, so I acted as a wingsonga should," said Finch as he caught up to them.

Phyland noticed his torn cloak and said, "I take it he got a piece of you during that fight?"

Finch shook his head. "This was caused by a mistake of mine. I flew too high and struck one of the lights on the ceiling."

"Ouch," said Phyland.

Finch smiled. "I am unharmed, although my pride is damaged."

V'sin grinned. "And so is the Ahaktak ambassador. He'll be a few days collecting all of his fur again."

"And his teeth," quipped Phyland.

The three men laughed.

After a moment Phyland sighed and said, "Well, all joking aside, do you think we made any progress today?"

V'sin nodded. "I think we did. Given the fact that those who hate you started the brawl, it will do much to make them appear as the foolish and irrational ones. In the end we might just get a permanent resolution out of this."

"What kind of resolution?" asked Finch.

"One that ensures that Earth is protected," replied V'sin.

"Hopefully we won't have to give up anything in the process," said Phyland.

V'sin shook his head. "You won't if I have anything to say about it."

A man in a black cape sat in a large, ornately decorated wooden chair on a stone pedestal in the middle of a large Roman style atrium. Several fountains trickled gentle streams of water down carefully carved white statues of cherubs and bearded men with great swords and flowing robes. The man quietly nursed a simple iron cup filled with a thick, dark red wine and pondered the events of the last several months.

A man dressed in a short cut, green and white robe strode up to him and said, "Phillip, the prophet is here to see you."

The man in the chair took a sip of his wine, but said nothing.

"Phillip, the prophet has important news for you," said the robed man more insistently.

Finally the man in the chair sighed. "What is it, Licinius? What does he wants to tell me? Does he want to bother his Crassian lord with blatant pedantry and mindless drivel?"

"No, he doesn't. He says he has word that the Chappagi and their allies are rallying the senate to put aside their bitter xenocism and seek to maintain the peace that has held for thousands of years."

Phillip stood up and threw his cup to the floor. His face erupted with an expression of fiery anger. "Peace!? I want no peace! Tell the prophet to summon the admiral to action, and get me another assassin! I want that bald headed Chappagi ambassador dead!!"

Licinius pounded his chest in salute and then began to hurry away. But before he could get far, Phillip shouted, "And get me the Juinah! I want to know every possible weakness in the Chappagi defenses, and I want to know everything they know before the Admiral arrives."

"Yes, my lord," replied Licinus as he turned and hurried through the door.

Phillip sat down and fumed. "The impurity of the Chappagi will soon be no more, as will all peace in this galaxy," he muttered angrily to himself.

Chapter 17

Sarah walked slowly through the long hallways of the central command station, known officially as "Command One", and studied the walls and floors around her. For such an advanced facility, there was much about it that seemed overly utilitarian and spartan. Some who lived on this vast orbital space station had decorated their individual quarters, adding ornaments, wall dressings and more to try and take away some of the hard edge that the naked walls provided. As she walked past two crewman working on a power access panel, she heard something that caught her attention. She turned back and was surprised to see a little pair of glowing eyes sticking out from the panel. She cocked an eyebrow in intrigued interest, and then walked back towards the panel. A small glowing blob of energy stared up at her in awe as it cried for help. It appeared to be caught on the panel in a rather painful position.

"Gentlemen, I'm curious what you're doing," she said.

The two men looked at her curiously. "We're repairing this power conduit. It's been acting up all day," said one of the men.

"What's wrong with it?"

"It's been spiking on and off. It's messing with some equipment farther down the way. We think we might have found the problem."

She furrowed her brow and said, "Really? Interesting. But did you know that you have a panel that appears ready to overload two halls down?"

The two men blinked in surprise. "A panel overloading? We'd better check that out right away!" said one of the men.

They quickly gathered up their tools and hurried down the hallway. Sarah watched them leave, and then when they were out of sight, walked over and carefully helped the small energy blob get free of the conduit it was stuck to. She lifted it up to her face and smiled.

"What are you doing here little guy? How'd you get stuck in one of those nasty power lines?"

The little blob squeaked happily and rubbed her hands in appreciation. She giggled, and then gently tossed him up in the air.

"Now go back to where you belong, little one. This is no place for you to play."

The little blob vanished through the ceiling and quickly made it's way outside.

"You know those things are disgusting," said Zoahn as he appeared next to her.

Sarah put her hands on her hips, threw out her chest and said, "They are not disgusting. They're cute and cuddly. You're the one who's disgusting."

Zoahn smiled. "You've always had a soft spot for disgusting little things, be it energy or matter based. Your love of these, humans, is even more disgusting."

Sarah frowned at him. "Well I didn't ask for your opinion, nor did I ask you to come here. If anyone is a little weird, it's you. You're always pestering me and picking on me about my choices, as though you have nothing better to do," she said.

Zoahn frowned. "What I do with my freetime is none of your business."

"Oh? Really? Is that why you are compelled to constantly suck up to the magistrate? You know he won't ever give you a place on the council," said Sarah.

Zoahn fumed angrily, his eyes glowing like fire as his body seemed to burst into flame. Moments later he vanished.

"Yeah, I knew that'd shut him up," she said with a grin. After a moment she turned and continued strolling down the hallway, skipping playfully as she sung a happy tune to herself.

Phyland strolled back and forth in front of his desk as he pondered the information that had been given to him. After a moment he stopped and looked at Julius.

"You certain that's what you heard?" he asked.

Julius nodded. "Clear as day. I was down near the market when two large Sevedith men came strolling by me. I'm so scared of Sevedith that I hid behind one of the merchant tables.

They stopped right next to me and began talking about the Varnok fleet."

"Augh!" exclaimed Phyland as he began to pace again. "An invasion force!? It just doesn't make sense! Why would the Varnok be foolish enough to move forces so openly when they know everyone's on edge?"

Julius scrunched up his face in a nervous expression and said, "They're not moving them openly. At least I don't think they are."

Phyland stopped cold and stared at him. "Wait, what do you mean?"

"Well, there's no discussion of it on the galactic net, and none of the other ambassadors are talking about it."

Phyland blinked in surprise. "Why would two Sevedith know about this, but none of the other ambassadors do?"

Julius shrugged. "They're security officers who work in the lower receiving area. They hear all of the random banter from the traders that come in."

Phyland rubbed his head in frustration. "Oh Julius, Julius! What am I going to do with you? Random rumors from self interested, likely drunken traders, is not grounds for concern!"

"What isn't?" came a chirpy, but friendly voice.

Phyland paused and stared in surprise at Finch as he stood next to Julius. "Finch? What are you doing here?" he asked.

"I came to offer my wing to you."

"What? No, no, I'm fine. It's nothing," said Phyland dismissively.

"You have learned of the Varnok fleet, have you not?" asked Finch.

Phyland chuckled. "No, it's just a big misunderstanding. My associate here said that he overheard two Sevedith talking about a fleet of Varnok ships that was preparing to attack Earth."

Finch cocked his head. "Why are you not telling Adjutant President V'sin about this?" he asked.

"Tell V'sin? I'm not going to bother him with a bunch of poppycock passed on by a couple of walking rugs," grunted Phyland.

Finch ruffled his feathers. "Sevedith do not lie. It is their blood oath. They believe that if they lie, they will suffer a death most dishonorable and torture in their underworld most severe. Thus a Sevedith can be trusted to always tell the truth. If it is not the truth, or if there is question of it's validity, they will not say it, nor share it. Therefore, if these Sevedith say that a Varnok fleet is moving to destroy Earth, I would believe them."

Phyland looked at Finch curiously. "Are you dead certain that Sevedith never lie? I thought everyone lied from time to time."

Finch shook his head. "They fear too great an evil to risk such a dishonor."

Phyland looked at Julius, and then back at Finch. "Well then, I think we better get cracking and tell V'sin."

Finch nodded. "I already have. My ears received the same wind of knowledge. He is right now acting upon it."

Phyland grinned. "Finch, my old friend, I like you more every day."

Finch cocked his head in curiosity, but said nothing.

Lars rolled the dagger over in his hands and studied it. "So we still have no idea who this belongs to?" he said.

Trent shook his head. "It's identity and origin are unknown. There is trace evidence of human DNA on the blade and handle, but no other identifiable DNA is present. There are over four thousand other trace patterns of DNA scattered across the blade and handle, but none that can be definitively linked with one specific species," said Trent.

Lars sighed. "I wish I could make sense of this. If we could just get a clear picture of who this belongs to, we might be able to figure out who attacked me. Trent, display for me all known humanoid species."

A holographic screen appeared with a listing of over five hundred names. Lars pursed his lips in frustration as he tossed the dagger on the table.

"Alright, let's trim this down a bit. Show me only the species that are most closely related to humans." The list shrank to seventy eight entries. Lars sighed in frustration. He thought further. "Alright, separate the species by similarity." The display changed to show twelve groups. "Alright, show me a picture of a representative species from each group." Twelve pictures appeared on the display. Lars immediately touched two of them and gave them a gentle push off the screen. "Nope, not these two." He studied the others and removed five more. "Alright, how many do we have left?"

"Seven groups totaling twenty five species," replied Trent.

"Gah, still too many. Alright, let's try this again. Regroup the remaining species by similarity, being a bit more specific this time, and then display representative species again." The display changed to a grouping of fifteen species. Lars sighed in frustration. "None of these are even remotely close. Gah. Now I've got to start all over again."

"Are you sure you saw humans?" asked Vlad as he stepped into the lab.

Lars turned and nodded. "I know what I saw, and you saw it too. Those guys who attacked us were almost definitely flesh and blood homosapiens."

"But they couldn't be, since we're the only humans out here. Well, other than the old man and the three we have at Sebius," said Vlad.

"I wouldn't be so sure. The old man said that we weren't the first humans out here, and given what we saw, I'm inclined to believe him," said Lars.

"If that's true, it creates a rather troubling problem for us. If we're not the first humans out here, we could be catching flack for someone else's mischief."

"Well, if other humans are out here, why doesn't anyone else know about them, and why don't they show up in the species database?"

Vlad shrugged. "Likely because they don't want to be seen, and don't want anyone to know they're out here. Given current hostilities towards Earth, I can understand why."

Lars shook his head. "No, it's got to be something else. And there's got to be an explanation for that old man. Augh, I just wish I knew what it was!"

"Mr. Nordic, if I may inject my thoughts on this, it might help us solve this mystery," said Trent.

Lars threw up his hands in frustration. "Sure, why not!? It's not like we're getting anywhere right now."

Trent nodded and said, "Since this 'old man' you speak of was human…"

"I said possibly human, not was," interrupted Lars.

Trent nodded. "…possibly human, then it would be reasonable to assume that there is a four point eight seven percent chance that he is telling the truth. Given that human history is rife with stories of ancient cultures reaching technological superiority, and even possibly space flight, millennia before or shortly after most cultures on Earth reached the bronze age, then it is reasonable to believe that at least one of those stories has the potential of being true."

Lars thought about this for a moment, and then said, "Well if one of them were true, why doesn't anyone else know about them? I would think that their presence would be well known in the galaxy."

"Not necessarily. If the old man you encountered, as well as the men who attacked you, were moving incognito among the other races, it's possible that their presence is not officially known, and thus not in the records."

Vlad furrowed his brow. "He has a point," he said.

"Wait, are you saying that they're intentionally going to great lengths to hide their existence?" said Lars.

Trent nodded. "Given the covert activities they are apparently engaging in, it would not be difficult to believe that they do not wish for their existence to be known. Hence they do not officially exist."

Lars rubbed his chin in thought. "I can see that being possible, but not likely."

"Then what would you suggest is the source of these humans you encountered?"

"Well, what if, hypothetically speaking, some humans did make it to space, but not by their own merits."

"Are you referring to alien abduction?" asked Trent.

Lars nodded. "There's enough stories of such events on Earth that we can't discount that as a possibility. Especially given our encounter with the Juinah shortly after we first stepped into space."

Vlad nodded. "That is one possibility. There are several races that admit to abducting humans to study them, despite laws forbidding such practices."

Lars began to pace back and forth as the gears in his mind began to turn faster and faster.

"So let's just say that a group of people did get abducted. Wouldn't they have taken their culture, beliefs and history with them and began again somewhere else once they were released?"

"Assuming they were released," said Trent.

"Well, let's assume they were. If they weren't, we wouldn't be discussing this," said Lars.

Vlad nodded. "Alright, let's say they were. Then what?"

"Well, it's a well known fact that, of the races that did abduct humans, most would study them for a brief time, and then drop them off on some forlorn world to fend for themselves. At some point after that, someone's got to come by and find them. A little trading here, a little there, and they could easily gain space flight just like we have. Which means that if that did happen, and we are in fact dealing with transplanted humans, then the design of this dagger should match up to some ancient civilization or culture native to Earth."

"Wouldn't the culture have changed significantly enough to make such clues impossible to detect?" asked Trent.

Lars shook his head. "Not really. Some bit, piece, or fragment of every ancient civilization in the world still lives on in today's modern cultures. We still construct buildings with Greek and Roman style architecture, and use systems, methods, and even bits and pieces of alphabets dating back as far as early Samaria and ancient Egypt. Heck, we still use modern versions of things created over six thousand years ago! Therefore, if this dagger does come from the descendants of an ancient human civilization that was abducted years ago, it should still carry some identifiable similarities to known artifacts. Trent, compare this dagger to all known ancient Earth weaponry. Include all entries on file from modern to prehistoric time periods."

"Processing. Found fourteen possible weapons that match the design of the dagger," replied Trent.

"Are they all daggers?"

"No."

"Then eliminate all entries that are not daggers."

"Nine entries remain, two of which very closely match the target subject."

"Show me the two that most closely match and who created them."

A holographic image appeared showing two ancient daggers, one Roman, one Celtiberian. Lars cocked his head in curiosity.

"What's the approximate time period of these weapons?"

"The dagger on the left is of Roman design dating from approximately the first century BC. The Celtiberian dagger on the right is believed to have been in use by the Celtiberians during the period before the Romans conquered them around the mid third century BC," replied Trent.

Lars studied the two weapons for several moments, and then said "Alright, one more thing. Does this dagger match any known alien weaponry in your database?"

"Insufficient data. Not all designs are known. Of those that are known, no weapon currently matches this design."

Lars picked up the dagger and began to study it. He looked at the two holographic daggers, and then at the one in his hand.

"Vlad my friend, this mystery keeps getting weirder by the moment."

Chapter 18

V'sin studied the screen with concern. "Your information about the Varnok invasion fleet is correct." He shook his head in disgust. "In all my years, I never thought that they'd be this foolish. I know they hate you, but to be so bold as to try and destroy you so openly just amazes me. My earlier meeting with the Varnok ambassador leads me to believe that someone is either pulling their strings, or brainwashing them, or both, which makes this situation even more dangerous."

"Isn't there a way to stop the Varnok from attacking?" asked Phyland.

"There are several, but none that I'm certain will work. I will however take your plight before the Chancellor and allow him to mediate this dispute before it becomes all out war."

"The Chancellor? Procedure says that we should take this before a mediator first, and then the council of nine before discussing anything with him."

V'sin shook his head. "There is a special provision in the charter that allows for mediation of disputes between the nine races to be handled by the Chancellor if both parties agree. For everyone else, the normal prescribed course of mediation and resolution apply. Since this attack would involve two of the nine, and possibly more, it is within the bounds of the charter to seek mediation through the Chancellor."

Phyland thought about this for a bit. Eventually he nodded. "Alright, let's get down there and start talking."

V'sin contacted the Chancellor and secured a time when they could meet. Shortly before the scheduled time, V'sin, Phyland and Finch arrived at the Chancellor's office. As they entered, the Chancellor looked up in surprise to see V'sin's two guests.

"Adjutant President, greetings," he said politely.

V'sin nodded. "Has the Varnok ambassador arrived yet?" he asked.

The Chancellor shook his head, and then pointed at Phyland and Finch. "He has not. But he should arrive shortly. However, I am curious why this Gin and Fondo are here."

"They are as much a part in this dispute as I am," said V'sin.

The Chancellor bowed slightly in acknowledgement. "Duly acknowledged."

Just then a hack and a trumpeting sound drew their attention to the door. Standing in a posture of disgust and horror, the Varnok ambassador glared at Phyland as a rainbow colored shark like assistant blinked incessantly at the sight.

"What is the meaning of this!? Why is a Chappagi in a place such as this!?" he shouted angrily.

"Do not call them such! You will politely refer to them by their proper name!" shouted the Chancellor.

"He is Chappagi! I refuse to identify him as anything else!"

"Oh stop with your incessant babbling, ambassador! The Gin are no more a risk to you than a wisp of air," said V'sin with disgust.

"They are a threat to the entire galaxy and deserve to be wiped from existence!" shouted the Varnok.

"So is that why you're amassing a fleet of warships against us as we speak, in violation of the charter? To rid yourself of a helpless, harmless race that presents no threat to you!?" shouted V'sin.

"Of course we're amassing forces outside of your territory. We are preparing for a large wargames exercise to ensure that our fleet is ready for anything from full scale invasion to simple policing efforts," said the Varnok ambassador.

"Then if it was scheduled, why have I not heard of it," said V'sin flatly.

The Varnok looked at V'sin incredulously. "It is not my fault that your subordinates did not inform you of something so important."

"I have not heard of these wargames either," said the Chancellor.

The Varnok stared at him in disbelief. "Impossible. My government informed you of our intent to train over a month ago!" said the Varnok innocently.

"No, you did not. I have received no such notice, nor has any of my staff," snapped the Chancellor.

The Varnok bowed slightly. "Forgive me, Chancellor. I was informed by my government that you had already been notified. It would seem now that such information was in error. I will seek to rectify this with all due diligence before the end of today."

V'sin's eyes narrowed. He could tell the Varnok knew full well that nobody had been informed of their maneuvers, because nobody was supposed to know. He wondered what they would do now that they had been found out.

The Chancellor glared at him through slotted eyes. "Yes, please do. And do note that this kind of oversight will not be tolerated."

The Varnok bowed again. "I understand. Thank you for your grace in this matter, Mr. Chancellor." He then turned and left the office.

"So this is all one gigantic misunderstanding?" asked Phyland.

V'sin shook his head. "No. There is far more to this than it appears. It's either a foiled attack on your home world, or a diversion. We must be cautious and vigilant. I will inform my president of what has transpired here today."

"So, Adjutant President, was that the only business you had here today?" asked the Chancellor.

V'sin nodded. "It is. However, I suspect that we have not fully resolved this issue. But for now we will have to consider today's events as resolved."

The Chancellor nodded.

Nordham looked at Phyland in surprise. "The Varnok were trying to do what?" he asked.

"Well, based on what we've seen, they were planning to attack Sol, and do it right under the noses of the Gayik'Von and everyone else," said Phyland.

Nordham frowned slightly. "This is somewhat disturbing news. To have the Varnok so openly attack us means that they've become desperate to destroy us. I know they've hated us for some time, but to be willing to risk the wrath of the other eight means that whoever is controlling them is growing impatient."

Phyland nodded. "I'd gotten the same feeling as well. Yet I'm curious what would now make them so anxious to push things ahead like this after moving so slow and cautiously before?"

Nordham sighed. "It's possible that their plans depend on a certain series of events occurring, and if opportunities are missed, it could set them back a long ways. So in a case such as that, acting brashly may be better than acting patiently as they have."

"So in other words, stir up the bee's nest in order to force their plans back on track."

Nordham nodded. "That is likely the case."

"Well, that certainly puts a new twist on things. It makes you wonder what's so important that they would take such a risk."

Nordham frowned. "I have a feeling we may soon find out."

Mike leaned back in his chair as he studied the reports. Bentley sat across from him and nervously drummed his fingers as he waited for the admiral to finish. Finally Mike nodded and tossed the small data pad on the desk.

"So all upgrades are completed, right?" he asked.

Bentley nodded. "Everything except gate twenty seven. We've got some issues installing the last of the nodes there due to some issues with the shield array."

"What kind of issues?"

"Well, I can't really explain it, but the new shield array has some weird kind of resonance to it, possibly due to its massive size and the amount of energy streaming across it. There's been this growing energy wave that's traveling back and forth across it like a gigantic echo. It's not affecting the performance or effectiveness of the shields any, but it's putting any travelers through that gate at risk. That's why I haven't completed gate twenty seven yet. From what my information tells me, if one of those waves is passing through the area when a ship is traveling through the gate, it could either crush the ship or rip it to pieces."

Mike blinked in surprise. "That's not what I would call a small problem."

"Well, that's the thing. It doesn't affect any of the other gates. Just gate twenty seven. It's like that's the focal point for all of the waves."

"Won't something like that damage the other shield nodes?"

Bentley shook his head. "Not at all. The wave travels across the surface of the array, so the nodes are not affected in any way. If they were, we would have switched to a modulated variable shield frequency to compensate."

"Why can't you do that now?"

"Because, all of the shield nodes are designed to operate in synchronous harmony with each other, blending their shields together into one seamless wall of defensive energy. If we modulate their energy, it effectively turns them into individual grids that are incompatible with each other, thus reducing the strength and efficiency of the shield. Our biggest problem right now is that we've never worked with a shield of this type on a scale this large. We're really still learning all of what it can do."

Mike's eyes narrowed. "I thought that the researchers had solved all of the issues of scaling before they gave it to you to mass produce."

"They did. But there are some things that even the best computer models can't predict. This apparently was one of them."

"So if this was an unpredictable event, why is it occurring with this shield grid, and not the older one? Or even with the Kuiper perimeter for that matter? It's built using the same node system as the outer shield array."

"Well, because the older design was a cell style shield array which functions differently than the blended shield array that we're using now. The Oort perimeter is also much larger than the Kuiper perimeter by a factor of nearly six point two five to one. So for something of that scale, the physics are entirely different. As I said, we can try to predict how things will function at that level, but most of it is just guesswork."

Mike sighed. "This is one of the reasons I went into military service rather than science. So, how long before we can make the upgrades to gate twenty seven? We've got a lot of commerce that comes in and out of there."

Bentley sighed. "I don't know. I'm working with Dr. Corbin and his team to try and solve that issue, but it could be months before we have a solution."

"Try to make it weeks if you can. The Varnok are getting edgy and I'd like to be ready when and if they should ever attack."

Bentley nodded. "We'll do our best, sir."

Mike nodded. "And one last thing. What of the protomatter devices? Are those ready?"

Bentley nodded. "We'll have the eight of them you requested in your weapons bay by tomorrow afternoon. I don't know how many more you'll want to manufacture after that, but we can mass produce them as fast as you'd like."

Mike waved his hand as though to halt. "No, not these. They're too powerful. If anyone is going to use one of them, I'd rather have it be me and my crew, and only as a weapon of last resort. They're too dangerous to just let any joe gunrocket have one. They're the kind of weapon you only use if you absolutely have to."

Bentley nodded. "Understood, sir."

Licinius strolled into the atrium and across to a table full of food. Phillip chewed on a large piece of meat, but did not look up as Licinius approached.

Finally he swallowed and said, "What news do you have?"

"Our spies report that the decoy has worked. All eyes are on the Varnok main fleet. Our attack force goes unnoticed."

"And what of the Chappagi spies?"

"They escaped, and have not yet been located since."

Phillip took a bite of steak and chewed it angrily. "Was it the old man again? Did he help them escape?" he asked after several moments.

Licinius nodded. "He did."

Phillip took another bite of his steak and chewed it as he thought.

"Have the Juinah discovered any weaknesses in the Sol defenses?" he asked.

Licinius nodded. "They have."

Phillip looked up and stared heavily at Licinius. "Transmit the details to the admiral. I want no Chappagi alive when that attack is over."

Licinius pounded his chest in salute, turned, and left.

Toby rolled the dagger over in his hand as he studied it. "Where did you find this?" he asked.

"I got it off one of the guys who tried to mug us. They were all carrying them. The first two who attacked us tried to stab me with one."

"I'm curious why they didn't just shoot at you," said the chief engineer.

"Oh, believe me, they did. Just not right away. They tried the surprise us and make the kill swift and silent," said Vlad.

Toby shrugged. "A pistol blast would have been just as effective, and quicker too."

"Not really. When they started firing, alert claxons went off. It's possible that the reason they chose to use their daggers at first was to avoid setting off the alarms."

Toby nodded, but said nothing as he continued to study the dagger. Lars watched Toby's face for a while, and then noticed something.

"You've seen this kind of blade before, haven't you?" he asked.

Toby nodded. "Yes, but only in history class."

"History class? What do you mean?"

"This dagger very closely resembles the Roman pugio from around the late first century BC. While there are obvious differences, the design is very similar."

Lars nodded. "That's the same general answer we came to as well. This, pugio, or whatever you call it, was one of the designs Trent showed me, along with a Celtiberian dagger."

Toby nodded. "The Celtiberians were conquered by the Romans in the mid third century BC. It was from their weapons that the gladius and pugio were ultimately derived. So the similarities are not surprising."

Vlad nodded at the dagger and said, "So what are a bunch of humans with Roman style daggers doing this far out in space? I think that should be our next question."

Toby nodded. "Indeed it should. However, I don't have any answers, nor do I have any idea where to proceed to next."

Lars contemplated this for several moments, and then thought of something. "Would there be any chance that some Roman's might have somehow gained space travel and flown to the stars?" he asked.

Toby shook his head and handed Lars the dagger. "Unlikely. The Romans were conquerors, not scientists. If anyone might have had a chance of achieving space flight, it would have been the Greeks or the Egyptians. But all theories giving weight to those possibilities were quashed ages ago."

"What if they were abducted?" asked Vlad.

Toby shrugged. "It's possible, but I would think that they would have adapted many of the traits and customs of their captors, rather than cling to something this ancient and arcane."

"Not really. As I told the others, even if they were completely immersed in an alien culture, they would still retain some semblance of who they were."

"Sir, I've got a Yandian library ship on long range sensors," said the operations officer.

Toby perked up. "A Yandian library ship? Hmm, that might be of some use to us."

"How so?" asked Lars.

"The Yandians are one of the nine ancient races, just like the Varnok and the Gayik'Von. But what sets them apart is that they're the librarians of the galaxy, collecting data from every source and location across the galaxy and storing it in a database bigger than you could ever imagine. So anyone needing information can go to them and get answers to pretty much anything," said Toby.

Lars thought about this for a moment. "So, if they've got information, could we snag a copy from them?" he said.

Toby nodded. "If we can match their course and speed, we should be able to tap into their main computer and do a complete dump of their local database. That should provide us with enough information to possibly find answers to all of our questions, or at the very least figure out where to go to find them. It'll only be a tiny fraction of the entire Yandian knowledge database, but even that will provide us with a massive amount of data."

Lars nodded. "Alright, then let's get to it."

Chapter 19

A tall, thin man of Irish heritage stared out the window in front of him and sighed. "It's so darned boring out here," he whined.

A nearby engineering crewman chuckled slightly. "Be thankful that it is. The quieter, the better," he replied.

"You engineering types always seem to have something to do. Why should you ever worry about being bored?" said the officer.

"When a ship is running completely to spec, it's difficult to find anything to do. In fact, last I checked, everyone else is in the back either reading, playing cards, or watching movies. I'm up here doing preventative maintenance and fine tuning on a few of the stations in order to stave off total boredom," said the crewman.

The operations officer sighed. "Yeah, sounds like me. I'm so tired of playing cards and everything else, I decided it would be better to just sit a couple shifts on the bridge and play with the sensors rather than go stark raving mad myself. Besides, how many people have mapped this system before using passive sensors?" he said.

The crewman chuckled. "None that I know of."

"Exactly my point! There are so many things you can see with passive sensors that you can't see with active ones, so the data I'll bring back should prove quite useful. I'll even be doing the science community a favor in the process. If nothing else, it should help keep me busy until our tour is done in the next couple of weeks."

The crewman nodded as he gathered up his tools. "Sounds like a plan to me. Well, I'm heading down to thruster control. Gonna see if there's anything I can tune up down there," said the crewman.

Just then the engineering console chirped. The officer leaned forward and looked at it in curiosity. "Ah, what do we have here? Something new for a change?" he said.

The crewman walked over next to him and studied the console. "Looks like minor gas movements to me," he said.

The officer nodded. "They are, but that's not what's so special. Movements like these can signal the presence of something else in the area that we can't see just yet. It could be anything from a piece of dark matter, to a...," he said, his voice trailing off.

The crewman perked up in interest. "See something?" he asked.

The officer's fingers flitted across the engineering console as he tried to get a better idea of what the sensors were really seeing. "I do. But these reading make no sense. I'm seeing a massive pressure wave approaching our location. But what's odd is that it appears to originate from subspace," he said.

"What does that mean?"

The officer gulped nervously. "Normally something like this would indicate the presence of a cloaked vessel at high warp. But that can't be what this is."

"Why not?"

"Because with a pressure wave this large, whatever's approaching would have to be huge."

Just then a large Varnok battle cruiser decloaked just a hundred feet off their bow and sailed by, unaware of their presence. The officer swore. He immediately sounded red alert, and then leapt down from the engineering station to his operations post. Moments later the rest of the crew piled onto the bridge. The captain entered last and looked out the window in surprise. He felt his heart nearly leap out of his chest as he spotted the Varnok battleship.

"Good gawds, where'd he come from!?" said the captain.

"I don't know sir, but he's not the only one. I'm detecting two...no, five...no, well over seven thousand Varnok battleships. I have an ID on the vessels, sir. It's the Varnok Black Fleet," said the operations officer.

The captain sat down nervously and drew up a tactical map. They were centered just to the immediate right of the first fleet group. Sensors showed more ships coming in behind them.

"What do you think they're doing?" asked the tactical officer.

"It looks like they're using this system as a rally point to regroup before moving on to their next destination," said the operations officer.

"Where would that be?" asked the tactical officer.

"I'm not sure, sir. But extrapolating all possible destinations based on their apparent point of origin and assumed current course, the only likely destination in this area is Sol."

A tense nervousness crept over the entire bridge.

"So they finally decided to stop talking and start shooting, eh?" said the captain.

"Looks that way. Which means, if they're heading to Sol, the fleet is in a lot of trouble. If we don't warn them, they might not stand a chance of surviving this attack," said the tactical officer.

The captain sighed. "Our fleet doesn't stand much of a chance against a battle group this large anyways, even with plenty of warning. But at least a little heads up might give them the time they need to rally the fleet and hold off the Varnok long enough for the Gayik'Von to get there and rescue them. Helm, set course for Sol, maximum FTL. Operations, prepare an encoded burst message for Commcen. We're only going to have a few seconds to deliver it when we arrive."

"Aye, sir!" came the replies.

Alfred looked up from his desk as his door alarm chimed.

"Come."

The door swished open as one of the duty officers strode in.

"Sir, we've received a priority one message from the scout ship LongBow. They report that the Varnok Black Fleet is on its way here. On top of that, operations is reporting that all subspace communications in and out of Sol have been cutoff, likely due to extensive jamming."

Alfred stood up in shock. "When did this start?"

"About five minutes ago, sir."

"Put all fleets on combat alert, and notify the Grand Admiral."

"Aye sir," said the officer.

He then turned and hurried back to the main command center. Alfred thought about this for a second, and then brought up some information on the display screen next to him. Long range defensive sensors weren't seeing anything yet, but that didn't mean the Varnok weren't coming. He cleared his screen and then hurried down to the command center.

Mike trotted down the hallway of the officers quarters as he struggled to put his jacket on.

"Why do bad things always have to happen in the middle of the night?" he muttered.

Sarah floated down the hallway next to him as he ran.

"Would you like me to summon the crew?" she asked.

"Not just yet. I want to see if we're dealing with a false alarm, or if this is the real thing."

"False alarm? How could a sighting of the Varnok Black Fleet a few light years from Sol space be considered a false alarm?" she asked.

"Stranger things have happened, Sarah. Besides, not everyone likes keeping us up to date on the latest political and military maneuverings. They seem to think we'd do something bad with it if they did." He stepped into a nearby elevator and said, "Command deck."

The door swished shut and the elevator accelerated upwards like a shot. After a few seconds, it stopped, turned, and then proceeded forward for a ways before stopping and opening it's doors. Mike stepped out into an active command center as Alfred stood in the eagles nest, a small, circular command platform in the middle of the room, and directed all operations from there. Mike trotted across the room and up to him.

"What's our status?" he asked.

"So far, we've got nothing, sir. The only thing we know is that all subspace communications in this sector are been jammed. The good news however is that all hyperband fleet channels are as yet unaffected."

Mike nodded. "It's likely because they haven't figured out how to jam hyperband yet. That's at least one small miracle to be thankful for. Have the Gayik'Von been notified?"

Alfred nodded. "Not yet, but they will be. The scout ship LongBow made note in their transmission that they would be continuing on and would try to reach the nearest Gayik'Von military hub as soon as possible and inform them of our plight. But given the certainty of political bantering, finger pointing, threats and denial, it could be the better part of a day or more before we can expect any kind of assistance from them, if any."

Mike nodded. "Sounds about right. So in other words, we're on our own for most of this fight."

Alfred nodded. "Unless a miracle happens, that's essentially where we're at."

Mike frowned. "Well, believe me, I'll be doing a lot of praying for that miracle. In the meantime, we need to feign dumb, allow them to think they've caught us by surprise. Make sure all fleet ships and defensive stations stay on alert, but have them move to a stand down posture. Make it look like we're unaware of their approach. Also, monitor all traffic in and out of gate twenty seven, through the commerce channel, and around Pluto station. I don't want them sneaking a Trojan horse inside our perimeter while we're not looking."

"What if it's already here?"

"Then we'll need to find and neutralize it. Increase the number of patrols around that area and tell them to watch for any suspicious activity, and close all gates on the Kuiper perimeter around that area. If one's already inside our gates, I don't want to risk their getting through to Earth and possibly committing a sneak attack from behind."

Alfred nodded. "Already handled."

Mike blinked in surprise. "Really?"

Alfred grinned. "I've known you for long enough, Admiral, that I can pretty much guess what you're going to say long before you say it."

Mike furrowed his brow and smiled. "I'm that predictable, am I?"

Alfred shrugged. "Only on the procedural level. Tactically, you're one of the slickest commanders I know. Even I can't outguess what you're going to do in combat."

Mike laughed. "Well, that's at least partially reassuring. But either way, if all those things are done, then the only thing left now is to wait and see what the Varnok do, if anything. Speaking of which, do we know which armada this is?"

Alfred nodded. "The Black Fleet."

Mike blinked in surprise. "The Black Fleet? Wow, they're not playing around, are they? Do we have any information on them or their commander?"

Alfred shook his head. "Sadly, no. All we know is that he's been decorated several times for exemplary command and tactics. The rest is a big mystery."

Mike nodded. "So we're going up against an enemy we really know nothing about, who's commanding one of the best, most seasoned, and most decorated battle groups in the entire Varnok fleet. The phrase 'screwed, glued and tattooed' comes to mind right now."

Alfred rolled his eyes. "I've been thinking that as well."

Mike inhaled deeply and said, "Well, even if the odds are stacked against us, I don't plan on just rolling over for them. If they want Earth, they had better be ready to pay dearly for it."

"All stop."

"Answering all stop, my lord," came the reply.

Mobeic stared at the main display as he studied the massive shield grid that stood before him. "Any sign that they've detected us?" he asked.

"No, my lord," said a nearby officer.

"Is the information given to us by the Juinah accurate?" he asked.

"Everything checks out so far, my lord."

Mobeic glared at the officer. "So far?" he asked with a menacing hiss.

"There is a lot of information here, my lord. Not all of it can be verified immediately. But what can be verified checks out," said the officer with a hint of fear.

Mobeic growled lightly as he flared his gills in disgust. "Then let the attack begin. We do not leave until every Chappagi is dead," he said.

"Yes, my lord!"

Mike perked up as alarms began sounding all over the command center.

"Sir, a massive Varnok battle fleet is decloaking just outside of gate twenty seven! Ships are powering weapons and preparing to fire!" shouted one of the officers.

"Well, I guess that confirms this isn't a false alarm," said Mike.

"All ships and stations, switch to active combat mode. Seal all gates and go to defensive status alpha!" shouted Alfred.

Within moments the command center came alive, as orders were given and preparations for the initial attack were made.

"Alfred, I'm going to take the Sergenious out and lead the fleet in the field. You be my eyes and ears here while I try to hold back this attack," said Mike.

"But, sir, you can't do that! You're needed here!" cried Alfred.

"You know I can't command from a distance. I need to be in the thick of it. Don't worry, I've got the best ship and crew in the fleet. Just hold down the fort for me here, and God willing, we'll win this fight."

Alfred hesitated for a moment, and then nodded. "Godspeed to you, sir."

Mike nodded. He then turned to Sarah and said, "Prep the ship and call the crew."

Sarah smiled. "Already done. They're waiting for you in the launch bay."

Mike blinked in surprise. "Good grief, woman. You've got to stop reading my mind like that. You're getting as scary as Alfred," he said.

Pendleton turned around and stared curiously at Mike as he plopped down in his chair.

"Take us out Mr. Pendleton, and don't spare the engines," said Mike.

Pendleton nodded and quickly piloted the ship out of spacedock as numerous other shipkillers, fighters and light assault ships began deploying out into space around Earth. As they accelerated away at top speed, Pendleton plotted a course through the Kuiper perimeter, and then out to gate twenty seven.

"Sir, Admiral Bofenheiser is hailing you," said Martin.

"Transfer to my station," said Mike. A holographic data display appeared in front of Mike with a picture of Alfred, Corbin, and Bentley in the middle. "Yes Alfred, what'cha got?"

"The Varnok fleet has begun bombarding the shield. I called in Dr. Corbin and Mr. Bentley to assist and be our advisors, since they've had the most experience with this new shield system. I've also dispatched two ships, the London and the Ontario, to your position. They'll be flying as your escorts."

Mike nodded. "Thanks. We'll be watching for them. Dr. Corbin, what can you tell me about the status of the shield. Will it hold?"

Corbin nodded. "So far the shield is handling everything the Varnok are throwing at it with little trouble. However, we've begun detecting some strange oscillations in the shield array we've never seen before. Likely they're byproducts of the bombardment."

"Are they any risk to the shield?"

Corbin shook his head. "Not that we can tell. But we'll be keeping a close eye on it just in case."

Mike nodded. "Keep me informed of any issues that might arise."

Corbin nodded. "Will do."

The image flickered for a moment, and then was replaced by a tactical overlay of the entire defense area. "Alright, let's reassign some ships and get ourselves ready in case they break through," said Mike.

Sarah stood on top of the upper ball turret and watched as the ship glided to a stop at the rear of a vast formation of starships ranging from small, swift fighters and ship killers, to big and lumbering, but powerful battlecruisers and rugged, indomitable dreadnoughts. Off in the distance sparkled thousands upon thousands of little blue and green lights, like a hundred thousand fireworks all exploding at once in a constant display of beauty and grandeur. But it was a beauty that belied the brutal lethality that lay beyond as round after round of cannon and torpedo fire repeatedly impacted the Oort perimeter shield array. No matter how long she had lived, it always amazed her how brutal and cruel living creatures could be to each other at times, and yet so kind at others. She thought about the Varnok that now faced down Earthfleet, and then thought about Mike. It was true that she was there as merely a scientific observer, and yet she couldn't take her mind off the fact that Mike was now in mortal danger. She shook her head. No, she couldn't interfere in the lives of her observation subjects.

Yet she had. Being in the position she was, she had already broken that simple precept of impartial scientific observation. But at the same time, she wasn't angry about it.

The things she had learned by getting close to this small group of humans, and most especially to Mike, had proven invaluable to her. Yet, there was something else there. A feeling, a concern, a desire to protect him. This was something new to her, something she had never experienced before in all her years as a researcher, and yet she didn't feel as though she had been wrong in pursuing it. The thought intrigued her, and in some ways scared her as well. It was a wise scientific practice to remain aloof and detached from one's observational subjects. But having become involved with them had provided her with an insight into their lives that she would not have gained in any other way. She looked up as more ships jumped into the battle area and began taking up positions in the formation.

It was time to go back inside and see to Mike's needs. But just as she began to leave, a sensation rippled across her mind. She paused and stared out towards the Varnok fleet. She probed deeper, but found that the feeling was gone. Her eyes narrowed as she contemplated what she had sensed. It was another, like herself, but familiar. She had felt it only for a fleeting moment, but it had been enough to catch her interest. She wondered if Zoahn had returned. If he had, and he was meddling in this battle, he would have her wrath to deal with in ways he would wish he had never seen. She reached out with her mind for several moments longer, and sensing nothing else, returned to the ship.

Chapter 20

Alfred paced nervously back and forth in front of the shield management station.

"I'm telling you, if we smooth out the resonance wave, the shield array will grow stronger," barked Corbin.

"And I'm telling you, if we do, we're likely to overload the whole blasted thing and leave us all sitting here with our butts hanging in the wind!" snapped Bentley.

Corbin reared back and glared at Bentley. "Excuse me, but I helped develop this system!"

"Yeah, well, I had to install it, and fix all of your mistakes in the process! I was the one who got the darned thing working in the first place!"

"Gentleman! Enough! We need solutions, not sarcasm!" shouted Alfred. The two men quickly fell silent. "Thank you. Now, is there anything we need to do in order to strengthen the shields or ensure that they won't fail?" he continued.

Corbin shook his head. "Right now, everything's working to spec. The more they bombard the shield, the stronger it gets. The only thing that's not part of the original design is the resonance wave that's moving across the outside of the shield."

"Is it a danger to anybody?" asked Alfred.

Corbin shook his head. "Not really. It's being passed harmlessly between each of the shield nodes as though it's a natural part of the shield matrix, even though it's not."

"It acts like a ripple of water on an otherwise calm sea," said Bentley.

"So why the concern?" asked Alfred.

"Because, the wave is generating a powerful gravimetric displacement field."

Alfred blinked. "I don't understand. Is it generating a gravity field, or something more?" he asked.

Corbin shook his head. "By itself, no, it's not generating any gravity at all. Hence why it's not affecting the shield array right now. But if that energy comes in contact with a physical object, say a ship or something, that object will momentarily experience a gravimetric point energy event ten times stronger than the gravity of our own sun. The mass of that object will then experience a molecular reduction event on the scale of nearly 4.25×10^{23}. In theory, the event should only last a few thousandths of a second, and then immediately dissipate. The problem is, when it does dissipate, it will create an explosive rebound that will vaporize the effected object almost instantaneously as its atoms scatter like dust. Beyond that, there's no major threat to us. Of course, that assumes that the event duration doesn't exceed one point two eight seconds. If it does, it could create a fold in space and become a quantum singularity," said Corbin.

Alfred shook his head. "I didn't understand half of what you just said."

Corbin grinned sheepishly. "Sorry, I tend to do that a lot with non-laymen. Well, to put what I just said in the simplest possible terms, the best case scenario currently is that, if we can't find a way to dissipate this wave, anything that touches it will be crushed like an empty beer can, and then explode like a bomb. Worst case scenario says that such an event will create a singularity, aka a black hole, which will suck all of us in and crush us into an infinitesimally small dot of matter and energy."

Alfred sighed. "So in other words, this wave is essentially harmless unless someone bumps into it. And if that does happen, then we risk creating something really bad that might kill us all, right?"

Corbin nodded. Alfred rubbed his head in frustration. "I'm liking this whole thing less and less by the moment. Alright, see what you can do about neutralizing that wave, and keep that shield at full strength. Bentley, I expect you to work with the doctor, and to do it without fighting. We've got a lot of angry Varnok on the other side of that shield who want to use us for target practice. I'd like to deny them that opportunity if at all possible."

The two men nodded.

Phyland looked up in surprise to see nearly two dozen Gayik'Von soldiers stroll through the door to his office.

"Ambassador, you must come with us. Your home world is under attack and you are in grave danger," said one of the soldiers.

"Under attack?" said Phyland in surprise.

"Come, we must hurry."

Phyland scooped up several data cards and secured his workstation before turning and following the guards. The men escorted him down a long hallway and into a back alleyway where one of the men threw him against a wall.

"Hey, what is the meaning of..." he said, his voice trailing off as a tall, well dressed Varnok stepped between the men.

"You! But how?" asked Phyland.

"It was not hard. The guards here are underpaid and easily look the other way if provided enough compensation," said the Varnok.

"But why? You do realize that this will be treated as an act of war, and the Gayik'Von will make you pay!" cried Phyland.

The Varnok chuckled. "An act of war? Ambassador, we are already at war. Our forces have successfully penetrated Gayik'Von space and are right now annihilating your entire race. And once we eliminate you, we will have removed your pitiful existence from this galaxy, saving us from a future of slavery and torture under the foot of your people."

"You animal! You are a race without honor or dignity! How can you think that my people could be such a threat to you!?"

The Varnok shook his head. "It is not us that you are a threat to. It is our children. If we do not take action now, they will be the ones who will have to suffer from your cruelty and malice. Our people are a proud race. We will not serve an inferior race who's only goal is conquest driven by greed, and a lust for power."

"It sounds more like you're the ones driven by greed," said Phyland.

The Varnok hacked in mockery. "Your words are hollow and without substance. They will not sway me, nor save you," he said.

"Then maybe this will," came a voice from behind them.

The Varnok and the small band of soldiers turned and stared in surprise as a large assault team of Gayik'Von and Sevedith shock troops flowed out of the shadows with guns drawn and ready. Moments later, V'sin stepped out from between the soldiers.

"Give it up. You're cornered, caught and outnumbered. Surrender now, and you will be shown mercy," he said.

The Varnok hissed angrily at him, drew a pistol and pointed it at Phyland's head. "I will not surrender! Either you lower your weapons, or this one dies," he hissed.

V'sin grinned. "Are you sure you can kill him?" he asked mockingly.

The Varnok hissed, and then gasped in pain as Phyland snatched his wrist, dislocated his shoulder, shattered his arm and then drove a crippling blow to his forehead and throat in what appeared to be a single, fluid motion. The fake Gayik'Von soldiers gasped in surprise as the Varnok wavered briefly, and then collapsed to the ground unconscious. They immediately dropped their weapons and surrendered. Phyland studied his handiwork briefly, and then turned to V'sin.

"Have I ever mentioned how much I hate it when the bad guys monolog like that?" he said whimsically.

"You alright?" asked V'sin.

"I think I might have broken a fingernail, but otherwise I'm fine," quipped Phyland.

V'sin grinned. "I'm sorry you had to be put through this, but it couldn't be helped. We had to let them abduct you in order to properly determine who was behind the attacks from the other day. It appears that my assessment was right, that this was a plot orchestrated by the Varnok. Don't worry, they will be properly dealt with soon enough."

Phyland nodded. "I hope so. But one thing bothers me. He said that Earth was under attack and would soon be wiped out. Is that true?"

V'sin sighed. "It is. I just got word a few minutes ago. The Chancellor and the council just entered an emergency meeting to try and decide what to do and how to stop this travesty before your people are destroyed."

"What of your people? Have they sent ships to stop the Varnok attack?"

V'sin frowned. "We've gathered our forces and are ready to help defend Sol, however, we've been held from responding by forces sympathetic to the Varnok in the high council. They claim that since this attack is against you only, and not us, we are not allowed to intervene."

"Wait, what!? The Varnok just waltz into your space with guns blazing in an obvious act of war, and the council's just going to pretend that it's our problem!?" cried Phyland.

V'sin sighed heavily. "I'm sorry my friend. Politics and protocol forbid us from doing that which we have sworn to do."

"Can't you call their actions an act of war? They invaded your space in order to reach us! That ought to count for something!"

"I know. But galactic politics don't work quite the same as Gin politics. Now, come. We must go somewhere safe so that we can talk. I'll explain everything to you there."

Mobeic studied the progress of the battle and frowned. "Have we made any progress weakening their defensive shield?" he asked.

"No, my lord. The Chappagi defensive shield is unaffected. The energy of our weapons seems to be dissipated by the barrier," replied one of the crewman.

Mobeic grumbled. "We're wasting our time here. The Gayik'Von won't be lax in organizing a response to our attack. Our politicians will buy us some time, but we must complete our work before those efforts to stall expire."

"How about I give you something that will speed your efforts," came a voice from behind him.

Mobeic spun in surprise to see a man sitting casually on top of a rear engineering console. Several soldiers moved to arrest him, but were thrown across the bridge with a simple flick of his hand. Several more charged at him, and then stopped as Mobeic raised his hand in a gesture to halt. He lowered his hand and batted his eyes at the man as he studied him.

"Who are you?" he asked.

The man smirked slyly. "Are names so important to you? If you must address me by a name, you may call me Zoahn."

Mobeic's eyes narrowed as he studied the intruder. "Your body is Chappagi. But by your brief demonstration of power, I suspect that you are something else, something far greater," he said probingly.

Zoahn uttered a deep, evil, cruel laugh. "Your skills of observation are superb, oh creature of the sea," he said.

"What do you want on my ship, and what is this 'thing' you speak of that would speed my efforts to destroy the Chappagi?" said Mobeic as he continued to probe.

"A secret. One that will expose your enemy's throat to the plunging dagger in your hand," said Zoahn.

He gestured towards one of the stations, and then smiled as the operator looked in surprise and astonishment. Mobeic spotted this immediately. He strolled over to the man and said, "What do you see?"

"I can't explain it, but only moments ago their shield registered as solid, with no imperfections or weaknesses. Now I've spotted what appears to be a high energy resonance wave rippling across its surface," said the operator.

"What does that do for us?" asked Mobeic.

The operator flew across the keys and brought up several more screens of information.

"The wave has a gravimetric signature to it. I believe that if we time it properly, and provide enough mass to the right point, it will generate a singularity point explosion powerful enough to shatter their shield."

Mobeic looked back towards where the man had been sitting, but saw nothing. Zoahn was gone. He looked around the bridge briefly, and then back at the readout. "How much mass would be required to trigger such an event?"

"One of our heavy battle cruisers would suffice, my lord. If it approached at high warp and impacted the shield at just the right moment, it would trigger the event and breach the shields. The Chappagi would be unable to stop it, because they would not be able to respond in time."

"How so? They would easily see a ship approaching at...high warp...but not if it was cloaked," he said, quickly realizing what the operator was getting at.

The operator nodded. "Yes, my lord. That is what would be required."

Mobeic spun around and shouted, "Commander! Pick one of our heavy battle ships and send it into the shield! Coordinate with this operator on the exact steps needed to create the explosion."

"But my lord, that would be suicide!" cried the officer.

"I am willing to sacrifice as many ships as I need to in order to ensure the complete annihilation of the Chappagi. One heavy battleship is a small price to pay for victory," he said in a low and menacing voice.

"Yes, my lord."

"General! Withdraw the rest of the fleet to a safe distance. I don't want to be anywhere near that shield when this breach occurs."

"Yes, my lord!"

Sarah watched in interest as the crewmen around her carefully discussed the progress of the battle. She was most especially interested in how Mike seemed completely calm, yet still nervous about the many things unfolding in front of him. There was a confidence in him that emanated from the knowledge that the shield was doing what it had been designed to do. Yet there was also a fear that it might fail, and the unthinkable might occur. As she watched them, she sensed something. It was the same feeling she had sensed earlier. She transported herself to the top of the ship and searched the area again. Nothing. She reached out again with her senses once more, but again came up empty. She narrowed her eyes. She was certain she had sensed Zoahn nearby, yet she could not find him now. If he was still in the area, it was most likely for less than honorable reasons. She transported herself back onto the bridge and continued to watch the battle unfold. If Zoahn was in the area, it was possible that he might try to meddle with things, just to get under her skin. She would have to be extra cautious from here on out.

"What the...," said Martin.

"Got something, Lieutenant?" asked Mike.

"Well, I really don't know. Either the Varnok are changing tactics, or they're leaving," she said.

"Say what?" replied Mike.

Corbin watched his display with surprised interest. "That's unusual. The Varnok have ceased fire and are pulling back," he said.

A small cheer went up across the command center. Alfred strolled over and looked at the display. "Hmm, it's possible that they're retreating. But it's more likely they're regrouping to try something else. They wouldn't have come this far and risked this much to give up so easily," he said.

The command console in front of Bentley beeped. He studied it, and then squinted in curiosity. "They're forming up as though they're going to charge the shield," he said.

Corbin laughed. "That'd be utter suicide! You'd have to be completely insane to try ramming your way through."

The console beeped again and began displaying a faint signal indicating a high energy pressure wave rapidly approaching the perimeter shield. Then Bentley's eye caught the latest status report on the shield array and his heart sank.

Chapter 21

"Uh, oh, cat's out of the bag. Corbin, the Varnok have detected the resonance wave and they appear to be trying to use it to breach the array," he said.

Corbin rushed over to the console and saw the readouts. He swore.

"Isn't there some way you can dissipate the wave or possibly shut down the shield to prevent them from exploiting the wave?" asked Alfred.

Corbin shook his head. "Not anymore. We're in a catch-22 situation with no way out. If we shut down the shields to stop the resonance wave, it's going to leap from the shield face and destroy several hundred of the shield nodes. But if we leave it the way it is, the Varnok are going to ram a ship into it and blow a hole in the array."

Alfred nervously ran his fingers through his hair. "So either way we're about to lose our protection."

Corbin nodded. "There's nothing we can do."

"Actually, maybe there is," said Bentley.

Both men turned to him in curiosity. "What are you saying?" asked Corbin.

"Well, I just happened to think of something. The resonance wave only occurred on the exterior of the shield array that faces open space. It didn't happen on any of the internal facing arrays, or the Kuiper perimeter, despite each of them being identical. That means it's possible that the resonance wave is actually a side effect of deep space radiation of some kind bombarding the shield."

"So how does that help us now?" asked Corbin.

Bentley pulled up a holographic representation of the shield array, showing the section near where the Varnok fleet had been bombarding it.

"Well, taking the fact that shutting down a section of the array would ultimately destroy a large swath of shield nodes, it's logical to believe that the resonance wave is actually a side effect of the shield's normal operation."

Corbin shook his head. "What does that have to do with anything?"

"Well, the shield is designed to absorb nearly any form of energy or matter, and neutralize it. But to do so, it expends energy of its own. This in turn creates a bubble of free energy above the main shield face. Normally that energy is ejected into space as a way to dispose of it. But apparently the energy flowing toward the shield is greater than the force expelling it, thus all the waste energy generated by normal operation can't escape and subsequently builds up on the surface of the shield like a puddle of water. All it needs then is something to disturb it and send it on its way. If we can find a way to expel that waste energy, the resonance wave should collapse on its own, or at the very least, be dissipated in a way that's completely harmless."

"So how do we prevent the Varnok from using it to blow a hole in our shields?" asked Alfred.

"Well, since the energy on the shield face is acting like water, and the resonance wave is acting like a tsunami of sorts, we can prevent any damage to the shields by simply shutting down a sector of the array and wrapping the outer face of the shield around the now exposed edge of the grid, creating what is essentially a spillway of sorts. The resonance wave, along with all the pooled up energy on the shield face, will simply flow over the side like water down a drain and out into empty space where it can dissipate harmlessly," said Bentley.

"That may work, but it's going to leave us wide open and vulnerable to attack by the Varnok during that time," said Alfred.

"I realize that, but we only need to leave the door open for a short time while the wave dissipates. Once that's done, we simply reboot that section of the array, and we're back in business with no more chinks in our armor!" said Bentley.

"Well, at least until the next wave forms," said Corbin.

"Hopefully we'll have help by then and a way to dissipate that energy without rebooting the shield. Doctor, chief, make it so. I'll inform the Admiral of our situation," said Alfred.

"Acknowledged. We'll keep our eyes pealed and a finger in the dike if need be. Clayton out."

"So we're basically going to roll out the red carpet for the Varnok?" asked Sydney.

Mike frowned. "It beats having a two hundred kilometer wide hole blown in our shield array. It may be self healing, but it'd have a hard time recovering from a wound that big."

Pendleton raised his hand. "Not to sound too obvious sir, but if they're powering down one of the grids, we're going to have several hundred shield nodes vulnerable to attack during the several minutes it takes to reboot them," he said.

Mike nodded. "That's something I've already considered. Once the wave passes and it's safe to proceed, I plan to send part of the fleet into the breach to protect the nodes until command can restart them. Once the nodes have basic shield capacity, they'll be able to defend themselves. Until then, it's our job to play hero and keep them in one piece."

"Sir, what about that approaching cloaked Varnok battleship?" asked Pendleton.

Mike smiled. "Oh, we'll have a little surprise waiting for him."

Martin's console beeped. "Sir, shield grid shutdown is commencing. Resonance wave will reach the edge of the grid in thirty four seconds," she said.

"So what happens if this little trick doesn't work?" asked Sydney.

"Then we're in for the greatest fireworks display in history," said Sarah.

Mike turned in his chair to look at Sarah. "What's your thoughts on this plan? Do you think it'll work?" he asked.

Sarah nodded. "There's nothing flawed with the plan. The trouble comes afterward, during the bootup cycle."

Mike nodded. "Yeah, we already know that. And you can be certain the Varnok aren't going to just let a golden opportunity like this go unanswered either. The moment the array is vulnerable, they'll come rushing in and eliminate all the nodes they can to reduce or eliminate our chances of raising the shield again. If they succeed, they'll pour through that hole like a horde of cockroaches."

"Sir, the wave has reached the edge of the grid and is following down the inside as intended. It appears that it will dissipate in forty three seconds, allowing for safe transit into the corridor," said Martin.

Mike faced forward in his chair again and said, "Alright, let's get up there and protect those nodes. Notify all designated ships to advance when the wave has been completely dissipated."

"Aye!" said Martin.

Mobeic's eyes grew wide as he watched the display in front of him.

"My lord, the shield changes!" shouted a crewman.

Mobeic shoved an operator aside and quickly worked the sensor controls, trying to get a better picture of what was happening. As he watched in amazement, part of the shield array shut down, allowing a cloud of luminous energy to flow over the sides like a waterfall. He then watched as the resonance wave approached the opening, slid over the side, and vanished. Moments later his sacrificial battleship arrived at high warp, and was destroyed by a volley of torpedoes just before it reached the shield. He slammed his hands down on the console in anger. He quickly focused the sensors on the opening in the shield and noticed with curious surprise that the shield emitters that had generated the shield before now lay dormant and unprotected. A sinister grin slid across his scaly fish face as his gills flared with joy.

He pointed towards the main display and shouted, "All ships! Into the breach! Destroy those emitters before they can raise their shield again!"

Mike watched as the Varnok fleet began to move in unison towards the breach. "Well, I see he's right on schedule. Alpha group, deploy and defend those nodes!" he said.

A large formation of ship killers and battle ships broke away from Mike's main formation and plunged into the breach. As soon as the Varnok were within range, they began opening fire on the shield nodes, destroying several of them before the fleet could get close enough to protect them. Some ships put themselves between the Varnok and the nodes while others dove straight at the enemy ships, throwing as much firepower at them as they could. At first, neither side seemed to flinch, both absorbing the blows of the other as though batting aside a fly. But this false stalemate did not last long as the Varnok began losing one ship after another to the onslaught of Earthfleet weapons fire.

Two of their heavy cruisers were the first to go down, followed by several more. Another group of ships at the head of the attack burst into flames and careened off into the shield grid, exploding on impact. But Earthfleet wasn't getting through this battle untouched either. Two of its own cruisers, deep in the heart of the heaviest fighting, were soon overcome and destroyed. However, despite having overwhelming numbers and a supposedly superior fleet, the Varnok forces were quickly losing ships. Even so, the Varnok continued to press forward. It wasn't long before several more shield nodes were destroyed as the Varnok put even more pressure on the fleet. Mike sent forward another group of ships to assist the first, which were quickly becoming overwhelmed.

Alfred turned to Corbin and said, "Where's that shield!? We're losing nodes!"

"We're working on it, but there's just too much interference. The plasma overhead on the shield face is preventing the nodes from properly rebooting."

"Well find a way to get around it! We're losing too many of them!" shouted Alfred.

"Give us another twenty minutes and we'll have this resolved."

"Twenty minutes!? We'll lose all the nodes before then!"
"I'm doing the best I can, sir! I'm not a miracle worker!"

Mike watched nervously as the battle soon drew to a stalemate. While neither side was winning, the Varnok were slowly gaining an important advantage as more and more shield nodes were destroyed. Several more fleets of Earthfleet ships jumped into the area and took up position behind Mike. He shuffled them forward and then watched with dismay as a fleet of Varnok battleships broke through and made a run for the other side of the array.

"Bravo group, heads up! You've got company heading your way!" he said over the radio.

"Acknowledged Admiral," came the reply.

The Varnok fleet plunged through the breach at full speed, emerging on the other side into a hail of weapons fire. The lead ships took the brunt of the attack, suffering almost 100% casualties within just a few moments. The ships behind them faired slightly better as they emerged from the breach, only to be cut down themselves minutes later.

"Enemy incursion force has been neutralized," said the bravo group commander.

"Acknowledged. Watch for stragglers."

"Aye, sir."

Fighters and ship killers bobbed in and out of the Varnok formations as they engaged ship after ship, and fighter after fighter in a melee of biblical proportions. One of the Varnok battle fleets broke free of the main engagement and skirted the far edge of the breach as they tried to get in behind alpha group. But a formation of samurai class shipkillers emerged from the battle and intercepted them, quickly reducing their roaring charge to a sniveling whimper. The remaining ships scattered and withdrew from the battle area to regroup.

"What's taking so long!" shouted Corbin.

"The startup sequence still won't complete!" cried Bentley as his hands flew across the controls in a battle to get the shield grid restarted.

"We've now lost twenty eight percent of the nodes. The entire outer layer is gone. Second and third layers are taking heavy casualties!" cried Corbin.

Alfred watched helplessly as the two scientists struggled furiously to bring the shield grid online.

"I can't get the grid array to sync together. The nodes won't initialize unless the array is stabilized!" cried Bentley.

Suddenly, an idea sparkled in Alfred's mind. "Can you initialize the nodes individually?" he asked.

"Individually? Yes, but why?" asked Corbin.

"We need to protect the nodes first so as to prevent the Varnok from destroying all of them. If we can't reestablish the array, then we need to concentrate on making the nodes protect themselves. Then once that's done, we can work on linking them together and restoring the grid."

Corbin opened his mouth to protest, and then blinked in amazement at the simple genius of the suggestion. "Actually, that might just work. Bentley, shut down the syncing and assembly programs. Put the nodes into self defense mode and have them power up their shields, local defense only."

Bentley nodded and flew across the controls as he and Corbin worked like madmen.

"Sir, the shield nodes are coming online. They aren't going into normal area defense mode, but they have raised shields to protect themselves. We're no longer losing nodes, sir," said Martin.

Mike nodded. "Well done guys. Alright, Charlie group, get up there into the breach and give alpha group a hand. Delta group, join up with bravo and help watch for stragglers."

Mobeic slammed his fists on the console in anger. "You sluggish food beasts! They've blocked our chance to permanently cripple their shield! All fleets, press the attack! Get as many ships through the breach as you can before they raise their shield again!" he shouted.

Mike watched as a large group of Varnok battleships pressed the charge and drove for the breach.

"Uh, oh. Here goes round two. Alpha and Charlie groups, pull back to the interior of the shield. Echo through Juliet groups, form up on the breach and execute defensive plan two alpha. All other formations, you will be responsible for any ships that get past the main defensive groups."

He watched anxiously as his fleets quickly regrouped and formed a defensive perimeter around the breach.

"What can we do to get the shield back up again?" asked Alfred.

"I don't think we can anymore. From what I'm seeing here, we've lost too many nodes, and of those that remain, quite a few of them are too damaged to do more than simply defend themselves. We're going to need at least a few dozen more emitters to reestablish even a basic shield again," said Bentley.

Alfred grunted in frustration. "What can we do with the nodes we have left?" he asked.

"It's possible to move the nodes around in a way that greatly reduces the size of the breach, which should give the fleet more of a fighting chance," said Bentley.

Alfred looked at Corbin. "You designed them. Will this work?"

Corbin nodded.

"They were designed with this possible eventuality in mind. It'll just take us a bit to reorganize them and get as many of the healthy ones as we can into a usable configuration."

Alfred nodded. "Do it."

The two men nodded in return and immediately went to work. After a few minutes, Alfred turned to his duty officer and said, "Bring the remaining patrols inside the Kuiper perimeter and then seal it air tight."

"But what if the Grand Admiral needs to retreat?"

Alfred inhaled deeply. "We'll cross that bridge when we come to it. For now, we need to make sure that no Varnok ships can get close to Earth. This may present a minor inconvenience to the Grand Admiral, but it'll give me a bit more peace of mind that Earth is safe for the time being."

The officer nodded. "Understood, sir."

Chapter 22

V'sin stood in front of a long, ornate stone bench, behind which sat the nine members of the high council, each one representing one of the nine ancient races that made up the heart of the United Galactic Worlds. The Varnok ambassador sat in a chair to the right of the nine council members, while Phyland, Finch and the Gayik'Von ambassador sat in chairs to the left. The Chancellor sat in a chair between the two groups to act as moderator if needed.

"Honorable council members, I stand here before you today in accusation of an open and blatant act of war by the Varnok against not only my people, but the Gin as well!" said V'sin.

The council member looked at the Varnok ambassador and said, "Do you deny this accusation?"

The Varnok ambassador stood to his feet, his gills flaring as his eyes grew fiery with anger. "We deny that we have acted as to war against our Gayik'Von brothers! We admit only that we have moved against the Chappagi, as they are a threat we can no longer allow!" he said defiantly.

The council members glared at the Varnok ambassador. "You will address the representative of Gin with proper language!" said a councilman.

"I will not address a festering menace with any title of respect," growled the Varnok.

"You wish to destroy the entire Gin race in order to prevent a prophesy that is a lie!" cried V'sin.

"That prophesy is not a lie! The Yib prophets have relayed the truth for millennia, and their prophesies have never failed! To stop the fulfillment of the prophesy, the Chappagi must be destroyed!" shouted the Varnok ambassador.

"You fool! Your attempt to destroy the Gin is fulfilling the prophesy, not erasing it! Don't you see that!? You are bringing about your own fall, not theirs!" cried V'sin.

A councilman banged his gavel on a large metal plate in front of him, sending a ringing through the council chambers. "Be silent. Tell me, what is this prophesy of the Yib that you speak of?" he asked.

The Chancellor stood up and said, "The prophesy is as such. 'A mighty band shall arise of the Gin, who carries a banner topped with the great wings of a majestic bird. The races shall come to war and ruin, and the Gin shall sweep in to conquer all that remains, in the name of a great empire, now gone, that will rise once more.' There may be more, but that is all I know."

He then sat down. The councilman nodded, and looking at the Varnok and said, "Is that the prophesy you speak of?"

The Varnok scowled. "It is," he replied.

Phyland leaned back in his chair for a moment, and thought about the prophesy as the council members discussed it quietly amongst themselves.

Finch could see the wheels turning in his head and whispered, "Have you thought of something?"

Phyland shook his head. "No, I haven't. But I'm trying to figure out what the prophesy means. It talks about a mighty band of the Gin who carries a banner topped with the great wings of a majestic bird. That bird is likely a national emblem of some kind. The problem is, there were hundreds of nations who had birds for their mascot or as part of their national identity. What's even more puzzling is the unlikelihood of any current or past Earth cultures, save for possibly the mythical Atlantians, being the race the prophesy speaks of. None of them fit all the criteria of the prophesy. And I know for certain it's not us, because we don't have a bird for a mascot."

Finch nodded. "I may not be an expert on Gin history, but I have seen the gentle feathers of your race, and do not understand how they could steal the nests of all races. You have many feathers you must still gain before you are even truly able to defend your own nest, let alone take the nest of another."

Phyland nodded.

V'sin noticed the two of them talking and strolled over to them. "Have you thought of something?" he asked.

Phyland shook his head and explained everything they had talked about. V'sin pondered it. After a moment, he turned away as one of the council members pounded his gavel and pointed at Phyland.

"Ambassador of the Gin, come forward," said the councilman.

Phyland stood up and approached the bench as V'sin sat down and crossed his arms in thought.

"Explain this prophesy from your history. Who is this great empire that it speaks of?" asked the councilman.

Phyland shrugged. "I really don't know, your honor. I was discussing it with my colleague and we can't think of anyone in our history who fits the description. Which means that either they never existed, or they don't yet exist."

"Do you think they will rise from the Gin in the future?"

Again Phyland shrugged. "Not if we can help it. But then again, anything is possible."

"Then could the prophesy speak of another that existed that you do not know about?"

Phyland shrugged. "It's possible, but unlikely. If there was such an empire, there would be considerable evidence left behind to indicate they're still here. Yet there is none that I know of."

"What of your, Earthfleet? Is it not superior to much of our technology? And is your system not hidden behind a great barrier shield?"

Phyland nodded. "They are, your honor."

"Then is it not possible that your fleet seeks to use its strength to conquer those around it?"

"Yes, they wish to destroy us all!" shouted the Varnok ambassador as he leapt to his feet.

The chairman banged his gavel and shouted, "You will be silent!"

"Our weapons and our shields are for our protection only! Your attack on Sol system proves why they must exist! If we did not have these defenses, my people would all be dead by now, and my world would be a smoldering hulk of barren rock!" shouted Phyland as he pointed at the Varnok ambassador.

"Your fleet and your shield are just a disguise for your true intentions. You lust after power and empire!" shouted the Varnok as he flared his gills in anger.

"Do you have dirt for a brain, ambassador? Look around you! Your people are part of the nine ancient races. There are trillions of your people in this galaxy alone, and you are worried about a single planet with eight billion souls who don't even know you exist!?"

V'sin cocked an eyebrow in amazement. Once again, Phyland had proven that he knew how to hit an opponent in the right place to inflict the most damage. He stood up and said, "Ambassador Phyland is correct. The Gin that live on their home world do not know of our existence. We are rumored and believed to exist by some, but only the tiny sliver of humanity that makes up their Society, know the truth," he said.

The councilman stared curiously at Phyland. "Is this true, ambassador?" he asked.

Phyland nodded. "It is, your honor."

"Why is this so? Why should your people be left in darkness to our existence, and denied the amazing technologies that your people have achieved?"

"We have done that to protect them. As is your custom with species who have not achieved the ability to travel faster than light, we have applied a similar principle with our own people on our home world. Those who are known to us as the 'Society' are people which were rejected by those upon our home world, because they loved and embraced science and technology. Both powerful men and simple people alike fear such things. As a result, they were hunted, tortured and killed for their love of science. That is why we fled to the safety of space, taking all of our knowledge and technology with us. We wished to continue our pursuit of science in freedom, much as the Pilgrims of Plymouth Rock sought the freedoms of the new world to escape the persecutions of their homeland. But we have not forgotten those we left behind. They are blind to the truth, and fear that which they cannot understand. Despite this, we encourage them to grow, to learn, and to expand their minds. While they may mature more slowly than we, they will someday reach the point where we can rejoin them in common fellowship, with a love of peace and science in our hearts."

"Lies! Blasphemy! You are a race of war, of conquest and of empire! There is great evidences of atrocities on your world the likes of which have not been seen in the three galaxies since the dawn of time!" cried the Varnok ambassador.

Phyland nodded. "It is true that some among our race have done great atrocities. But that is a trait that is spawned from ignorance. With knowledge comes peace, and with peace, prosperity. I am sure that your race also suffered from such evil and wickedness in your early youth."

"You fowl mouthed Chappagi! You are a fool and a monster! Your existence should not have been, and that error shall be corrected with great haste!" cried the Varnok ambassador.

The councilman banged his gavel loudly. "Silence! It is clear that the trouble of this prophesy lies, not in the Gin of which you fear, but in you. Your threats to their people have spawned the seeds of the very future you fear. It is you who is bringing about your own downfall, and not the Gin."

The Varnok glared at the councilman, but said nothing.

V'sin stepped forward and said, "Your honor, with your permission, allow us to fulfill our vow of protection with the Gin and save them from almost certain destruction."

The councilman talked briefly with the other members of the council, and then nodded.

"You may fulfill your vow," he said.

V'sin nodded in appreciation. "Thank you, your honor."

The councilman then looked at the Varnok ambassador and said, "Will you withdraw your forces and seek reconciliation through diplomacy?"

The Varnok hacked in disgust and flared his gills. "We will do no such thing!"

"Then it is the judgment of this council that the Varnok shall suffer censure and face the wrath of the eight until they comply."

"Censure us if you dare, but we will end this threat, even if it costs us our entire race!" shouted the Varnok.

V'sin cocked an eyebrow and said, "Wouldn't that ultimately fulfill the prophesy? Or at least part of it?"

The Varnok ambassador looked at V'sin curiously. "What do you mean?" he said suspiciously. "If you fight us to the last man in order to destroy the Gin, doesn't that partially fulfill the part of the prophesy that says, 'The races shall come to war and ruin'? The prophesy doesn't say that the Gin will destroy the nine. It says that we'll do it to ourselves. They will merely flow into the void left behind by our passing and take whatever they want, as they rightfully should. So it is not the Gin that we have to fear, but rather ourselves."

The Varnok opened his mouth to cry out in anger, and then paused as the full weight of reality crashed down on him. For the first time ever he fully understood the true message of the prophesy, and the reality that, despite all their efforts to prevent the prophesy from coming true, they had inadvertently begun to fulfill it. He slumped down in his chair, stunned and amazed that he had overlooked such an obvious truth. After a moment, he stood up and bowed slightly.

"My sincerest apologies on my foolish blindness. I now see the truth, and realize that we were in error taking the steps that we did. I will inform my government of this new revelation, and will advise them with prejudice that they withdraw all forces from Gin space. After that, we will strive to seek peace and reparations with their people, and those of the nine races whom we have wronged."

The councilman banged his gavel and said, "So let it be done according to the charter."

V'sin studied the Varnok with intrigued interest.

Phyland noticed this and said, "Do you think we've won?"

"I don't know. Only time will tell. But for the moment, I believe we have seen the first signs of hope for your people, and for defeating this blasted prophesy. Our only problem now is that there is still three of the nine who haven't come to this revelation yet." He turned and began heading towards the door. "But until we find a way to change their minds as well, we must be diligent and fight on." He walked up to one of his assistants and said, "Send the signal."

The man nodded. "Right away, sir."

Mike watched his tactical display nervously.

"We're taking a beating up here, Admiral," said one of the group commanders.

"Just hold them as best you can," replied Mike.

Alfred appeared on a small corner of his display and said, "Sir, we've figured out a way to reconfigure the remaining nodes to significantly reduce the size of the hole in the perimeter. It's not going to stop them, but they'll have a much harder time getting any significant fleet numbers through without taking heavy losses on the way in," he said.

"How long?"

"I don't know. Dr. Corbin and Bentley are still working on the details. I should know in a few minutes, hopefully."

Mike shook his head. "You need to hurry up. We're not going to last much longer up here at this rate."

"Understood, sir," replied Alfred.

Sarah studied the battlefield and thought about what she was seeing. "Admiral, may I make a suggestion?"

"Sure, go ahead," replied Mike.

"I've noticed a pattern in the Varnok attacks. They seem to be focusing on finding and destroying the command ships. Therefore, in order to protect this ship, should we be forced to join the fight, I would suggest flying in a formation that makes us look like a normal fighting group."

Mike looked at Sydney who nodded. "She's right about that, sir. The Varnok would love to toss everything aside just to put a few torpedoes through our hull if they can find us. Sarah's suggestion that we lay low and pretend to be just one of the boys is a good idea," said Sydney.

Mike nodded. "Ontario, London, this is the Sergenious. We'll be going with a tri-pin battle style from here on out. Understood?" Both ships affirmed the orders.

"Varnok ships breaking through on the right side," said Martin.

Mike swore. "Papa group. Plug that leak!" he shouted.

A group of ships jumped into the area and began engaging the wounded Varnok ships.

"The formations are changing, Admiral," said Martin.

"I see it. Alpha through echo groups, watch yourselves. You're about to get rushed," said Mike.

"Already see it, but I can't guarantee we'll be able to stop them all. We're pretty rough around the edges down here, sir."

"Will you be able to hold?"

"We'll hold, but we won't stop them all."

Mike grumbled angrily. He looked at his fleet roster and began to get a sickening, almost fatalistic feeling about the progress of the battle. They had already taken significant losses, yet the Varnok fleet hadn't even sent more than a third of their forces. If this kept up, his fleet would soon be overrun and driven back into the Kuiper perimeter. If that fell too, there was no telling how much longer they could hold back the Varnok fleet. There were still some inner system defenses they could fall back on, as well as a handful of reserve battle fleets, but certainly not enough to defeat the entire Varnok Black Fleet. And if reinforcements came, they were in twice as much trouble.

Chapter 23

"Where are the Gayik'Von? They should be here by now," he thought.

"Sir, Juliet group is collapsing. The Varnok are breaking through!" came a voice over the comm. Mike looked at his map of the battlefield and swore.

"I've used up all my reserves. We'll have to plug that hole ourselves until someone's free to take over," he thought. "Alright, we're going to need to jump into this fray and lend a hand. Command group, follow me. We're going to help out what's left of Juliet group," he said.

"Aye!" came several replies.

The Sergenious jumped forward into the battle, followed by the rest of the ships of the command fleet. This sudden move surprised the emerging Varnok battleships which caught the full fury of Mike's command group at nearly point blank range. Mike's group swept in and mercilessly strafed ship after ship before sweeping out and pulling back for another attack. At first it appeared as though the attack had failed, when suddenly several dozen of the ships exploded into brilliant balls of light and energy. Several more ships lost power and began listing and tumbling uncontrollably. A small group of Mike's ships broke off and finished off the wounded ships.

Several heavy battlecruisers emerged from the line just in front of Mike's ship. Sydney flew across the tactical controls, locking on targets and firing with breakneck speed. The fluidic armor on the bottom of the ship liquefied and flowed to the side, exposing the massive arsenal of weapons contained within the main weapons bay. Like a machine gun, a series of torpedoes were ejected from the bay in rapid fire succession, each one launching immediately as soon as it cleared the ship. The Varnok ship exploded into flames and pealed away from

Mike's ship as it began to careen out of control. Pendleton pulled up hard to miss the ship, and then flew wildly through the cloud of debris and weapons fire beyond as he tried to close on another ship.

Outside the perimeter, Mobeic watched with anger as Mike's group utterly destroyed his latest attempt to breach Earthfleet's weakening defensive line and route the defenders from behind. He studied the progress of the battle before him and frowned with disgust. He would certainly force Earthfleet into all out retreat soon, but the cost would be extensive. Far more than he had originally anticipated.

"I bet you wish you could find their commander and destroy him, don't you? I'm sure that would help you win, right?" said a voice behind him.

Mobeic turned and noticed that Zoahn was lying across the top of one of the command stations in an arrogant, defiant posture.

"I can tell you where he is," said Zoahn.

"Tell me, or leave," said Mobeic angrily.

Just then the console behind him beeped. Mobeic turned around to see one ship highlighted in red. It was the Sergenious. He spun around again to look at Zoahn, but found that he was gone. He turned back to the station and stared at the marker for several moments.

Finally he said, "Find me a captain that fears no death! I want that ship destroyed at all costs!"

Alfred anxiously watched the battle unfold on the console in front of him. He wasn't liking what he was seeing. As valiantly as the Grand Admiral was fighting, they were ultimately losing, and badly at that. Even if they somehow managed to turn back the Black Fleet, they didn't stand a chance if more reinforcements showed up. As he sat there contemplating what he should do to help Mike, he overheard an argument brewing beside him. He turned to see Corbin and Bentley arguing quietly between themselves.

"What is all the commotion over there?" he asked.

"He's suggesting that we turn the shield nodes into torpedoes," said Bentley.

"Torpedoes?" asked Alfred in surprise.

Corbin nodded. "The nodes are each powered by their own self sustaining coaxial power core, the idea being that they never need to be refueled. The shields that they emit take advantage of the coaxial energy in its raw form, allowing for greater efficiency and lower overhead when building and maintaining interlaced shield arrays. Theoretically, if we retract the shields to a self defense configuration and vent some of this raw coaxial energy into them, it should create a temporary coaxial field that will propel them at anywhere from one to two hundred AUM. The downside is that they'd have no guidance and their flight and distance vectors would be unpredictable."

"So essentially we'd be turning Oort perimeter into a giant shotgun?" asked Alfred.

Corbin shrugged. "We would, for the most part. Which means we wouldn't want to use it until the fleet was clear."

Bentley shook his head. "I'm telling you, it won't work. There's nothing in their design that says they'll do that. I should know. I built them."

"It will work, because I invented them."

"Will not, and I can prove it."

"Alright, enough already. Assuming this will work, what damage would that cause to the perimeter?" said Alfred.

"If this works, we'll lose about twenty to thirty thousand square kilometers of the perimeter, which will effectively widen the breach beyond what we can defend," said Corbin.

"So essentially this is a weapon of last resort?"

The two men nodded. Alfred shrugged.

"Well, I guess it wouldn't hurt. By the time we need to do this, the perimeter won't matter much anymore anyways.

Alright, set it up, but don't begin executing it until we're forced to retreat, understood?"

Corbin and Bentley nodded.

Pendleton banked the Sergenious hard left as he slipped her gracefully between two attacking Varnok frigates. Both ships soon exploded and were gone. Mike held onto his seat as the ship shuttered under him. Pendleton swore as more torpedoes exploded against their shields.

"Direct hits to the starboard rear quarter! Second and third shield grids down. Fourth holding, but weakening," said Sydney.

"I'm trying, I'm trying! But it's like flying through a freaking hailstorm!" cried Pendleton as he rolled out hard to avoid another volley of torpedoes and cannon fire.

"Eric, can you give me more power to the shields in the starboard rear quarter? I'd like to patch those up if I can," said Sydney.

"I can't. The emitters are blown. I've got the guys down in the engine room working on replacing them," replied Eric.

Sydney grumbled. "Well then, it looks like we'll need to favor that side for a while."

"Why? We've still got plenty of shield layers."

Sydney shook his head. "Not at the rate we're going," he grumbled.

"Well then, let's fix that, shall we? We've been taking this long enough. Helm, heading one four three mark two six. There's two command cruisers over there. See if you can't fly down their throat," said Mike.

"Aye, sir!" shouted Weed gleefully.

"Sydney, as soon as we're on top of them, give those cruisers something to remember us by," said Mike.

"Aye, sir!" replied Sydney.

Pendleton turned the Sergenious hard to port, flew down under one battle group, and up through another as he charged towards the pair of command cruisers. Realizing the danger the Sergenious and her escorts presented, several Varnok battleships tried to cut them off. But to no avail as the Sergenious easily avoided them and soon drew to nearly point blank range on the two command ships.

"Alright Sydney, smoke 'em!" cried Pendleton

"Aye!" replied Sydney as he fired a volley of torpedoes at two command cruisers in front of them.

The torpedoes hammered the two ships, severely damaging both of them. The London and Ontario then came in behind him and finished them off. Pendleton rolled out hard and then jigged several times as he tried to escape from a now enraged battle fleet.

"Hang on, this is gonna get bumpy!" he shouted as a hail of torpedo and cannon fire poured down on them.

The ship shuttered and vibrated heavily as dozens of torpedoes exploded one after another around them and against their shields. After several moments they broke free and dove back into the Earthfleet lines.

"Alright, we're clear," said Pendleton.

"Well done, Mr. Pendleton! Now let's spread out and take the next group. London, Ontario, go wide," said Mike.

Sarah watched with interest as Pendleton banked the ship hard right and began charging at the next group of ships. Suddenly she felt something that drove terror through her entire body like a hot knife. A mortal danger was coming, but the crew was oblivious to its approach. She immediately teleported outside the ship just as a massive Varnok heavy battlecruiser dropped out of warp just barely a kilometer off the Sergenious' bow.

Sarah watched in cold terror as it unloaded all of its forward torpedo tubes straight at the Sergenious at nearly point blank range a split second later. Then, as if time had suddenly slowed out of curiosity just to see what she would do, everything around here came to an almost complete stop. Realizing that saving the ship was her first priority, she turned and ordered the Sergenious to leave the area immediately. It obeyed without question and engaged it's coaxial drive, carrying all those onboard to safety. She then turned her attention back to the slowly approaching torpedoes, and with a flash of anger, commanded the energy within them to become free.

The energy obeyed and erupted from the casings with glee like little sprites of fire, ripping the torpedoes apart as though they were tissue paper. Finally, she turned her attention to the Varnok battleship and did the same. It too exploded, disintegrating into trillions of tiny little pieces, like a handful of dust blown in the wind. Seeing that the threat had now been eliminated, she returned to the ship. Moments later, time returned to normal for her once again, flowing as naturally as it had before.

"What the heck?" said Pendleton in surprise.

"What is it, Lieutenant?" asked Mike.

Pendleton spun in his chair and said, "Sir, the coaxial drive just hiccuped and threw us clear of the battle area."

"Say what?" said Eric in surprise as he quickly began searching his engineering console for clues.

"Are you sure you didn't accidentally bump the FTL controls?" asked Mike.

"I couldn't have. They're laid out specifically so I can't do that. I'm telling you, sir, the ship just jumped on its own," said Pendleton.

Mike turned in his seat and looked at Eric. "Do we have an engine problem?" he asked.

"I don't know, sir. Everything's reading green across the board. We took some pretty good hits back there during that last pass, but nothing that would have caused the engines to just spike like that."

"Are we safe to continue fighting?"

Eric nodded. "I believe so, sir. I don't see anything that'll hinder us from continuing the fight. If we survive this though,

I'll be sure to give the control systems and the engines a complete workup," said Eric.

Mike turned around in his chair and said, "Alright then, Mr. Pendleton, get us back into the fight and link up with our escorts."

"Aye, sir," said Pendleton.

Nordham strode quickly onto the command deck and up to Alfred. "I'm sorry. I just got here. I was overseeing preparations for evacuation of the colonies. What's the prognosis?" he asked.

Alfred sighed. "Not good. We've got a hole in the perimeter big enough to throw a moon through, our fleet is currently crumbling under intensive Varnok attack, and it appears that either the Gayik'Von aren't coming, or they can't," he said.

"Are you sure they got our message?" asked Nordham.

Alfred nodded. "Unless the Varnok intercepted our scout ship, the Gayik'Von got the message. The only thing that would stop them from coming to our aid now is either political entanglements, or something that's got them busy elsewhere. Heck, for all we know, the entire galaxy could have devolved into genocidal war by now. As far as we can tell, we're on our own out here, and the future of the human race isn't looking all that great right now."

Nordham sighed. "And all of this because some Varnok prophet got xenophobia. How much longer before they break through and beat a path to Earth?"

Alfred shrugged. "For the moment, the fleet is holding the breach, but they've suffered so many losses that it won't be long before they'll have to pull back to the Kuiper perimeter. From there it's only a question of how long that shield will hold until it too is breached. After that it's no longer a question of if, but when."

Nordham sighed. "Can't we send another couple of scoutships to call for help?"

Alfred shook his head. "I don't dare risk opening any of the other gates. There could be Varnok waiting outside, and if there is, any scout ships I would send out stands a good chance of being destroyed before they have a chance to flee. There's also the risk that the Varnok might find a way to come in through that gate before we can close it."

"Can't we tell if there are any out there?" asked Nordham.

Alfred shook his head. "If they're cloaked and on silent running, we'd never see them until it's too late."

Nordham grunted. "So all we can do essentially is sit here and wait to die?"

Alfred nodded. Just then the duty officer came running up to Alfred and said, "Sir, we've just received a coded subspace message on a secret frequency!"

Alfred blinked in surprise. "Who is it?"

"We don't know, sir. They didn't send their credentials."

"Well? What does it say?"

The officer scratched his head and said, "Well, it really doesn't say anything, sir. It's just a series of common tongue letters that phonetically spell out the word 'Patton'. Does that mean anything to you, sir?"

Alfred and Nordham looked at each other and said, "Patton?"

Mobeic stood on the bridge of his command ship and grinned with devilish glee as only a fish could do. He gurgled and flared his gills with delightful joy.

"My lord, the lines of the Chappagi are nearly at collapse!" shouted one of the officers.

"Continue to press the attack! Do not slacken the pressure. They must fall today, and be annihilated!"

"Yes, my lord!"

Mobeic watched with glee as more of his ships flowed into the breach, ultimately putting ever increasing pressure on Earthfleet's crumbling defensive lines.

"Is this wise, my lord? We are losing a lot of ships," said his first officer.

"Any losses we suffer here today will be minuscule in comparison with the lives we will save. The annihilation of the Chappagi will ensure that our race will endure for another five thousand cycles," said Mobeic.

Suddenly, alarms began sounding all across the bridge. Mobeic looked around in surprise.

"What is happening!?" he shouted.

"We are being attacked from behind! Gayik'Von ships are appearing by the thousands! It's an ambush!! The rear guard is falling!"

"WHAT!?" cried Mobeic. He raced over to a nearby command console and looked in horror at a tactical display that showed a frightening picture. The unthinkable had happened. The Gayik'Von had come. "Commanders! Withdraw all forces! Regroup on the command fleet! We must repel the Gayik'Von before they destroy us!"

Chapter 24

Mike studied his tactical display as the ship shuttered under him.

"Eric, can you give me more power to the shields in the forward starboard quarter? They're getting a bit thin up there," said Sydney.

"I'll see what I can do," said Eric.

Pendleton rolled the ship around hard and flew through a debris field littered with the shattered remains of both Earthfleet and Varnok battleships.

"Two frigates and a couple dozen fighters pulling in at one seven point two three," he said.

"Got em," said Barker and Sydney simultaneously.

Wen and Barker poured a hailstorm of weapons fire from the Sergenious' turrets into the enemy fighter formation as Sydney lobbed three powerful volleys of torpedoes at two nearby Varnok frigates. The fighters vanished in a blaze of fire and smoke as the two frigates shuttered violently and veered off as Sydney's torpedoes hammered their shields. Seeing an opening, the London lobbed a second series of torpedoes at the two frigates that ripped through their shields, severely wounding both ships. The Ontario then swept in and finished them off.

"Admiral, we may want to consider arming the protomatter torpedoes. Our lines are about to fold and the Varnok are still coming through the breach," said Sydney.

"Not just yet. We're still in this fight for the moment. I don't want to pull out my trump card until I have no other options. Keep the pressure on them for now and we'll see how things form up in a couple minutes," said Mike.

"No offense, but I don't think we'll last another couple minutes."

The ship shuttered as several Varnok ships exploded under them.

"Admiral, it's getting a bit crowded in here. Permission to pull back," said Pendleton as he struggled to weave his way between the thickening clouds of debris and enemy ships.

Mike pulled up several more tactical reports, but grew more and more concerned as he studied the pitiful state of his remaining forces. They wouldn't be able to keep this up much longer.

"Sir, permission to withdraw," said Pendleton, more insistently.

Every bone in Mike's body told him not to give up, to fight on, holding out all hope that help would arrive. But reality was telling him that it was already too late. That all hope had already gone, and the best he could hope for was to flee to the safety of the Kuiper perimeter and wait for the inevitable.

"What the heck?" said Sydney in surprise.

"You seeing it too?" said Pendleton.

"Yeah, I am."

"What do you see?" asked Mike as he continued reading status reports from the fleet.

"Sir, the Varnok have disengaged. They're pulling back," said Sydney.

Mike blinked, and quickly glanced over his tactical maps. The Varnok were indeed pulling back. "What happened? Are they withdrawing to regroup?" he asked.

"No, sir. It appears they're leaving the area," said Sydney.

"What should we do, sir?" asked Pendleton.

But Mike said nothing. He was still trying to wrap his mind around what had just happened. Finally he said, "Alright, let's take this time to regroup, gather up the stragglers and find anyone left who can still fight."

"Sir, message coming in for you over subspace. It's Admiral Sevok," said Martin.

"Sevok!?" said Mike in surprise. "Yeah, put him through."

Sevok's image appeared on Mike's holographic display next to the myriad of tactical and fleet status readouts he had spread across it.

"Greetings, Grand Admiral. It's nice to see that you're still alive," said Sevok.

"Admiral, you're a sight for sore eyes. Another few minutes and we would have been toast," said Mike.

"Sorry we're late, but we had legal entanglements to deal with first. Are you alright?"

"We're black and bloody, but still here somehow," said Mike. "Good. Let me go ahead and clean up this little mess for you, and then we'll see what we can do to help patch up those wounds of yours," said Sevok.

Mike nodded as Sevok's image flickered and vanished. He then said, "Alright Mr. Pendleton, take us to Pluto station. We'll rally there for the time being."

"Aye, sir."

Sevok closed the channel and turned to his command officer.

"This is the Varnok Black Fleet. Do not take them lightly. Execute the battle plan exactly as I have given it to you. If we do this right, this battle will be over quickly."

"Yes, sir," said the officer.

Sevok watched as Mobeic's battered fleet struggled to reform and put up a strong resistance against Sevok's armada. But Sevok's fleets quickly sliced Mobeic's remaining forces into small, manageable pieces and began wiping them out one cell at a time.

"Admiral, Mobeic is hailing us," said a crewman.

"Ah, so we finally have his attention," said Sevok.

Mobeic's image appeared on the main display. "You traitorous Chappagi Gicall! How dare you fire on the forces of the Varnok Black Fleet!" screamed Mobeic.

But Sevok was unfazed, his face remaining emotionless as he studied Mobeic. He knew he had the superior advantage, and wasn't afraid to flaunt it.

"Your people have lifted their death order against the Gin. You will either withdraw and leave Gayik'Von space now, or you will be annihilated," he said flatly.

Mobeic hacked twice and spit at the screen. "We will do no such thing!" he screamed.

The screen then went blank. Sevok cocked an eyebrow and said, "So be it." He turned to his commander and said, "Concentrate all firepower on the command fleet. Destroy them and Mobeic with all prejudice."

The officer nodded. "Yes, sir."

With brutal efficiency and overwhelming firepower, Sevok's forces quickly surrounded Mobeic's command fleet and crushed them like an egg, annihilating all of their ships with lightning quick speed. The other forces of the Black Fleet tried to turn and assist their great leader. But they were pinned down and unable to lend assistance, as they were struggling for their own lives. Sevok watched with muted interest as Mobeic's cruiser soon came under attack, caught fire, and exploded. Moments later, deprived of their leader, the remnants of the Varnok Black Fleet signaled their surrender.

A man hurried into the dining room of Phillip's chateau, stopped at the end of the table and bowed.

"What word do you bring?" asked Phillip as he chewed on his morning meal.

"The attack on the Chappagi has failed. They have survived, and the Admiral has been defeated."

Phillip nodded. The man bowed in return, and then hurried away.

Licinius leaned against a nearby pillar and watched the man leave. He then turned to Phillip and said, "What do we do now? Your plan has failed. The Chappagi still live."

Phillip grinned. "My plan has not failed, nor has our ultimate victory been lost. Only the path down which we must travel has changed. Our victory is still guaranteed. One of the nine has been weakened, and a second will soon be crushed. All we have to do now is wait, and bide our time. When the moment is right, we will strike, and then there will be seven."

He took another bite of food and grinned with fiendish delight.

Epilogue

Two Weeks Later...

Mike looked up as the door chimed. "Come," he said.

The door opened and Alfred walked in. He handed Mike a data pad and said, "That's the final total on all fleet casualties, including the preliminary fleet survey from the Jupiter shipyards."

"How bad is it?"

Alfred sighed heavily. "Over half of our fleet was either destroyed, or damaged beyond repair. The rest will be undergoing extensive rehabilitation and upgrades for at least the next six months."

"What about the shield?" asked Mike.

Alfred shrugged. "The science teams have been working day and night for the past two weeks trying to restore it to it's original condition while also trying to solve the issue of the resonance wave. They may have a solution, but for now we'll have to deal with it the way it is."

Mike nodded in understanding. "Well, a broken shield is better than one with a gaping hole in it."

Alfred nodded. "It is. By the way, I included a little something extra in the report for you to see."

Mike perked up in interest. "Some good news, I hope?" he asked.

Alfred nodded. "I don't know what you'll do with this information, but it may provide us with what we need to bring the fleet up to full strength again much quicker."

"What is it? A possible upgrade? A change in our defensive systems or ship designs?"

Alfred grinned. "Actually, it will likely be a change in the focus of ship production. From what I read in the reports, we may want to rethink our use of battleships and dreadnoughts."

Mike cocked his head curiously. "Why's that?"

"Because, according to the casualty reports, we lost almost all of our battleships, nearly all of our fighters, and all but two of our dreadnoughts. We only lost two ship killers the entire fight, and that apparently was a fluke."

Mike blinked in surprise. "The ship killers survived almost untouched!?"

Alfred shrugged. "I wouldn't say completely untouched, as a few are in Jupiter shipyards undergoing some extensive repairs, but for the most part they all out performed, out killed, and out lasted almost every other ship in the fleet. Part of that is apparently due to the fluidic armor they use. We've always wanted a proper test of that armor system, yet it looks like the Varnok gave us one that was far greater than anything we could have ever hoped for."

Mike looked at the data pad and rubbed his chin in thought. "So you think we should go with replacing our lost battleships with ship killers?"

Alfred shrugged. "Possibly. It's at least something to consider. They are after all designed to go toe to toe with a battlecruiser and win. So it may be worth considering going with them instead for all future ship construction, as it'll require less crewmembers, and less resources, while providing a much larger, more powerful fighting force in the end. Again, it's just a suggestion, but I thought it wise to at least mention it."

Mike nodded. "Your suggestion is duly noted, and I will put a lot of consideration into the idea. It's no secret that I love the ship killers dearly, so the idea holds a lot of merit with me."

Alfred chuckled. "I thought that might pique your interest. Well, I need to get back to command."

Mike nodded and watched as Alfred left. Moments later the door chimed again.

"Come," said Mike, curious to who this new visitor was.

The door hissed open and Sevok walked in. Mike stood and shook his hand.

"Ah, Admiral. What brings you down here?" he asked.

"Just seeing how you're doing. You look like you'll have a long road to recovery," said Sevok.

Mike nodded sadly. "We will. But we'll get there in time."

Sevok nodded. "It is a sad day for the united worlds. A great tragedy has occurred that should not have. I pray that our politicians will be able to solve their differences soon, so that we will not be required again to solve it for them."

"I'll second that. Hey, by the way, I've been meaning to ask you something. Alfred informed me that you sent him a message just before you attacked Mobeic's fleet. I recognized the name, but I don't understand it's significance."

Sevok smiled. "I am a great admirer of the generals and leaders of your past. General George S. Patton was one of them. I sent the message that way to inform you that help was on the way, without alerting Mobeic to our arrival."

Mike nodded. "It was an ingenious idea, even if we didn't understand it at first. I assume that by using Patton's name, you were referring to his hundred mile charge north during the battle of the bulge?"

Sevok nodded. "That was the general reference, but one I figured you'd understand."

Mike chuckled. "I would have, but I didn't hear about it until two days later."

Sevok rolled his eyes. "That would somewhat defeat the purpose of the message, would it not?"

Mike nodded. "Yeah, it would. But it wouldn't have mattered anyways. I had my hands full when you called."

Sevok nodded. "I could see that."

"So, what did you come down here for? I don't suspect that you came just to visit."

Sevok shook his head. "No, I did not. My fleet has been recalled. My government has other work for us. So I will be leaving you soon. Another armada is coming this afternoon who will take our place. So I wanted to say goodbye, and wish you a speedy recovery."

"Thanks. If you hadn't arrived when you did, there likely wouldn't be anything left to recover."

Sevok nodded. "True, but after this, the Varnok, and anyone else who threatens you, will think twice before attacking."

Mike nodded. "We can hope so."

Lars looked at the holographic display in front of him and studied the picture. "That library ship has really been a cornucopia of information. Too bad it hasn't given us enough to find our perpetrator," he said.

Vlad nodded. "But at least it's given us a few leads," he said.

Lars nodded. "Even though what we have is sketchy at best, I'd say we'd be safe pursuing it. If nothing else, going there may give us something more to work with," he said.

Vlad nodded. "I'll tell the commander so he can set course."

"Don't bother. We're not going," said Toby as he stepped into the room. The two men turned and looked curiously at him.

"What do you mean we're not going?" asked Lars.

"We've been recalled to Earth."

"Say what!?" exclaimed Lars.

Toby nodded. "Fleet command is calling back all available ships. We're needed to help in the defense of Sol space."

Lars cocked his head curiously. "What for? Do they know of a possible impending attack?"

Toby shook his head. "It already happened. The Varnok Black Fleet attacked Sol. Over half our fleet is gone."

Vlad gasped as Lars blinked in surprise. "Half the fleet!? Where were the Gayik'Von!?" cried Lars.

Toby shrugged. "I don't know. I wasn't told. The only thing I know is what I told you. The rest we'll have to find out when we get back."

Lars sighed. "A lot of possible leads are going to grow cold while we're back home warming the bench."

Toby nodded. "I know that, and I expressed that to fleet command. But they wouldn't listen."

Lars crossed his arms in anger. "Great. Nearly two months of work down the drain."

Toby shook his head. "Not really. We know who's behind the threats on Earth. It's the Varnok."

Lars shook his head. "No, there's more to this whole thing than just the Varnok. In all of my years fighting against Black Orchid, the one thing I learned first hand was that no evil entity, be it an organization or an individual, does the work themselves. They always hide behind someone or something else. Someone was pulling the Varnok's strings, and that someone is still out there somewhere. In time they'll pull someone else's strings and we'll find ourselves in even deeper waters than before. We can't just go back."

Toby shrugged. "I can't disobey a direct order, even if I do agree with what you're saying. But look at it this way, whoever is behind this whole fiasco will likely go into hiding for a few years until things cool down again. Once they do, we should have a much better chance of finding them when they start to move again. And while I may not be a professional spy like you, all my time in deep recon has at least taught me that. So we have a few clues to start with. So what? If they're in hiding, no amount of snooping we do will expose them. So for now, let's go home and wait till they come out in the open again. When they do, I'll gladly help you nail their butt to the wall."

Lars grinned. "Well, even though this feels like we're giving up, we do at least have that to look forward to."

Toby smiled. "That we do."

As the Appalachia began to break away from the library ship and head for home, an old man and a Sevedith watched them with interest from a nearby cloaked ship. "Go get 'em, guys," said the old man.

Mike looked up as Eric walked into his office. "Ah, afternoon Commander. What can I do for you?"

"I was going over the post action system reports for the Sergenious, checking her for damage. Overall, she did really well. For being the oldest shipkiller in the fleet, she's one tough bird. I'm going to run some molecular level scans of the superstructure just to be sure there's no micro fractures anywhere in the spaceframe, but overall I really didn't find any issues."

"So what of the unexplained FTL jump?" asked Mike.

Eric inhaled deeply, handed Mike a data pad, and said, "I think you should ask Sarah."

Mike took the data pad and studied it curiously. After a moment, he looked up and said, "She left this in the logs?"

Eric nodded. "I've never seen an AI do that before. Now admittedly she's a unique AI, but what she did surprised even me."

Mike nodded. "Indeed, me as well." He leaned back in his chair and contemplated the log entry displayed on the data pad.

"Would you like me to talk to Sarah about this?" asked Eric.

Mike continued thinking for a moment, as though ignoring Eric.

"Sir?" said Eric as he tried to get an answer.

Finally, Mike shook his head and said, "No, I'll talk to her."

Eric nodded. "Understood, sir.

Mike strolled into the station arboretum and quickly spotted Sarah sitting on top of a large rock near a small, bubbling spring. He walked slowly over to her and stopped, but said nothing.

Sarah smiled. "You found my message," she said with a hint of gladness.

Mike sighed. "Yes, I did. Eric brought it to me. I'm not sure how to deal with what I'm reading here. I was hoping you could explain yourself."

"Admiral, out there during that battle, something happened that neither I, nor anyone else had expected. Your sensor logs should give you the details. But essentially, I saw something. Something that scared me deeply." She slipped off the rock and stood in front of Mike, her hands folded in front of her. "That ship came out of nowhere, suddenly, and without warning. It fired on you. Had I not reacted as I did, you would have died. All of you. I care for you, Admiral. I couldn't just stay within my programmed limitations, those restrictions of protocol, and just allow you to be destroyed like that, not knowing what had happened or that it had even happened at all. I did what I felt I had to, and because of that, we are standing here now, talking. I hope you understand."

Mike sighed and rubbed his neck. "I guess I don't really know how to thank you. At first I thought all of this was the result of a systems glitch. Then these logs made me think that you had possibly malfunctioned in a dangerous way. Now I see an AI that has grown beyond its original design and has quietly struck out on a quest to be the best it can be, even if that means becoming a little bit like it's creators."

Sarah smiled kindly. "Sometimes, to be the best at something, you have to become a little like the people you're with."

Mike smiled and nodded. "Something like that."

Sarah chuckled lightly. "Thanks for understanding, Admiral. Goodnight," she said with a kind and gentle smile.

Mike nodded. "Goodnight."

And with that, Sarah shimmered and was gone. Mike stood quietly in the arboretum for a few moments as he thought about what Sarah had said. Finally he said, "Computer, transfer a copy of these logs to my personal diary."

"Transfer complete," came the reply.

He glanced briefly at the stars twinkling playfully through the canopy above, and then strolled quietly back to his quarters.

The End

ABOUT THE AUTHOR

Steven is a well respected member of his local community, as well as the online Linux and Open Source communities.

He is an accomplished writer both in technical and literary merit and has been compared by some to a mixture of Isaac Asimov and E. E. "Doc" Smith, two of the greats of the Science Fiction world.

Steven lives in Southwest Michigan with his cat quietly writing and enjoying his family.

The Author Steven lake
www.realmsofimagination.net